Keller knew it was dangerous surgery. The Army did it a dozen times daily, but still it was dangerous. It could not be otherwise, messing with your brain. His palms dampened at the thought.

"It's hard work," the medics warned him. "It's not a free ride. If you're an Angel there's an attitude you have to cultivate. *Wu-nien*. You know what that means, Mr. Keller? It means you're a machine. You don't think, you look. You don't look where you want, you look where it matters. You *are* a camera. You're not there to *do* the work. You *are* the work."

Keller understood perfectly. Byron had already taught him a little Angel Zen. *To see without desire. The perfect mirror.*

"You won't be Raymond Keller anymore. What you want, what you care about, you have to learn to leave it all behind. You're a pair of eyes, a pair of ears. That's all."

Keller thought it sounded pretty good.

That night, for the first time in a month, he slept without dreaming. In the morning, they wheeled him into surgery.

MEMORY WIRE

ROBERT
CHARLES
WILSON

BANTAM BOOKS
NEW YORK • TORONTO • LONDON • SYDNEY • AUCKLAND

MEMORY WIRE
A Bantam Spectra Book / January 1988
2 printings through March 1990

ISBN 0-553-26853-8

Published simultaneously in the United States and Canada

Bantam Books are published by Bantam Books, a division of
Bantam Doubleday Dell Publishing Group, Inc. Its trademark,
consisting of the words ''Bantam Books'' and the portrayal of a
rooster, is Registered in U.S. Patent and Trademark Office and in
other countries. Marca Registrada. Bantam Books, 666 Fifth
Avenue, New York, New York 10103.

PRINTED IN THE UNITED STATES OF AMERICA

RAI   0 9 8 7 6 5 4 3 2

PART 1

BURIED
HISTORY

CHAPTER 1

1. Because of the monomolecular wires twined deep into his cerebral cortex, Raymond Keller's memories often announced themselves as scents. He would smell dust and concrete and think, seconds later, of the water-rationed conduit suburb in which he had spent his childhood. *Gasoline,* he would think, and be back in his father's oily garage, chain-lifting an antique internal combustion engine.

Tonight—standing in the kitchen of his Los Angeles apartment with a glass of water in his hand—he smelled the hot granular earth of a manioc field in Brazil, and knew the memory would be a bad one.

He put aside the glass with a deliberate motion and moved to the translucent outer wall of the living room. The sky beyond it was dark and starless; across the long bow of the harbor, the scattered lights of the boat barrios flickered.

The memory trick was one side effect of his Angel wiring. There were others, mostly minor. He had grown accustomed to it, or so he told himself. The biosynthetic wires grown under his skull were microscopic and immunosuppressive; in terms of tissue displacement or body weight, they hardly existed. But, Keller thought moodily, the body knows. Leiberman, the Network M.D., had told him so. "The imperial flesh," Leiberman had said. "Poke it, it responds."

He closed his eyes and sighed.

In the flickering retinal darkness, bright lines of tracer fire stitched out

Helpless, he watched Megan Lindsey die one more time.

Keller was periodically employed as a Recording Angel by the news and documentary arm of the largest satellite video network operating out of the western United States. In the course of his work he had sold burned-out krytrons in the Oslo weapons market, he had endured the terrors of the joychip underground. But he knew what he guessed most Angels knew: the real terrors are internal.

Wu-nien, he told himself. No-thought. In the silence of his apartment, the memory fading—after midnight now —he practiced the lonely rigors of Angel discipline.

When he had achieved a measure of calm, he emptied the card windows of his wallet and placed the plastic rectangles side by side on the slab of smoked glass that was the surface of his coffee table.

Pacific Credit Exchange, the Military Registrar, California DMV. A handful more. Some of them featured his photo in two or three dimensions: a man in his mid-thirties frowning out from the photographs with an expression Megan had once described as "the blessed innocence of failed comprehension." He wore nonprescription eyeglasses and his hair was cut back to stubble. The name embossed or printed on each card was Grossman, William Francis.

The cards were insubstantial, Keller thought: soap bubbles. A year ago they had meant a good deal to him. They had represented a new life, a new identity, yet another chance to outrun the juggernaut of his past. When the Network issued him the ID, part payment for his dangerous and prolonged penetration of the joychip covens, Keller had in effect invented William Grossman: a mild, inoffensive man with modest pleasures and no ambitions. He had created a past for him—parents, a school, lovers. He had coached himself in this artificial history until he was convinced he could in some sense *become* William Francis Grossman, and for months it seemed to work. He told the Network he didn't work for them anymore.

For a time it seemed as if he had found a way back into the world.

But lately, gazing out the walls of Grossman's luxury apartment at the coastline stretching north to the Santa Monicas, he had felt the old fears creeping back. And now—terrible memories still flickering in the lights of the tidal barrios—he knew it was the end of Grossman.

He stacked the cards carefully, picked them up, fanned them out. They were artificial and a cheat.

Tomorrow, he thought, I will burn them.

He would go back to the Network. He would light up the wires in his head. He would be an Angel again.

2.   In the morning Keller traveled to the Network building in the city core and met his contact there, an independent producer named Vasquez. Vasquez sat in a large private office with polarized windows and vertical blinds, and the angle of vision the windows allowed was intentionally oblique, so that one saw only the blueness of the ocean and not the shabby patchwork of the Floats.

Vasquez regarded him with a mild curiosity and said, "I thought you didn't do this anymore."

The work Keller did was sublegal, his contacts with the Network strictly sub rosa. He worked without contract, and so he was, to a degree, at the mercy of Vasquez. But he was also good at his work; he knew it; Vasquez knew it. "I changed my mind," he said.

Keller outlined the proposition his friend Byron Ostler had made him a couple of weeks ago.

The Network executive nodded. At first, as Keller spoke, Vasquez seemed excited; then a patina of concern came across his face. "What you're proposing," he said, "would be dangerous."

Keller admitted it would be.

"Maybe more dangerous than you think," Vasquez persisted. "Not everybody can be bought off. There are too many competing interests. The military, the government, the Brazilians—"

"I appreciate that. I can handle it." Keller sat forward in his chair. "No one has footage like this. You know how valuable it would be."

They talked a while longer. As Vasquez relented, his excitement crept back. Keller had known it would: Vasquez was already embarked on an investigation of the oneirolith trade and the deal was too tempting to refuse. Keller held out for a little more money than he ordinarily received; Vasquez agreed easily.

He was committed now. No pulling out. The idea was faintly but suddenly disturbing.

Vasquez withdrew a notepad from his desk, scribbled on it, lifted the sheet of paper and handed it across the desk. "Give this to Leiberman. Go this afternoon. He'll make time for you. I'll arrange it."

Keller nodded.

The appointment with Leiberman was for three. At lunch Keller met Byron Ostler at a waterfront café down the coast highway, a high patio overlooking the boat barrios, *barcos viviendas* in Gypsy colors sprawling between the mainland and the distant tidal dam. Byron was alone, waiting. But he would have been impossible to miss even in a crowded room. His thick archaic eyeglasses, round as coins, sat on his pinched face like a challenge or a rebuke. His hair fell down over his shoulders in white cascades. He wore an old khaki jacket threadbare at the collar and loose around his narrow throat. He looked, Keller thought with some amusement, like a painting by El Greco of a consumptive jockey.

"Ray," Byron said, and the smile widened fractionally.

"I'm still Grossman," Keller said.

"Oh?"

"For a few hours." He pulled up a chair.

"So it's on? You're making the trip?"

"Looks that way," Keller said.

Byron chuckled softly.

Keller ordered a sandwich from the bored day waitress. "Something's funny?"

"You," Byron said. "Me. That there's two of us crazy enough to go back."

"You said it was arranged. You said—"

"I know. It is. Safe passage guaranteed. Still . . . there's this *irony* in it."

Byron had a right to talk. Byron had been there. Byron had been Keller's platoon Angel all those years ago; he would show you—if he was in the mood—the pale blue Eye tattoo on his skinny forearm, washed over with blond hair now, fading but intact.

Keller, after the war, had had his own tattoo removed. Leiberman had performed the skin graft. It was a good job: only a rigorous microscan would reveal the seams. Byron was a 'lith chemist long since gone underground out in the Floats; he could afford to keep his Eye insignia. Keller, a private Angel, could not.

Both of us outlaws, Keller thought. But so different.

"It's only a place," Keller said.

"The Basin," Byron said. "The River—Rio Mar, the River Sea. The Amazon, Ray. Heart of Weirdness."

Keller smiled steadily. "Bullshit."

"You plugged in yet?"

"Not for a couple of hours."

"So . . . your last meal as a human being."

The waitress brought his sandwich, and Keller looked at it without enthusiasm. "Is that how you think of it?"

"I did your job once."

"Yours is better?"

He shrugged.

"Drug pusher," Keller said.

"Not exactly."

Keller ate, and Byron continued to grin until Keller began to find the grin an irritation, a kind of insult. It *is* bullshit, he thought suddenly—the grin, the swagger, the faded khaki; all of it, all hype.

"Don't repress," Byron said. "Tell me what you're gritting your teeth about."

Because he was irritated, and because the friendship was old enough and sturdy enough, he did so.

"Maybe," Byron conceded. "Maybe I'm a fake. You include yourself in that, Ray? The walking eye? The man who had his humanity shot off in the war?"

Keller winced. "I include myself," he said.

"But of course. Objectivity—yes? How could you *not* include yourself?"

"At least you don't deny it."

"Wouldn't dream of it," Byron said. "But you're wrong, you know, if you believe that about Teresa."

"I haven't met Teresa."

"It's for her sake. All this is for her sake."

Keller put his card in the table slot and stood up.

"Think about it," Byron said, lost now in some thought of his own. "Everything moves in circles. The Wheel, Ray. Everything returns."

3. Leiberman's office was a shabbily genteel building in the Hollywood Hills, pastel stucco and a discreet sign: it could be mistaken for an abortion clinic. It was, of course, much more than that. Leiberman was the Network's neurotechnician of last resort: implanting vapid actors with digital prompters to whisper their dialogue to them; boosting their stage presence or neutralizing their stage fright with his pharmacopoeia of narrow-gauge psychochemicals; sometimes installing AV blanks for Angels like Keller . . . performing any medical work that must not suffer the scrutiny of the legal guard dogs. In Leiberman's office no real

records were kept; no names, no credit lines, no phone numbers.

Inside, Leiberman's secretary smiled at him. He handed her the note, his passport. Her eyes glittered icily. "Go on in," she said.

The inner office was Leiberman's workroom, a glass-and-chromium chamber, surgical instruments dangling on coiled wires from the ceiling. Leiberman greeted him and ushered him to a chair. Leiberman was plump, bald, grossly physical; his surgical smock was tight across his belly. "This shouldn't take long," he said. "Remove your shirt. Sit."

The access socket was embedded between Keller's shoulders next to the spine, a couple of millimeters under the derma. "Army workmanship," Leiberman clucked, exposing and sponging that bit of metal; but it was only professional rhetoric: the socket did its job. On his first visit, Leiberman had run a deep neurological scan and admitted that the actual wirework was excellent: biosynthetic tendrils much thinner than hairs sampling Keller's visual cortex, his auditory ganglia. He had never needed upgrading or repair. Leiberman's job was to seal and unseal the skin, keep the socket sterile, and install a passive AV memory to store Keller's data.

"Fine new ones these days," Leiberman said. He removed the AV memory from a sterile perspex pack. It was smaller than Keller remembered, a snowflake between the prongs of Leiberman's tweezers. "You can get up to two years continuous realtime on one of these—audio and video. And it's sturdier into the bargain. New materials. Well, you know."

Keller sat with his head immobilized in a skull clamp while Leiberman worked. Installing the memory, the testing of it, sent little back-EMF blips surging into Keller's brain. His visual cortex lit up: impossible mandalas blossomed and flared on his eyelids. The subdued anger that had been riding him since lunch began abruptly to fade. Surrendering to the process, he thought, that was what it was all about. It was surrender that had saved him. In this cool ice envelope, Camera Eye, Recording Angel, he was preserved from the ravages of real memory.

He relaxed and watched the misfiring of his visual ganglia, cascades of blue electric fire. The vision consumed all of Keller's attention until Leiberman withdrew his tools and the surgical studio snapped back into focus.

"You're fixed," Leiberman said.

He was. He felt it. Nothing specific, simply an aura of heightened awareness that was not even physiological: only the knowledge that he was an Angel again, that everything he saw and heard was being quietly recorded on the molecular memory Leiberman had installed.

He turned to look at the neurosurgeon, and it was a different motion now, a pan-and-sweep, coolly professional.

Leiberman frowned. "Don't stare," he said. "It's impolite."

4. Keller's neural harness had been installed at an Army staging base in Santarem during the long Brazilian conflict. Keller had been shipped in from frontline action along the contested highway BR-364 in Rondonia, in a condition the military doctors called "emotional dysfunction." He had surprised them by asking for Angel duty.

Every combat unit had an Angel. It was Army policy. The Angel performed essentially the same role in an infantry platoon that the black box, the flight recorder, performed in the cockpit of a passenger airliner—"box" was one of the politer epithets for a Recording Angel. Byron Ostler, Keller's own platoon Angel, had explained it to him one time. Because an Angel was in effect the ultimate intelligence unit, carrying an unimpeachable record of combat action, Angels were entitled to certain benefits. They were not obliged to do heavy physical work. In combat they were scrupulously defended by their fellow soldiers. They wore special protective clothing, and other people humped their supplies for them.

They were shunned, of course, socially. But they were also exempt from the hard equations of triage: it was Med Corps policy that Recording Angels received priority medical attention.

If they died, their bodies were recovered.

In all these customs and regulations there was no concern for the individual Angel, only for his neural harness, his AV memory, his ultimate debriefability . . . but that was okay, Keller thought. That was just Army.

The hospital at Santarem was a very loose unit. The nurses were civilians, the doctors volunteers. The building was makeshift, an ambling single-story structure electronically sealed against insect traffic. Keller lay in a ward with twenty strangers united by their fear of the impending surgery. They read American paperbacks or looked at the Portuguese sex comics that arrived in box loads from São Paulo every Tuesday. They listened to the drone of troop carriers and the white hiss of the air-conditioning; they played cards. One by one they were wheeled away and came back wired.

Keller had known it was dangerous surgery. They all knew. The army did it a dozen times daily in installations like this, but still it was dangerous. It could not be otherwise, messing with your brain like that. The brain, Keller thought, was delicate, fragile. Thread it with those wires and you could lose something. Before he volunteered for Angel duty, Keller had purloined a medical text and checked it out. Theoretically it was simple: the "wires" were living biosynthetic tissue, designed to grow unobtrusively into the brain, built with tropisms that would carry them deep into the visual cortex. An automatic process. But the book referred also to the symptomology of implant failure, a long and daunting list. Partial or total loss of the visual field; dysphasia, aphasia; disorientation, memory loss; impairment of limbic function; flattening or disturbance of emotional affect. His palms dampened at the thought. Still, he had been deemed suitable for this work and had—it was elective—volunteered.

"It's hard work," the medics warned him. "It's not a free ride. Don't even think it. If you're an Angel, there's an attitude you have to cultivate. *Wu-nien*. You know what that means, Mr. Keller? It means you're a machine. You don't think, you look. You don't look where you want, you look where it matters. You *are* a camera, right? You're not there to *do* the work. You *are* the work."

Keller had understood perfectly. Byron had already

taught him a little Angel Zen. *To see without desire. The perfect mirror.*

"You won't be Raymond Keller anymore. What you want, what you care about, you have to learn to leave it all behind. You're a pair of eyes, a pair of ears. That's all."

He thought it sounded pretty good.

That night, for the first time in a month, he slept without dreaming. In the morning they wheeled him into surgery.

5. Back in Grossman's apartment Keller fixed himself a light meal. He needed to drop a few pounds, make himself lean, shed Grossman like a skin. When he had eaten, he gathered up the contents of the refrigerator and the kitchen cupboards, put them all into two shopping bags, sealed the bags, and carried them down the hallway to the building's communal annihilator. They vanished into the metal chute in a puff of actinic light.

Good-bye, Grossman.

He thought about burning his cards, decided to postpone the ritual. First he would call Lee Anne.

A sex agency had supplied him with Lee Anne. Buying sex on credit had been a novelty for him, but it seemed like something Grossman might do. He had hired Lee Anne on a short-term contract and expanded it to long.

She appeared on the telephone monitor as immaculately groomed as ever. How she managed this daily perfection in response to an impromptu phone call was a mystery to him: some kind of digital enhancement, maybe. She was beautiful in a manner that was rigorously contemporary, her cheekbones suppressed, her face heart-shaped, her eyes blue inside bright orange rays of mascara. She smiled . . . pleased to see him, or professionally seeming to be.

"I'm going away," Keller said, already uncomfortable with the Grossman persona, wearing it this last time.

"For how long?"

"Long time," Keller said. "I have to cancel the contract."

She was silent a beat. "You should have told me."

"I'm sorry. There wasn't time."

"Well." She shrugged and smiled. "I wish we could have gone on. It was a good time. The best."

It was a lie, but so professional that Keller felt a sudden pang of regret. There had been nothing between them but commerce and gestures, but for one terrible moment Keller felt the overwhelming urge to confess, to pull out of his commitment to Vasquez, to tell her how unbearably lonely he had been these past ten years. Worse: he wanted to put his fist through the video screen, touch her somehow through this insect tangle of optics and wire.

The image left him shaking. He forced a smile, registered his regrets, and signed off with his fists clenched at his side.

Wu-nien, Keller thought as he burned the last of the cards.

His Angel basic had comprised a kind of roughshod Zen instruction. Selflessness, fearlessness, focus. His master sergeant had been a Roshi of the Rinzai School. There was talk of the Three Pillars: great faith, great doubt, great perseverance. They were setting aside the mind. Everyone was very solemn. They believed—Keller believed—that it just might be true, that satori might lurk, mysterious enlightenment, among the oxbow lakes and green heron islands of the Amazon.

Wu-nien. He was an Angel. He was Keller once more. It was the ultimate objectivity they had all striven for: *wu-nien, wu-hsin,* no-mind, no-thought; only seeing, vision apart from judgment, vision without desire. The perfect mirror.

It was like a place, Keller thought; a place without love or loneliness or fear. A calm and brightly illuminated place in which the only memory was AV memory, clean and mutable.

He called it the Ice Palace.

He had come to that place again.

CHAPTER 2

1.   From the balcony of her floating balsa, moored deep in the tangle of tidal industries and boat barrios that had grown up where the coast jogs eastward from Santa Barbara, Teresa Rafael watched an old woman approaching across a pontoon foot bridge from the east. She set aside her pencil and thought, *A customer.*

    She switched off the pencil and listened as its insect hum faded to stillness. She was an artist. A decade ago she had begun selling junk sculptures to the seaside galleries up Highway One—pinwheels oxyacetylene-welded to antique crankshafts, pachinko boards of rivets and sheet aluminum. Later, after Byron Ostler introduced her to the dreamstones, she took up softer media. Currently she was working on a crystal painting, a translucent plate less than an inch thick, shaping and shading its laminar depths with a homemade interference pencil. The piece, a landscape, was nearly complete. Green paddies stretched to a hazy horizon. The sky was a chalky shade of blue, and from it a flock of frail gossamer-winged people—a slightly darker blue than the sky—sailed down to a wooden pagoda by an irrigation canal.

It was something she had seen in a stone trance.

She looked up from her work as the door bell—an old cowbell on a twine pulley—sounded. Sighing again, she padded down and opened the door.

The old woman's face was familiar. "Mrs. Gupta," Teresa said. She encountered Mrs. Gupta periodically at the fruit and vegetable stalls out along the market canal. The suggestion of familiarity destroyed any hope she'd had of turning the woman away; she said resignedly, "Come in."

Mrs. Gupta shuffled inside, frail in a faded yellow sari. "I don't mean to disturb you." Her voice was faint, her accent bleached by years in the Floats. "It's just I heard . . . somebody said you do memories."

"I do, yes. Sometimes."

"Would you try? For me?" She peered up at Teresa through magnifying lenses set in wire. "I have money."

"It's all right . . . you don't have to pay."

"That's nice," Mrs. Gupta said placidly.

They went up to the workshop. Mrs. Gupta gazed enviously at the broad wooden floor, at the tall leaded windows Byron had liberated from a grain terminal out in the old city harbor. A balcony surrounded the second floor, and Teresa had hung spider ferns along the western wing of it; the ferns cooled and filtered the afternoon light. For the Floats her studio represented a luxury of space and air. She had subsidized it with cash from private sales; her artwork had been fashionable these last few seasons.

She could guess a great deal about Mrs. Gupta just by looking at her. A refugee, probably; probably one of the wave of displacees airlifted in from the Madras reactor accident decades ago. Since the unemployment riots of the twenties, the Floats had been in effect a borderless state, haven for refugees of all kinds, a collecting basin for the marginal people who could not survive in the crowded boom cities of the coast. People like Mrs. Gupta, Teresa thought.

People like me.

The old woman said, "May I see the stone?"

Teresa brought it out from the drawer of an ancient wicker desk. It was not an original stone but a copy, grown in Byron's overheated laboratory. Technically, her possession of it was a violation of federal and state law. But in the Floats such laws were seldom observed and almost never enforced.

Mrs. Gupta held it a moment in one arthritic brown hand. The stone had been polished but not faceted; it was an irregular octahedron the size of a grape. The peculiar latticing of its molecules drew the eye inward; the old woman stared. "People say they come from far away."

"Brazil," Teresa said.

"The sky," Mrs. Gupta said.

"Well, yes. It's true. The sky."

The old woman nodded and handed it back. "What should I do?"

"Nothing yet." Teresa pulled up a chair opposite her. "You want to remember?"

The old woman nodded. Her turtle eyes regarded Teresa gravely. "It's been a long time. I was married. Before Madras. His name was Jawarhalal. He died in the Event. I *do* remember—I spend a lot of time remembering. But time passes." She shrugged. "It gets dim."

"I'll do what I can," Teresa said. "But I can't promise. Do you understand?"

"Yes."

Teresa closed the stone in her fist.

She did not do this often. It was too much like a parlor trick, too much like something a charlatan might do for money. Word had spread through the Floats that she had the skill, and so once or twice a week, people like Mrs. Gupta would show up at her door. Old people. *Help me remember.* And so she would rescue some fraction of their lives from the rolling surf of oblivion. Their pleas were heartfelt and often heartbreaking, and Teresa could not bring herself to resist them.

Though of course there was a terrible irony in it.

She closed the gem in her left hand and with her right clasped Mrs. Gupta's dry, ancient fingers.

She closed her eyes.

The images erupted at once. They were distinct and colorful, and if it were not for the necessity of describing them to Mrs. Gupta, she might have allowed them to become more real: sights and sounds and odors. "A stony beach." She envisioned it from a position up the littoral. "There are people in the waves. Children. The stones go up into a sort of wall. Old stone buildings behind it—a temple of some kind."

She heard the rasp of the old woman's indrawn breath. "The beach at Mahabalipuram." Faintly: "We went there, yes. . . ."

She did not see Mrs. Gupta but felt her presence, a hovering sense of self. "You're there," she said. "You're wearing a blue sari. It feels like real silk. Very fine. Your hair is tied back. Wire glasses. And the mark on the forehead, the, uh—"

"Tika." It was a whisper.

"The wind is off the ocean," Teresa said. "The sky is clean and clear. It's not hot. The children are laughing. You have a shawl. . . ."

She could not say where they came from or how she derived them, but she paged through the memories for almost an hour, the beach at Mahabalipuram, the family *charpoy*, a holiday in New Delhi. It faded at last into a single stark vision of the fractured, blackened dome of the Madras reactor, a soldier wielding the butt of his rifle; she kept the image to herself. "I'm sorry," she said. "That's all."

Mrs. Gupta nodded and stood up. She was not visibly moved, but Teresa sensed the old woman's gratitude.

At the door Mrs. Gupta turned and said, "Is it true what they say about you?"

She stood warily in the foyer. "What do they say about me?"

"That you came out of the fire a dozen years ago. That you don't remember your childhood."

She nodded slowly. "Yes. It's true."

"You can't do what you did for me—use the stone to remember?"

"No," Teresa said.

Mrs. Gupta bobbed her head, accepting this strange intelligence. "May I come back? There are other things," she said, "other times—"

"Come back if you like," Teresa said. "But I should warn you. I'll be away for a while."

She closed the door.

That night she was full of anxiety.

By choice she lived alone. By choice she lived in the Floats. Since her gallery successes, she could have bought ID and moved to the coast, lived fashionably there for a while. But the pontoon city soothed her. It was a *barrio bajo*—a slum, but it was also *el otro barrio*—a separate world. In spite of or maybe because of this poverty, the Floats preserved a certain low-rent gentility she inevitably missed when she visited the mainland. The mainland world changed rapidly and often, and the most successful of its denizens were too often the most voracious—the predators. Here, the presumption of failure served as a great equalizer.

Too, she liked the nearness of the ocean. All this water had been locked in by the huge federal tidal dams, sheltered from the excesses of the sea but exposed to its gentler moods. On rainy days she would walk out along the concrete margins of the seawall and watch the clouds angle in from the western horizon. The ocean talked to her; sometimes— not tonight—it soothed her to sleep.

So why are you leaving?

She lay in bed and groped for an answer.

The journey she was contemplating might be danger- ous. She knew that. It would be a vacation, Wexler had told her, much deserved, and only incidentally a courier run. But Byron was more skeptical. They would be entering a realm, he said, in which nations and criminals had long since grown indistinguishable. "Hard money," Byron had said, "and hard people." For years the Exotic stones had been the pivot of progress, the world's single most valuable resource. They had capsized the sovereignty of nations and the supremacy of corporate empires; a protracted war had been waged over them. In this environment, smuggling— even the sort Cruz Wexler had planned—was more than a risky business.

But I have to go, she thought. She felt the pressure. She could not continue doing for people like Mrs. Gupta what she could not do for herself. She had unearthed, these last three years, a nugget of herself, and that was good; but it was insufficient and incomplete.

She was insane to go. In the Floats, because of her artwork and her affinity for the dreamstones, people sometimes called her crazy. "Crazy Teresa," they said.

They thought it was a joke. But tonight, lying sleepless in her bed, faint moonlight etching out the silhouettes of the spider plants across the floorboards, she wondered if it was.

When she did sleep, she dreamed of the child again.

The child was no older than ten. She was undernourished and ragged; she wore old denims gone at the knees, cheap athletic shoes tied with twine, a bowl haircut. She stood in limbo, somehow spotlit. Her arms and legs were thin. But it was her eyes Teresa would remember.

They were very wide, very old, terribly knowing.

Teresa, in her dream, was trapped by the pressure of those eyes. She wanted to turn away; she could not.

"Find me," the girl said. "Help me. Find me."

She woke up sweating. The darkness was expansive. She pulled her angular knees up to her breasts and hugged herself. It was at times like this that she felt most profoundly alone.

"All right," she said into the darkness.

The balsa rocked silently in the swell. The wind from the sea lifted gauze curtains like wings.

"All right." It was a whisper. "I'll do what you want. Just leave me alone."

2.   In the morning Byron came in a motor launch down a crowded market canal with the stranger, the man from the mainland. The stranger's name was Raymond Keller.

Teresa had agreed to accept a third person on their journey. She had, however, retained veto power over Byron's choice. It seemed now like a wise decision. Looking at Raymond Keller, she was not certain she wanted to spend much time with him.

She led both men up to the narrow balcony that surrounded her studio, to the wicker chairs there. Byron made introductions; she brought out iced bottles of Mexican beer; the three of them sat. Strange mixture, she thought. Byron, of course, looked displaced in almost any rational setting. He cultivated the look: outlaw 'lith chemist, wild veteran of the Brazilian War, scarred and tattooed and inscrutable behind his moon-shaped lenses.

This new man (Byron had said) was also a veteran. He wore an old flak jacket, carried a battered duffel—he looked the role. Perhaps too much so. She distrusted the opacity of his pale blue eyes, the way he scrutinized her when he thought she wasn't looking. She had seen too many of these people in the galleries, urban operators with an eye to the main chance. They came out of the dry conduit suburbs of the Valley as if from an assembly line, slick and soulless.

They talked in general terms about the war. Byron had been Keller's platoon Angel, he said, and then Keller had become an Angel himself. Unlike Byron, Keller had kept his wires. Keller worked for the Network and would be recording the journey in its entirety.

Byron had explained some of this before. "You understand," he'd said, "Ray does his own editing. Mostly he wants the footage of Pau Seco. If we appear at all in the material he hands over to the Network, names and faces are systematically altered. There's no threat to us."

"I don't understand," she had said, "why we need him."

"Because he's been there," Byron said. "Because he knows the territory. Because—up to a point—I trust him."

"You think Wexler is lying?"

"I think he's fallible," Byron had replied.

And now this man, this Angel, wired, was sitting and

regarding her with his distant blue eyes. It was strange to think about.

She excused herself and brought out a sketchpad and a carbon pencil from her studio. She gave them to Keller. "Ray," she said, "would you do me a favor?"

He hesitated, nodded.

"Draw me a picture," she said. "While we talk. Will you do that?"

"I'm not an artist."

"Doesn't matter."

He frowned at the blank page of the sketchpad. "Picture of what?"

"Yourself."

He gave her a long look but nodded yes.

She said, "I guess Byron's told you what we have planned."

"The basics. We all go down into the interior. We bring back a new stone."

She nodded. "It's more complicated, of course. Cruz Wexler is financing the trip. You know Wexler?"

"He runs some kind of institute up in Carmel."

Byron said, "He's been putting money into the 'lith underground for a long time. The news now is that there's a new kind of 'lith coming out of the Pau Seco mine. The theory is that the Pau Seco astrobleme was a single chunk of data-intensive memory, and that the core samples coming up now have been better preserved, less degraded over the centuries. Wexler's been trying to buy one through the standard black market—out the back door of the government labs—but the lid is on very tight. So he arranged the Pau Seco purchase direct from source. We are his couriers."

"Paid," Keller said.

"In my case," Byron said. "I stand to make money. Professionally speaking."

Teresa said, "I volunteered."

He turned his eyes on her. "It matters that much to you?"

She watched Keller's pencil move absently over the sketch paper. She nodded. "Yes. It does."

"Byron says you're a dreamstone addict."

"Addict is maybe the wrong word. For most people, you know, it's not a very satisfying drug."

"It makes visions," Keller said.

"It does more than that. You ever try it, Ray?"

He shook his head no.

She said, "It's powerful. Direct interaction with the mind. It's not a chemical, there's no chemical effect. The lab people can't explain it. But you touch a stone . . . worlds open for you. Can you understand that?"

"I don't know." He shrugged. "Maybe."

At least it was an honest answer. She had met plenty of 'lith chemists in the Floats and plenty of dealers, and their attitude toward the Exotic stones was too often purely exploitative. For them it *was* a drug, an item of contraband, a more esoteric variation on the Schedule One neuropeptides that had proven so popular in the coastal cities. That was the odd thing about the stones, she thought: something different for everyone. For the laboratory technicians they were data-intensive Rosetta Stones from the ancient stars, decodable and immensely profitable; for the chemists and their urban customers they were a new drug, a visionary diversion. . . .

And for me?

Well. A road, she thought. A destination.

She wondered if Raymond Keller was capable of understanding that.

She said, "I can't see making this trip with somebody I don't trust. Byron says you're a good guy, Ray. But I can't *know* that. Right? I can only guess. Intuition is all I have right now, you understand?"

He nodded.

She said, "So show me your picture."

He looked down at it as if it had slipped his mind. Picture? But his hands had been busily at work. That was what she wanted.

She took the sketchpad and held it in her lap. Surprisingly, the drawing displayed a certain amount of talent. It was a head-and-shoulders portrait, ragged but complete. It was also, she thought, immensely revealing. Keller had done the outline in hard angular strokes; the eyebrows were single slashes, the mouth an emotionless compaction of pencil carbon. Soulless, she thought. But the eyes redeemed him. Around the eyes Keller's pencil lines had softened; the pupils were deep and dimensional, the expression pained.

She thought, *He is not what he believes himself to be*. Hard, oh yes. But she looked at the eyes and thought, *Redeemable*.

It was enough.

"We leave in a couple of days," she said.

CHAPTER 3

The oneiroliths, the Exotic stones, had shaped Keller's past and created his history. What he had told Teresa was more or less true—he had never held one in his hand for more than a moment. But he dreamed of them persistently.

His dreams were jungle panoramas, condensed video scenarios in which he, Keller, was simultaneously narrator and protagonist. In some he was that anonymous *forao* who had stumbled out of the Brazilian hinterland clutching a strange gemstone, afraid of the visions it produced but anxious to sell it, frustrated when he could not, fearful when the stone was at last impounded by the Valverde government. In the dream he was tortured by FUNAI officials (though there was no real evidence of this) who demanded to know the precise location of the discovery. A nation, they explained, cannot be sustained indefinitely by gold and bauxite. Tell us, they said calmly, and plied him with electrodes.

Dissolve to aerial shot. *The Amazon:* jungle, farms, ranches, dams, wilderness mostly—the languid snake of the eponymous river brown and sunlit in it. He dreamed history in sepia tones: four times the Amazon Basin had repulsed the invasion of civilized men. It cast out, chastened and scythed by dysentery, the Portuguese *bandeirantes* who came in search of El Dorado. It allowed the Jesuits only a little more grace before it reclaimed their missions, lost to crumbling government support and the unassailable hugeness of the wilderness. Briefly, there had been the rubber boom, the jungle had been invaded for its latex groves— but the Malaysians grew better trees on more accessible plantations. And in the closing years of the twentieth century there had been a more prolonged effort to settle the interior: highways had been built, villages founded, oil wells and mines created; all fueled, however, by an international debt so enormous it could not be sustained. And so these small oases had come crashing down. Villages had gone to ghost towns, vines had crept across the roads.

Now a fifth invasion.

Montage shot. The tin-and-paper slums around Rio and São Paulo, reservoirs struck by lightning, pour out human rivers to the west. Machines penetrate the jungle or streak through the air above it.

The dreamstones, dubbed "oneiroliths" by a bemused Federal University geologist, were more valuable than even a greedy *forao* could have imagined. There was talk— hushed, then skeptical, finally awed—of their extraterrestrial origin. Carbon tests were of course meaningless; but the small stones must have lain a considerable time in the shallow soil of the Basin, relics of some astronomical impact vastly older than the *bandeirantes*. Moreover, the oneiroliths were not merely passive. They were encoded, deeply layered with information, every molecule a dictionary of atoms, a syntax of electrons. Their language was binary and universal. They contained a new physics, a new cybernetics; they hinted at wholly new technologies.

The implication was obvious. Control of the oneiroliths was control of the planet's economic and political future. In a century that had begun without fanfare twenty years earlier, the discovery was interpreted as a token, at last, of real change: the New Reconstruction, the industrial re-shaping of a global economy. For the first time since the ecological debates, the great powers focused their attention on the Brazilian hinterland. A new kind of *forao* began to invade the wilderness. The impact site—a deposit of frag-mentary stones miles broad and indefinitely deep—was staked and claimed according to ancient Brazilian mineral-rights laws.

There were of course obstacles to this millennium. The Valverde regime was in political trouble. Insurgents had captured a provincial capital; there was the possibility that vital roads might be endangered.

Intervention was called for. A methodical war was undertaken.

Here, Keller's nightmares became more personal.

His second night in the Floats a storm came up, sheets of tepid rain off the ocean, and Keller sat drinking with Byron Ostler under the tin eaves of Byron's bamboo patio. The water here was dense with balsas and boat shanties, twining among the open waterways the locals called canals. It was an artists' neighborhood, boat shacks lit up with Chinese lanterns, silhouettes of windwheels churning against the watery glow of the urban mainland; there was only the faint rocking of the floorboards to remind him that they were balanced a half mile out over the continental shelf, precar-ious on a foundation of pontoons and anchors.

Byron talked about Teresa, drinking Mexican beer from a squat bottle and plugging memory cards into a music generator. Keller, listening, gazed out across a canal of dark water.

"She's not in danger," Byron said. "I believe that. *We're* not in danger. Wexler has it all set up." He pulled at his beer. "Any sign of danger, Ray, I would bring her back. No question. But it was her project from the beginning. She was with Wexler in Carmel when he set up the trip—she may have helped talk him into it.''

Maybe, Keller thought. But she had impressed him mainly with her fragility. Something in the broad set of her mouth, the curious downturn of her eyes. If Byron claimed to care for her, Keller thought, then maybe he should have found a way out of this. He said, ''Still—''

''I *know*.'' The 'lith chemist stood up and tossed his empty bottle into the dark canal beyond the railing of his float shack. ''Whatever you mean to say, Ray, I thought of it, all right? It matters to me what happens to her. It really does. But she *needs* to go. She has this thing about the stones. She needs to go farther . . . deeper. . . .''

Keller said, ''You sold it to her.''

There was a silence, and Keller was briefly afraid he might have overstepped the bounds of this old, awkward friendship. But then Byron said quietly, ''I didn't sell it to her. I gave it to her.''

Keller gazed patiently across the water.

''Three years ago,'' the chemist said. ''You didn't see her, Ray. She was making money hawking scrap metal to the galleries and spending it all on lab opiates. Synthetic enkephalins. Very, very bad. She came to me with a wad of cash in her hand, and her hand was, you know, like a claw, anorexic. 'You sell 'liths,' she said. I said yeah. I got to know her a little. She showed me where she lived— a corner of an old bulk-oil terminal in the harbor slums, stick furniture and a Mason jar full of pills. I brought in a doctor to look at her. He said her neuropeptides were seriously unbalanced. She was courting death. I mean that. Dancing with it. I said, 'You'll die.' She didn't even answer; she just nodded—it was true, so what. But the stone was a new thing for her. One more drug, I guess she thought, but it didn't turn out that way. She took it in her hand—''

''Visions,'' Keller said.

''It doesn't work for everybody. For her it was all there. New worlds. She wanted to get it down somehow. I bought her the tools for these crystal paintings she's been doing, trance landscapes. We weaned her off the enkephalins until her neurochemistry settled down, and she's been clean ever since.'' He held up a bony hand. "Three *years*."

"The stones did that?"

"I guess they did. Sometimes . . ." Byron smiled hollowly. "Sometimes I like to think I did it."

"But she's going to Pau Seco," Keller said.

The chemist peered out across the float shacks, the canal of dark seawater.

"It was a deal she made," he said softly. "I think that's all it ever was. I tried to check out her history, found out she doesn't have one. She came out of the big fire back in '37; she was only a kid, third-degree burns and no parents and traumatic memory loss. A refugee family took her in, named her—she didn't even have a name. And then she started on the pills. Killing herself, you know, but slowly. And the stones didn't change that. They touched something inside her, woke her up a little bit, but it was only ever a truce." He regarded Keller bleakly. "A little détente between Teresa and death. But the stones we have aren't whole, Ray. They're like pictures torn out of a magazine. Whatever she sees in there, she needs to see it more clearly."

Keller said, "She might not find what she wants. She might be going down there to die."

"Or live," Byron replied. His fists were clenched. He said firmly, "I believe that."

A little unsteadily, half drunk now, Byron led Keller back into the houseboat, to a lower level, sealed, underwater maybe—it was claustrophobic—through a dim stucco anteroom in which a single red light burned.

"Here," he said quietly, opening a second door. "You wanted to see it? Here."

It took a while for Keller's eyes to adjust.

There were vats and vats of dark fluid moving in the swell. The room was swelteringly hot. Must have a generator down here somewhere, Keller thought. Christ! It was almost spooky . . . a thousand ongoing gestations in those photophobic jars, silent and quite alien.

This was where Byron grew his dreamstones.

Keller recorded it all meticulously. He was an Angel;

it was his job. Everything he saw, everything he'd seen since the moment Leiberman installed his memory, was spooling down indelibly into his AV memory. Ultimately, the chip behind his spine would contain thousands of hours of raw experience, footage (it was still called "footage") no camera could ever capture.

Byron displayed his work with a flourish of drunken pride Keller could not assay for sincerity. "It's the same technology they use in the government labs. Just scaled down a little. The fluid in the vats is a supersaturated solution, only a little more complex than seawater. Given the medium, the rest is simple. The 'liths reproduce. 'Reproduce' is maybe not the correct word—they aren't technically living things—but I don't know what else you'd call it. The stone releases a transcriptaselike substance, which acts as a kind of seed crystal. New stones grow around it. Identical copies. You can't tell the new from the old. The technology for growing stones was among the first data downloaded from the first significant samples, which means whoever made these things devoted a lot of redundancy to it. The Exotics—whoever they are or were—wanted us to spread these things around."

He could hear the fascination in Byron's voice. Byron had come into the military a college draftee, and when he was excited, curiously, it was the working-class patois that dropped away—he began to use words like "redundancy."

In the fogged depths of the Chemware vats, Keller discerned the faint colors and cloudy shapes of new, nascent stones. Mineral life. He felt their strangeness like an aura.

"They're indestructible," Byron said. "They fracture along their axes of symmetry, but they cannot be burned, drilled, or dissolved. Theoretically, if you could collect all the Brazilian stones in one place, you could put them together like a puzzle. Topologically they're mostly orthorhombic or triclinic—those are the most common shapes. No one can say exactly what they're made of. The evidence is that they've been engineered—the substance of them has been engineered—down beyond the subatomic level. Complex micropotentials propagate along the axes of symmetry, which is how the lab people tap in. Their observable physical properties are very strange, and it has been suggested that they exist in several more than three dimensions."

"Serious medicine," Keller said.

"Serious indeed."

"You used it," Keller said, "to save her life."

He saw Byron's expression harden in the dim light. "You could say so."

"You care that much?"

There was a pause. He said, "I'm not drunk enough to have this conversation."

Keller persisted, "But you're worried about her."

"I'm worried about Brazil. This new stone. Not just that it's physically dangerous." He shook his head. "Sometimes I think it'll be okay. I really believe that. Maybe better than okay. We go down, we come back, she finds what she wants. Maybe we have a life together." He added faintly, defensively, "She might consider it. . . ."

"And if she doesn't find what she wants?"

"Then she might die. She might let herself die. This time I might not be able to stop her."

Keller slept half drunk, riding the swell in a bamboo-frame bed and dreaming of a manioc field in Rondonia. Large words circled like birds inside him. *Amnesia, agnosia, dysphasia, aphasia.* In the dream he could only see the left sides of things; when he spoke, the words came out skewed and hollow.

He woke at dawn with a halo of sweat on his pillow-case.

He bought lunch at a stall near the tidal dam. Byron arrived after noon, smiling blankly, and handed him an envelope containing his black-market ID, a passport, and a plane ticket to Brazil.

CHAPTER 4

1.   They arched up beyond the curvature of the Earth in an AeroBrazil jumpflight, briefly spaceborne; but the journey was not so much outward, Keller thought, as inward —into the Basin, into the strip mine of Pau Seco, into the past. Gliding down the arc of the trajectory, he wondered whether there was not some hidden momentum that had carried him here, his mind's own traitorous clambering into the abyss of memory.

The wheel, Byron had said. It was a bad and persistent thought.

The plane banked toward the floating runways of Guanabara Bay, past the statue of Christ the Savior threadbare and alone up windy Corvocado Mountain. Last time he came here, Keller had been a nineteen-year-old draftee riding a military transport, and the statue dominating the mountain-top had been his first signal that he was entering strange territory: this weatherbeaten Christ, granite eyes unfocused, hands raised in mute blessing over a city as big as the horizon. Seeing it again, Keller felt his fingers tighten against the armrests. He had vowed once that if he were allowed to leave this country, he would never come back . . . an old but fervent promise, and it echoed with painful irony in the roar of the aircraft cabin.

"You all right?" Teresa asked, and Keller managed to nod.

"Be fine," he said, thinking *wu-nien*, abstracting himself, retreating down the icy corridors of his cultivated aloofness—taking refuge there.

They had to wait overnight for their connection to the capital. Byron, extravagant with Wexler's credit line, had booked them a room in one of the bone-white hotels over-looking the bay. "Only the best," he said. But Keller had fixed his attention on Teresa, on her profile as she peered ahead through the window of the transit bus.

The image was spooling down into his memory chip, but most of this was wasted footage, trivial and hardly dramatic. Too, by the final edit she would have become a stranger, her features systematically altered beyond recognition: protecting his sources. Keller was, in his own word-less way, a journalist, and he understood the necessity of editing, of extracting significance from the raw ore of ex-perience. Still, the finished product never failed to surprise him. He had felt that way about the last Network project he had worked on, an exposé of the joywire underground. He had spent three months in hospitals, in lean-tos, in the grimmest recesses of the Floats. He had grown to know some of these men (almost always men, mostly combat veterans) who had accessed the deep reward centers of their brains and who burned out slowly, like wax candles, in the neglected corners of the urban nuclei. He thought sometimes that what he saw, the tertiary stages of their terrible ad-diction, must surely cauterize the wires in his own head, overload the circuits, defy memory. It had tested the limits of his *wu-nien,* his old Army training. He had cared perhaps too much about these people whose deaths had become inevitable.

The documentary aired in prime time and drew a respectable market share through the urban Pacific Rim. Keller's footage was embedded among statistics and interviews and a pious commentary. The documentary was not exploitative, and he was not ashamed of his work; still, he thought, it was amazing how these events lost their impact, translated through the flat glaze of a video screen. Even the deaths he had witnessed—digital traces of his immediate experience, enhanced and polished for the final cut—had become squalid but somehow inevitable, a logical consequence of the schematic flow of events.

It tested his faith. Faith, he thought, was not too strong a word. He believed in what he was doing; he was not cynical about his work. The joywire documentary had fueled the demand for publicly-funded rehab clinics; some lives had been saved. He believed in his objectivity, in his ability to become a dispassionate witness; he believed it was important.

And yet . . . in the face of such horror, wasn't "objectivity" itself a little monstrous?

He talked it over with Byron after the documentary aired. "You dignify it," Byron said, "with all these words. All the Angel Zen they taught you back in Santarem. But maybe that's not what it is. Maybe it's a side effect from the neural harness. Flat affect. Maybe you don't know how to care anymore, maybe you can only piss and moan over *whether* you care. Or maybe it's something else."

"What?"

Byron hesitated. "Fear," he said at last. "Cowardice."

No, Keller thought.

You cope, he thought, that's what matters. Some things were simply too terrible to bear. You *have* to look away, that's the truth of it . . . and if you cannot look away, you have to learn how to look for the sake of looking.

Vision without desire. The perfect mirror.

They rode an elevator up to their room, Byron pressed

his thumb against the lock, and through the window Keller once more confronted the Christ of Corvocado Mountain across the blue angle of the bay.

This country made you, the statue seemed to say. *This country is your mother and your father.*

Teresa moved to the window, obscuring the view. "We're wasting time here," she said. "We should have gone straight on to the capital."

"We're tourists," Byron said. "What does it matter? A day or two—"

"I can feel it," she said. Her eyes were distant. "Sounds crazy, right? But I know it's out there. Pau Seco. The place the stones come from. Buried out in the Basin all those centuries." She gave a small, involuntary shiver. "I want to go there."

"Soon enough," Byron said.

Keller nodded, uneasy now in spite of himself: *soon enough.*

2.   They rode a domestic flight into Brasilia.

It was the interior at last, the old white chess-piece city scoured by the winds of the *planalto,* set like an island in this sea of poverty and forest. For two decades hard currency had been rivering into the capital, and while it had done nothing to alleviate the squalor in the barrios and the box cities, it had in part paid for the scaling and renovation of this antique landmark, the last century's stern vision of the future. The chief industry of Brasilia was government; all these buildings were government buildings.

For a few days they lived like tourists in another big hotel, breakfast in the Continental Lounge, sunlight in the rooftop gardens. Keller, idle, found himself watching Teresa. She spent a lot of time in the pool—as if it reminded her of home, of the Floats or the distant ocean—moving through the water with an absentminded grace. And yet there was this alertness about her, somber and intent. He thought of the time she must have spent with the oneiroliths, artifacts from some unknowably distant world: as if some of that strangeness had rubbed off on her.

He watched her. He was aware of Byron watching her.

On the third day they caught a bus into the city and rode an elevator up the white glass tower of the SUDAM building, the monolithic Superintendency of the Amazon, the agency that controlled the development of the vast Brazilian hinterland. Byron had obtained from Cruz Wexler the name of a friendly SUDAM bureaucrat, Augusto Oliveira. Oliveira's receptionist downloaded their ID into her desktop processor and told them in unaccented English to wait, please, Mr. Oliveira was in conference.

They waited through most of the morning in the plush, relentlessly bright office. Keller had picked up some rough Portuguese during the war, and he spent a little time deciphering the legend on Oliveira's door; far as he could tell, it was DEPARTMENT OF MINES, MAPS, AND DOCUMENTS. Oliveira himself appeared shortly before noon. His inner office was a sanctuary of wall windows and broad, flat filing cabinets. Outside, a rack of cumulus clouds cruised above the microwave dishes that crowned the old white buildings.

Oliveira waved them into chairs and gazed at them aloofly. Byron cleared his throat and said, "We're from Cruz Wexler. He said you could get us—"

Oliveira's look became aggrieved. "Please," he said. "Don't mention that name here. I have no connection with Cruz Wexler." He added, "I know who you are."

"We want to get into Pau Seco," Byron said. "The rest of it doesn't matter."

"Everybody wants to get into Pau Seco. Obviously. Pau Seco."

"Is it possible?"

"It may be." Oliveira hooked his hands behind his back. "You want to own a plot, is that it? Dig in the dirt? Become *garimpeiros*?"

"Just visit," Byron said stiffly.

"Pau Seco is seldom visited. Journalists are forbidden. Foreigners of any kind are very unusual. Really, you're asking a lot."

"Wexler said—" Byron caught himself, glowered. "We were told it would be possible."

"Possible but dangerous."

Oliveira moved behind his desk, thumbed his intercom, and said something in Portuguese to his secretary. A cavernous silence fell over the room. Byron crossed his arms and leaned back, scowling. Oliveira watched calmly. Keller understood that the bureaucrat was savoring their discomfort now. In return he watched Oliveira closely: he did not doubt this footage would find its way on to the Network, set amidst some stern dicta regarding the corruption of government officials.

Oliveira gazed at them silently until his secretary arrived with a *cafezinho:* dense, fragrant coffee in a thimble-sized cup. He drank it back convulsively and said, "How much do you know about Pau Seco?"

"It's the mine," Teresa said, "where the oneiroliths come from."

"It's a hole in the jungle," Oliveira said, "where thirty thousand men are attempting to become wealthy. It's also a national security area. The military is in charge. Anarchy and martial law—both, you understand? Here, look."

He tapped a keyboard. Keller sat forward: the surface of Oliveira's desk had become a topological map, black contour lines on a field of gently glowing blue.

"The Pau Seco mine," Oliveira said.

The scale was immense.

"It's operated the way the gold mines at Serra Pelada were operated. Foreign powers came in very quickly back in the twenties, you understand? The land was surveyed, there were sophisticated interferographs made of the soil beneath. But in the end it was Brazil that prevailed. Our antique mineral-rights laws." Light from the liquid-crystal display played up the soft angles of Oliveira's face. Absorbed now, he swept his hand over the desktop. "This is where the Exotic deposits appear. All this territory. Ten square miles of mud and clay, progressively less rich from the core deposit, here. The government allots the land in units of four square meters. For a brief time, years ago, the plots were sold cheaply. Now they're auctioned. No one may own more than one, and it must be worked for the owner to retain title. Any given plot may produce nothing . . . but understand that even a small stone, a small onei-

rolith, is worth at least three hundred million cruzeiros."
He shrugged loftily. "Someday this may end. We may
decipher all there is to be deciphered from these artifacts.
The secrets of the universe, hm? And then Pau Seco will
go back to jungle and all the *garimpeiros* can go home.
Maybe that day is coming. But not yet. Every stone we
unearth sheds new light, reveals a little more of the puzzle.
Once its data have been abstracted, of course, the stone
loses its enormous value . . . it might be duplicated, it might
even find its way into the black market as a sort of drug."
He looked at Byron and smiled. "But I wouldn't know
about that. At Pau Seco the government buys the stones
directly from the *garimpeiros* and takes a commission against
their value on the international market. They may not be
sold or traded privately. The price we offer is competitive
. . . and there is the military to prevent smuggling."

Teresa's eyes were fixed on the top map. She said
contritely, "We'll need a permit to get in—"

"Get in! If you go to Pau Seco, you'll need a permit
to eat, a permit to sleep, a permit to piss—"

"Can you get us these permits?"

Oliveira became haughty. "It's been arranged." He
waved his hand: it was trivial, a nonissue. "But I want you
to be prepared. There are no hotels in Pau Seco, you understand? There is only mud and shit and disease. Are those
familiar words? You might get dirty."

"Wouldn't be the first time," Byron said.

Oliveira switched off the top map. The blue glow faded.
"No," he said. "I don't imagine it would."

His secretary gave them their documents on the way
out: thick sheafs of buff-colored paper with the SUDAM
stamp embossed on every leaf.

"Thank you for your patience," she said politely.

CHAPTER 5

1. The irony, Oliveira thought later, was that because Brazil had become essential to the world, it had been lost to the Brazilians.

It was inevitable from the moment the Valverde regime called on the Pacific Rim nations for military aid. They had come more than willingly. The Japanese, the Koreans, the Americans. They had come, and in an important way they had never left. Brazil controlled the resource that controlled the world . . . but the world controlled Brazil.

He felt no loyalty to the man who had approached him through the American embassy. Oberg was his name. A man with thinning hair and a faint, obscured Texas accent; a man who looked like a schoolteacher and who was, beyond doubt, something far less pleasant. Oberg worked for the

Agencies, the integrated complex of intelligence-gathering and enforcement bureaus that constituted a second and largely covert American government. Things being what they were, Oliveira owed the man a certain deference. But not loyalty.

But he felt no loyalty either to Cruz Wexler—a bourgeois cultist with highly-placed contacts in Brazil and an American's faith in the corruptibility of foreign governments. And certainly Oliveira owed nothing to the three innocents who had appeared in his office today.

And without loyalty, Oliveira thought as he punched up Oberg's telephone code—without loyalty there is no such thing as betrayal.

Oberg answered personally. His face was flat and oblique across the plane of Oliveira's video screen. In the room behind him Oliveira saw a stone window, a stand of mimosa. Oberg looked at Oliveira and said simply—a soft, suppressed twang in his voice—"They've come, then?"

"They were here. I gave them the documents."

"You're certain it was them? The man and the woman?"

"They fit the description. And one other."

Oberg seemed taken aback. "An American?"

Oliveira nodded casually and sketched out a description of Keller. Oberg scribbled notes. "I'll want a photograph," the Agency man said finally, "plus any information the man gave you."

The voice commanded obedience. Oliveira was a professional subaltern, and he understood the mechanism of command. It came naturally from men like Oberg. Oberg had the look of command: even over the telephone he seemed tensed, poised to spring. If we were dogs, Oliveira thought, I would have to offer my throat to him. "Surely," Oliveira said, performing the obeisance but resenting it, the necessity of it.

But Oberg had been surprised to hear about the third man, Keller. *You are not so omniscient after all,* he thought, watching as Oberg's image faded from the CRT. *You have something to learn yet.*

The thought produced a flicker of satisfaction. He rang his secretary and asked for a second *cafezinho.*

2.   Keller sat out on the walled portico of their hotel room, the evening of their last day in Brasilia, and watched the daytime traffic streaming out of the city, bureaucrats in boxlike Chinese automobiles and secretaries in crowded buses as the sun angled down toward the *planalto*.

After a time Teresa pushed through the beaded curtains and joined him. She had the documents in her hand, the papers they had brought back from Oliveira's office. The name on her documents was Teresa Maria Rafael, the name they had downloaded from her black-market ID: the name her adoptive family had given her, Byron had said, in the months after the fire.

She pulled up a chair next to him. Her expression was thoughtful—had been, Keller thought, since their encounter with Oliveira. "It's strange," she said finally. "When you think about it. I mean, that ordinary people do this."

Keller made a questioning noise.

"Well, it just struck me. You hear words like 'smuggler' and 'criminal.' It's like something out of the Network nightlies. But that's what we are, isn't it? Smugglers and criminals."

"In somebody's eyes," Keller agreed. "Does it scare you?"

"I think it does. Now that we're here. Back in the Floats it was Wexler's project. Wexler set it up, Wexler paid money, we were doing him a favor. Down here . . . it's just us, isn't it?" She looked away. "Oliveira scares me," she said. "There's something ugly about him. I don't trust him."

Keller waved at the sheaf of papers in her hand: "If he were trustworthy, he wouldn't have given us these."

"But not just him. There must be others like him. People who want to stop us."

"The enforcement agencies," Keller said. "The Brazilian government, at least potentially."

She said distantly, "It's the real world."

"Too real." He added, on impulse, "You can pull out, you know. It's not too late to buy a ticket home." He shrugged. "Maybe it would be wise."

She stood up and leaned out from the balcony with her elbows on the railing. The last light of the day seemed to surround and contain her. She shook her head. "I'm here for a reason. And I'm not fragile."

"You trust Wexler that much?"

She considered the question. "You don't know him," she said.

"Only what I've heard."

"He was at Harvard for years. Did you know that? He did serious work in cryptology. He did a little contract research before the security people cut him off, so he had access to some of the first Pau Seco stones. Everybody else was plugging them into microchips, you know, downloading data. They all thought it would be this tremendous revelation . . . wisdom from the stars. He thought so too. But he was more fascinated with the human interface. You touch it, it makes visions. Nobody could figure out how it worked, so nobody much cared: it was 'soft data.' But for him it was the only thing."

"Mysticism," Keller said.

"He got into that," she said, "yeah. This idea of wisdom. He says there's nothing on earth we can feel or touch that's truly alien, except the stones. The ultimate Other."

"He made a lot of money."

"He kept all his contacts in the government labs. The academic old-boy circuit. It's easy for him to get stones, or copies of stones, once they've been downloaded. So he controls a large part of the black market up the coast. So yes, he's made money . . . but I believe he's sincere."

Keller said, carefully neutral, "You believe what he says?"

"About the stones?" She shrugged. "I don't know."

"You've had the experience."

"For me," she said quietly, "it has always been more personal." The sun was down now; the sky above the city was a darkly radiant blue. She asked, "Is that possible, Ray? That you can look into something as alien as a dreamstone—look as far and hard as you can—and find yourself looking back?"

He recalled what Byron had told him: Teresa in a shack in the Floats, trading artwork for lab enkephalins. "I'm not fragile," she had said, but it seemed to Keller that she was: fragile and brittle as glass . . . except for this energy that came welling up from inside her, this restlessness.

He felt a twinge of fear for her, and that was bad: *adhyasa,* he thought, Angel sin. He stood up hastily. "Tomorrow we bus to Cuiaba," he said. "Best get some sleep."

The stars had come out above the dark margins of the *planalto.*

3. But she didn't sleep. Too much coffee, she thought, too much to think about. Instead she walked with Byron down the avenue outside the hotel, hoping to tire herself out.

Brasilia was quiet at night. She could hear the flickering buzz of the ancient potassium streetlights, the periodic rumble of a distant truck. Nobody in the streets but a few stray tourists, a few hookers poised at a public fountain. It was unreal, Teresa thought, empty, these antique white towers.

She asked Byron why he brought Keller along.

"We've talked about it. He knows the hinterland. A little protection . . ."

She said, "He's reliable? You trust him?"

"Yes." But his voice was more cautious.

"He's an Angel."

"So? I was an Angel."

"But you changed."

He took her arm. Overhead, in the faint light of the city, she could see the low clouds moving. Byron said, "I could have been like him. I know what it's like for him."

"What *is* it like?"

"You care?"

She shrugged.

He said, "It's like walking in a cloud. You're above everything. Above fear, above your body. Your body's a machine, you move it along, take it where it's supposed to go. Everything is very clear, very lucid, because there's no good or evil, no better or worse. You just look. Everything is what it is. No more, no less."

It stirred a memory in her. "I can see how that might be attractive."

"It is. But it wears you out. It's cold. It's like standing out on some mountain. You get scared to be so far above it all, scared you'll never get down again. And some don't."

"Like Ray?"

"Maybe like Ray."

"But you said you trusted him."

He shrugged. "I think it's always been a hard choice for him. He has some bad memories out of the war, so there's this incentive . . . the need to stay above it. But I think the truth is that he's not comfortable there. Some part of him wants to climb back down. Even after all this time." He looked at her. "This matters to you?"

"I was curious."

They turned back toward the hotel. "It would not be a good idea," Byron said, "to care too much about Ray Keller."

Teresa shrugged.

That night she dreamed again of the nameless girl in rags and twine shoes.

The girl looked at her from the depths of her huge brown eyes. As ever, Teresa was caught up in the urgency of that gaze. Darkness like smoke swirled around her; anxiety filled the turbulent air.

"Almost home now," the girl said faintly. "Almost home."

CHAPTER 6

1. Keller was ten years old when the discovery of the oneiroliths in the Amazon Basin made international headlines. He remembered leaning out the window of the single-bedroom apartment above his father's garage, aiming a polystyrene thread-rifle at a line of dung-brown hills while the TV droned on about "artifacts of extraterrestrial origin." It was a Sunday afternoon and the Public Works had turned on the water supply; his father was down on the tarmac soaping fiberglass car bodies. Keller paid only intermittent attention to the video screen because he knew the whole thing was a lie.

His father had told him so last night. His father sat in the big easy chair which dominated the shabby room and said, "It's bullshit, Ray. Mark my words." Keller thought his father looked disturbingly small in this oversized chair: it emphasized his leanness, the arthritic bulge of his finger joints and elbows, the sparseness of his hair. "Stones from outer space." His adult voice was rich with scorn and authority. He had migrated here from Colorado before Keller was born, had achieved what Keller understood, even then, was an unhappy and marginal life. "Christ almighty, what a crock." Who could doubt it?

His skepticism was short-lived. It was replaced very soon by boredom, and that was pretty much the reaction of the entire country. Interesting things came out of the oneiroliths over the next few years but they were all more or less abstruse: new mathematics, a subtler cosmology. Important but, in the raw, unspectacular. The profounder questions—where had the stones come from, who had left them, why?—went unanswered. In time, no one asked. Speculation was abandoned to cultists, science-fiction writers, and the tabloid newspapers. Out in the real world there were more important things to worry about. The Russians, for instance, smuggling wire missiles and military software to disenfranchised *posseiros* down in the Basin: where might all *that* lead?

"Grade-A bullshit," Keller's father had ruminated from the depths of his chair. Keller nodded to himself and fired his toy rifle thoughtfully at the bole of a palmetto. *Zing,* the rifle said.

Ten years later he had learned to fire a real rifle in a real jungle. Crudely grown crystal 'liths circulated freely among the combat troops in the Basin, and Keller was impressed the first time he saw one: a device, he thought, a kind of machine from another world. But when he held it in his hand, he was suddenly back in that dusty apartment with the smell of gasoline and ancient auto upholstery rivering through the window and the grating echo of his father's voice: *mark my words.* Except that Keller's father was three years in his grave now, a cancer statistic, and the memory was scaldingly vivid—a kind of resurrection. He dropped the stone as if it had moved in his hand, and backed away, gasping.

It had surprised him, that a memory could be so frightening.

The road to Cuiaba was littered with relics of the war. Teresa saw the broken shapes of war machines in the green valleys beside the road, and felt some echo of the violence that must have raged through here.

It was a relatively new road, Keller told her, only a little older than the war. The road was a ribbon of macadam that cut like a geographer's line through the province of Goias, swept on a spidery suspension bridge across the boiling water of the Araguaia and then into the deep Mato Grosso.

The world beyond the bus window startled and impressed her. Strange, she thought, to have come so far so quickly. The horizon was endlessly green as far as she could see, which, when the road wound up a hillside, was very far indeed. A wilderness, she thought. The idea had become stunningly real to her. A wilderness, a place where no cities were, an anarchy of nature. The landscape was as profoundly alien as anything she had seen in a stone trance. The few visible traces of human work—a blackened Army troop carrier showing its chitin through the riotous green, tanagers roosting on its gutted turrets—only reinforced the feeling.

Somewhere out here was the place where Keller had met Byron. Buried history. Somewhere out here, too, was the oneirolith mine. Cruz Wexler's gnosis, the alien, the Other (she had told Keller). And something more personal.

They traveled into the sunset and beyond it. The sky darkened; reading lamps blinked on overhead. Byron pulled his wool cap down over his eyes and slept. Keller was lost in a magazine he had brought from Brasilia. The bus was mostly empty; the other passengers were unhappy businessmen in wrinkled suits, a few Koreans with drugged expressions, snoring *posseiros* in the cheap rear seats. A few tourists . . . *like us,* she thought, and then, *but we're not.* She considered sleep but guessed it was impractical; she felt the pressure of the wilderness too acutely.

A little before midnight Keller reclined his seat and

dozed off. Smiling faintly, she found herself watching him: watching the way his face relaxed into sleep. He looked different, she thought, with all the daylight tension drained out of him.

She thought, *He's an Angel.*

Odd, how easy it was to forget that. Talk to him, she thought, and you could be talking to a million people. Everything he saw was spooling down into his mechanical memory, buried somewhere inside him. Remembering for the masses.

She wondered if he could turn it off . . . whether he would if he could.

She slept in spite of herself. When she woke in the heat of the morning, the wilderness was gone; the bus moved through a steaming box barrio, tin shacks riding up dirty little hills—the outskirts of Cuiaba, Keller said. "It's an ugly town. A meat town. The abattoir is the only real business." He wrinkled his nose. "You can smell it already."

"You were here before?"

"In the war," he said wearily. "It was a staging base. From here we rode carriers out along BR-364. Lots of guerilla activity in the farm towns out that way."

So it had been an Army town. That explained all the signs she had seen in English and in cursive Japanese: Bar & Grill, Live Sex Acts, *manga* outlets. The bus station itself was a cavernous concrete structure crowded with humanity. Old diesel buses filled it with their stinking fumes, and the names written on cardboard signs over the ticket windows were all strange to her: *Ouro Preto,* one said; *Ariquemes,* another. She shouldered her bag and they left the terminal, Byron leading them to some hotel Wexler had told him about; a man would meet them there, Wexler had promised. She felt lost, walking among these ancient colonial buildings. It was a bad neighborhood, more bars, ragged men sleeping on the fractured sidewalks. Down one alley near the hotel she saw a sign that intrigued her: CHURCH OF THE VALE DO AMENHECAR, it said, and in the dusty window beneath it there was the painted image of an upraised hand, a dreamstone radiating from the palm.

We are close now, she thought, and the pronoun

came so naturally to her that she did not notice its strangeness: *we*.

2. From here, as Keller understood the plan, they would cease to be tourists. They would pass, for a day or maybe two, into the *sertao* hinterland. They would be taken to Pau Seco by a truck driver, an expatriate Vietnamese named Ng.

But Ng wasn't at the hotel. No problem, Byron said. They were booked for three days. Ng would be here tomorrow, guaranteed. Day after at the latest.

Keller shrugged, spreading out his bedroll on the floor of the hotel room.

"Hotel" was a generous word. Cuiaba was not in any sense a tourist town. The building was a box of ancient stucco and rotting wood. Byron and Teresa each occupied one of the room's two tiny beds. Keller lay in the dark for a time, aware of the night noises; meat trucks moaning down the narrow streets, the empty distances between the old buildings. Aware, too, of the distance between himself and Teresa, between Byron and Teresa: distances that had become electric with implication.

He understood now—it had taken a few days—how profoundly Byron was in love with her.

Understood, too, that the feeling was not mutual.

It surprised him a little. A decade ago Byron had been the model Angel—slick, aloof, obscure behind protective lenses. It was the image he still projected, dealing dreamstones in the Floats. But with Teresa (Keller saw all this ruthlessly) he was another thing altogether: nervous, gazing at her when he thought she wouldn't see, almost fawning.

Strange, but maybe predictable. Byron had rescued her from a slow suicide: some sense of responsibility had to follow on that. Too, there was this aura of *unfinishedness* about her. She was drawn by strange tides. She had imbibed often and deeply at the well of the oneiroliths. Keller recognized that there was an allure in all this—night territory, dangerous and exotic. He understood the attraction.

Understood it, he thought, maybe too well.

His eyes strayed to the bed where she slept.

In spite of his doubts, in spite of his lapses, he had learned in the years since the war to practice scrupulously the art of *wu-nien*. And he had learned to recognize the threats to that condition. The threats were named Compassion, and Hate, and Desire, and Love. In Angel basic he had been taught to set these things aside as earnestly as a Buddhist monk sets aside the temptations of the flesh. But like the temptations of the flesh, they were difficult to suppress. Suppressed, they were prone to erupt—randomly, unexpectedly.

He lay in the cloistered darkness with his pulse whispering in his ears. In the dim city light through the curtains, he could make out the shape of her body under the blankets—the delicate geography of her.

You know better than to think what you're thinking.

He closed his eyes and worked to make his mind empty. A mirror bright, he thought, echoing the Shen-shiu poem they had all memorized in Angel basic: Carefully we wipe it clean / And let no dust alight.

But the dust *had* alighted, Keller realized. Feelings welled up in him that he had thought long cauterized.

Adhyasa, he thought bleakly. Angel sin.

He woke up wearily; Byron handed him a cup of coffee from the wall dispenser. By midmorning their truck driver still hadn't arrived. Teresa moved restlessly around the room in fatigue pants and a khaki shirt, hands in her pockets, brooding. "I want to go out," she said at last.

"We have to wait here," Byron said. "We have to be here when Ng shows up."

"We don't all have to stay."

Byron drew his head back, drummed his fingers thoughtfully. "Where do you want to go?"

"The church we passed. The dreamstone church."

"It's a Valley church," Byron said. "Jungle cults. You want to sacrifice a chicken? Maybe we can arrange it."

Keller remembered the Valley from the war. The Vale do Amenhecar was a Brazilian stone cult, one of the junk religions that had prospered since the discovery of the 'liths. It was a peasant's religion, wildly syncretic; they believed in sacred jaguars, the divinity of Christ, the imminent arrival of fleets of flying saucers.

"I want to see what it's like," Teresa said. She added quietly, "I have a right."

"It's not safe."

"None of this is safe." She turned to Keller. "You want to come along?"

He said yes without thinking about it.

Byron turned stiffly to the window. Over his shoulder Keller saw the rain sheeting down from a leaden sky. The streets were slick and black. "Go ahead," Byron said coolly. "Pick up some local color." He looked back at Keller, pained. "Why the hell not."

3.   She bought an umbrella at one of the sidewalk stalls and held it over them. It was hardly more than waxed paper, she thought, the color of a dahlia, but it kept the drizzle off.

Keller said, "He loves you, you know."

Byron, he meant. It took her by surprise. She peered at Keller—at his blue eyes, studiedly inscrutable. She said, "Is that an Angel question? Or are you really worried about him?"

"It wasn't a question," he said coolly. "And I guess it's none of my business. But you can't look at him and not know it."

Traffic flooded down the wet streets—electric carts, scooters, big Japanese cars. Keller hunkered down under the umbrella; he put his hand around her waist. She said carefully, "I love Byron. I do. I love him for what he's done. I'm not callous."

"There are all kinds of love."

"We were together a while. It didn't work out."

"He hasn't stopped caring."

"I'm grateful for that too. There are times when I've needed him. Maybe that's selfish—I don't know." She frowned, wondering at Keller's curiosity.

He said, "It just took me by surprise. I didn't know he could be so . . ." He groped for the word. "Single-minded."

"Obsessed, you mean. But we all are." They had reached the church now, candles burning behind dust-caked windows. "Obsessed," she said. "All three of us." She put her finger out, touched the painted icon of the dream-stone. She felt Keller's sympathy fade abruptly.

He took her hand and pulled it back. "You follow that thing," he said, "you could follow it a long way down."

"You know all about it, right?" He looked startled. But it was not an insult. She meant it. "Being an Angel must be like that. Byron talks about it sometimes. Seeing without feeling." She looked at him cautiously. "Seems like you followed it a long way down already."

A curtain came down over his face. "It's not the same."

She shrugged and opened the door.

The interior of the church was dark and empty. Long ago it must have been a Catholic church, buried here between the taller and newer buildings. Behind the altar there was a soot-dark stained-glass intaglio of the Virgin Mary with her hand upraised. The glass was illuminated faintly from below; no exterior light entered here.

An old woman stepped out from a back room. She regarded them with a crabbed expression and spoke in sibilant Portuguese. Keller translated: "She says tourists aren't permitted." *Igreja*, the old woman said. "It's a church."

"Tell her we want to use a stone."

Keller spoke haltingly. The old woman sighed and went into the back. Teresa sat down at one of the candlelit tables that had been installed where the pews might once have been. The woman returned with a tin lock-box clamped under her arm. She held the box protectively and extended her open hand, palm up. Keller gave her a hundred-cruzeiro note.

The old woman took up a station by the door as Teresa opened the box.

The stone inside was an nth generation copy, dark with contaminants; the angles were muted, the colors pale. It could not have been worth much more than Keller had paid for the privilege of touching it. Still . . .

So close now, Teresa thought.

She took the oneirolith in her hand.

It was always the same for her, this sense of an opening up, a clambering out of the shell of her body. With her eyes closed she felt suspended in an indefinite space. The room had fallen away on every side; her body felt numb and distant.

The phenomenon was mysterious; copious research had shed no real light. The current theory, Teresa understood, was that the oneiroliths acted somehow directly on the mind—the ghost in the crystal touching the ghost in her own architecture of blood and tissue. Maybe the Exotics had used the stones this way; maybe the visions they created were some skewed diffraction of that function, the human mind laboring over inhuman code.

It hardly mattered. What mattered were these persistent half dreams, the delicate blue-winged people in their impossible plenitude . . . their deserts and forests and farms and cities . . . and the human scenarios, too, almost as strange, a parade of ancestors. She felt their potency even through the medium of this crudely copied stone. Giddy with it, she reached for Keller's hand.

He pulled back.

"It's all right," she whispered, the sound of her own voice vague and distant. "It's just . . . I would like not to be alone." And opened her eyes a moment to see him.

Slowly, he nodded. Watching her—his eyes on hers with the intense scrutiny of a frightened animal—he reached his big hand across the table.

The contact was electric.

Old, powerful memories.

She saw Keller in Cuiaba a decade ago.

Keller the draftee. Keller riding in on a mottled green military transport from Rio. Keller and a couple of other recruits dispersed to a combat unit in this dusty meat town, dazed, an Army-issue thread-rifle slung over one shoulder and his duffel over the other.

His face was indistinct—an image glimpsed and ignored in mirrors—but cruelly young. He was stick thin, clean-shaven, made naive by a childhood in the simmering conduit suburbs. "The blessed innocence of failed comprehension"—Meg had said that.

Megan Lindsey was one of the women in his platoon. A Pfc like Keller, but she had some combat experience; she had been on patrol down the dangerous corridor of BR-364. "California-born," Byron said, "like you. Doesn't talk much. Attitude problem, some people say. I think she's just scared—and scared to show it."

Byron Ostler was the platoon Angel. Keller was fascinated by him, this white-haired gnome drafted out of an industrial-chemistry course at some midwestern agricultural campus, a year younger than Keller. Byron showed him the scar at the back of his neck. "Angel scar," he said. "Look for it." He regarded Keller through his protective lenses. "You should stay away from me, you know. If you run with the freaks, you *are* a freak. Plus, who knows what might get downloaded?" He flashed his tattoo. "The eyes of the Personnel Branch are upon you."

"They look at all these recordings?"

"Combat mainly. Running them in realtime is what you might call problematic. But you never know."

It didn't bother Keller. He was fascinated by Byron, and more fascinated by Meg. He maneuvered himself next to her in the mess hall, talked to her a little. She seemed grateful for the attention. Her family ran a bacteria farm up in the San Fernando Valley; she had been burned brown walking the enclosures every summer since she was ten, reading out fermentation gauges into a pocket recorder. She was lithe and small and her face was mobile, but Keller thought Byron was probably right: there was fear there, too, not far below the surface.

He watched her move in esoteric *katas* on the parade ground one tropical noon. Sheened with sweat, she achieved grace. Her khaki T-shirt dangled limply from her shoulders; the huge pockets of the fatigue pants blossomed at her hips. Her hair, cut into a military pageboy, gave back the vertical sunlight. Keller had never seen anything like her. He watched from the shade of a storage shed, letting the memory burn into him, admitting for the first time that he might have fallen in love with her. She moved like a scythe, and did not seem to see him until, moments later, sitting *zazen* in the damp heat, storm clouds rising up behind her from the Mato Grosso a horizon away, she looked at him . . . locked eyes with him, shocked him with a smile.

Because the compound at Cuiaba was overcrowded, Keller slept in a tent staked out between the halide lights and the barbed perimeter fence. She came from the women's bunker after lights-out that night, whispering his name in the dark, and although they had not planned it, neither was he surprised: the promise had been in her look. They made love inexpertly but passionately, traded childhood reminiscences in the hours before reveille.

When he asked her about her patrols out BR-364, she sat up abruptly, shivering in the dark. "You'll find out soon enough."

He apologized for asking. She ran her fingers through the stubble on his scalp. "Out there, Ray," she said, "it's easy to do things you're not proud of."

The platoon went out a couple of days later. A troop carrier dropped them off in the ragged farm country southeast of Ti Parana. Keller walked point some. Byron went into an Angel fugue, not talking much, looking intensely, gliding—Keller thought—above the deep currents of his fear. Meg walked with a white-knuckled grip on her threadrifle. The tension was high—there had been guerilla activity all through these pockmarked farm villages—but they did not actually see action until they stumbled into an ambush in a muddy manioc field somewhere in Rondonia. The noise was sudden and astounding. The sky lit up with the antiseptic glare of burning phosphorus. Keller heard the bang and whistle of cluster bombs on every side of him; without thinking, he went to his knees. The blood—

"No," he said, and pulled back his hand.

Teresa opened her eyes, shaken.

Keller was staring grimly back. Some of this had seeped through to him, she thought, powerful images leaping the gap between them. His own memories. "I'm sorry," she said hoarsely. She opened her hand and left the oneirolith on the table. The old Brazilian woman scuttled over with her tin box. *"Passou a hora."* Their time was up.

It left her depressed. They walked back to the hotel in the aftermath of the rain, a sour humidity rising from the streets. Down the mouth of an alley Teresa glimpsed a *posseiro* woman, in transit or homeless, squatting among her possessions and suckling a naked child. The child had a thatch of dark hair, big eyes, Indio features. The woman cradled the child's head in the crook of her arm and gazed down at him with an expression of unselfconscious affection that made Teresa turn away, suddenly weak. After what Keller had said about Byron, after what she had seen, she felt chastised. We are all down here hunting some grail, she thought, digging for it, scrabbling after it, not out of greed but out of our misplaced sincerity . . . and here was this illiterate woman crouched in an alley, certainly poor and probably homeless, but whole where they were broken (she felt it like a cold wind through her), healthy where they were crippled. It made her feel small; it made her feel ashamed.

The hotel lobby was full of stale warmth. In the room, Ng was waiting.

CHAPTER 7

When he was certain the Americans had left Brasilia, Stephen Oberg boarded a SUDAM flight directly to Pau Seco.

He had simply to flash his Agency card. SUDAM and the Brazilian government generally had been eager to cooperate. Technically—according to his documents—Oberg was a civilian employee of the DEA, but since the great amalgamation of the federal agencies in the thirties, the distinction had become obscure—his immediate superior was an NSA bureaucrat on lease to the security branch, and he was answerable to the Embassy.

The aircraft was crowded with peacekeepers in pea-green uniforms, talking among themselves in laconic Ariguaia Valley accents and oblivious to the dark ocean of forest below. Oberg propped his head on a pillow and pretended to sleep. He was 190 pounds, bulky in a gray suit, a plodding but methodical thinker. He was not given to fits of nerves, but he admitted that Brazil made him nervous.

There would have to be changes made. He had tried to impress that on the Agencies and on the government functionaries he had been introduced to in his brief time here. For years the mining of the Pau Seco artifact had been a relatively casual affair; smuggling happened mostly at the research facilities in America and the Asian states, where the oneiroliths were temptingly easy to duplicate. Smuggling from Pau Seco itself was problematic, and for years there had been no good reason to attempt it. The Eastern Bloc had periodically made its presence felt, but that was to be expected . . . tolerated, even, within limits. The exigencies of the balance of power. But times had changed.

Oberg had been at the government labs in Virginia when the first of the new stones came in late last year. Technically, the research team leader told him, these new stones were more "addressable"—they interfaced more successfully with the cryptanalytical programs running out of the building's big mainframes. "We're downloading all kinds of material," he said. "Ask for it, it's there. It's like an encyclopedia. A *bottomless* encyclopedia. But the effect on human volunteers . . ."

Oberg said, "It's different?"

"Very idiosyncratic. Very strange. You should see."

And so Oberg, who was the Agencies' liaison-in-place, had followed the voluble team leader down a hallway to the small pastel rooms where the human volunteers were kept. This was essential research, too, Oberg had been told, though it made him queasy to think of it. Perversely, there were data the computers could not evince from the stones, data accessible to the living mind alone. Everything that was known about the Exotics had come through this route. A blue-skinned people who inhabited, or had inhabited, a small planet of a distant star. Through human volunteers some little knowledge of their language and anthropology had been eked out. But it was sporadic work, and much of it was contradictory, overlaid with dreams and wishes, the excrescences of the human mind.

The volunteer was a man named Tavitch. Like most of their volunteers, he came from the federal prison at Vacaville. Tavitch was a soft-spoken middle-aged man who had murdered his wife and two children a week after he lost his job as a data-base manager, and who chose the Virginia facility as an alternative to amygdalectomy. His eyes were large and moist, his expression faintly petulant. He held one of the new deep-core oneiroliths in his hand.

"First time he touched it, he was practically comatose," the team leader burbled. "Oculogyric trance. Some kind of traumatic hypermnesia. But he's relatively lucid now."

Oberg folded his arms patiently. "Mr. Tavitch? Can you hear me?"

Tavitch looked up, though his expression was preoccupied.

"What do you see, Mr. Tavitch?"

There was a long pause. "Time," Tavitch said finally. "History."

It was eerie, unpleasant. Oberg looked at the team leader. The team leader shrugged and waved his hands: *go on*.

Oberg sighed inwardly. "History," he said. "Our history?"

"Our history," Tavitch said, "their history. Ours is newer. Oh, it shines! You should see it. It's like a river. A golden river of lives. Millions and millions, fading away back as many years." His eyes were glazed and patient. "They're all in there. . . ."

"Who?"

"Everybody," Tavitch said.

"Everybody?"

"The dead," Tavitch said calmly. "Lives tangled up like strings. The living too—more like fuses. Burning."

Oberg had shuddered. It was the instinctive revulsion he inevitably felt in that room. A sense of contamination. People assumed the oneiroliths had been tamed, that their familiarity had taken the edge off their strangeness. For Oberg, at least, it wasn't even remotely true. They were the product of an intelligence that was profoundly and dissonantly inhuman. You could tell by looking at them—the oily shine of them, the illusion of depth. Stone mechanism, he thought. Mineral life. It made him uneasy.

"*They're* in here too," Tavitch said, and his voice descended now into a minor key.

"Who, Mr. Tavitch?"

"Alma. Peter. Angela." The convict's face seemed to collapse into itself. Oberg was stunned. He thought the man might cry—Tavitch, the murderer, who had never demonstrated any sign of remorse. "They want to understand," Tavitch said, "but they don't . . . they *can't.* . . ."

Oberg left the room, repelled.

Alma, Peter, Angela.

They were Tavitch's family . . . the ones he had killed.

Later, over lunch in the sterile staff cafeteria, the team leader had tried to talk away the event. "You understand, we're working here with selected subjects. Criminals. Murderers, like Tavitch. So the work has a certain bias built into it. Conventional research hasn't given us everything we're looking for. We're very little closer to understanding who the so-called Exotics are, or how an oneirolith interacts with the mind—or why—than we were fifteen years ago."

"It's unnatural," Oberg had said. "It's ugly."

The team leader blinked. "I follow your concerns, Mr. Oberg. All I'm suggesting is moderation. Patience. Look at it from our point of view. Communication is what we're all concerned with here. And communication—of one kind or another—is what happened in that room with Tavitch. There's this prejudice against what's called 'the human interface,' the effect of the oneiroliths on the human mind. Well, obviously it's a difficult study. The effect is subjective. You can't measure it or calibrate it. So we do a limited kind of research, and we have to compete for funding with people who are downloading much harder data. You see what I'm driving at? I know you had a negative reaction to what happened today, but I wouldn't want that to affect the course of our work."

So it comes down to this, Oberg had thought: this man's career. "I don't control funding."

"You have influence."

"Only a little."

"Still, I'm convinced we're doing important work, vital work, with these new stones. No one wants to consider it, Mr. Oberg, but maybe the real message the Exotics left us isn't strictly linguistic. Maybe it's preverbal. Maybe it operates on the level of intuition . . . or emotion . . . or memory."

Memory. What was it Tavitch had said? Something about history. And the team leader had talked about hypermnesia, an involuntary upwelling of the past. To Oberg all of this seemed obviously, patently sinister. The past was the past, a burial place, the tomb of events, and better that way. Nobody cared about the past but priests and poets. You did a thing and you left it behind you. Hypermnesia, he thought, Tavitch's "history," was a light cast into places that by all rights should have been dark, hidden, buried.

Briefly, Oberg felt a wave of what the Army psych officers had called "depersonalization"—a sense of standing apart from himself, a disconnection. For one crystalline moment he understood that his horror of the alien stones might be purely personal, a pathology, a self-disgust as profound as he had seen in Tavitch this afternoon. A phobia of memory. He gazed at the bland, pale face of the man across the table and thought: if you'd seen what I've seen —if you'd done what I've done—

But it was a progression of logic he could not allow, and he thrust it from his mind. The oneiroliths were evil; there was no other possibility.

"Just trying to clarify our position," the team leader said.

"I understand," Oberg told him.

He woke from the reminiscence as if it had been a bad dream.

The aircraft was circling now, the sky lightening with dawn. The uniformed peacekeepers were mostly asleep. Oberg imagined he could feel it coming nearer—the source of the virus, the center of the infection. He did not think the analogy was unfair. It bred like a virus; it insinuated itself into the body—or at least the mind—like a virus. Like a virus, it had purposes of its own. Not human purposes.

He peered out the window and saw the dust of Pau Seco, pale in the morning light, rising from a canyon in the jungle.

CHAPTER 8

1. "It looks like hell," Keller said.

"It *is* hell," Ng said blithely. "But this isn't the worst of it."

They had come in along the broad highway from Cuiaba. Ng drove a battered Korean semi full of refrigerated meat —it was his day job, he said. He ran supplies to the box cities full of hopeful *foraos* and unlucky *formigas*. It paid okay, he said. He did not say what his night job was.

It was a long run from Cuiaba. Teresa and Byron napped in the rear of the huge cab; Keller sat up with Ng. Ng didn't talk much but Keller was able to confirm his suspicion that the man had been a soldier, one of the Vietnamese commandos who had fought in the Pacific Rim offensive. Keller had always been just a little scared of the Vietnamese. They were culled soldiers, tagged at birth and raised in the big military creches outside Danang. Their bodies produced chronically high levels of serotonin and norepinephrine, chronically low levels of monoamine oxidase. They were, in other words, aggressive, domineering, and desperate for excitement. It was there in the way Ng drove his rig: too fast, but with a tight, rapt smile. And when he turned a corner and the sleeve rode up his arm, Keller recognized the faint blue double-X etched under the skin—the Danang tattoo.

They approached Pau Seco a little after dawn. Keller saw the plume of dust on the horizon feathering toward the south. "Pau Seco?" he said, and Ng nodded. Within an hour they had reached the outskirts of the old town, the endemic poverty of Brazil but on a grander scale. Shacks rolled up and down these bread-loaf hills, all nearly identical, random configurations of corrugated tin, tarpaper, cardboard. Keller gazed at the emaciated men gathered by the road, who returned his gaze without curiosity as the big rig rumbled past.

"*Formigas*," Ng said. "Unlicensed miners. Most of them are not even that, actually. They come in the hope that they'll be hired into the mine. The *garimpeiros* are the men who own the land. They hire the *formigas* to do their work for them. For wages, or more likely a share of the income. If there is ever any income. But there are more of these people than there is work for them. Most of them spend their days in the laborers' compound hoping someone else dies. It's the best way to get work."

And then they topped a rise and Keller saw the mine itself.

Pau Seco, he thought. The ugly center of the world.

Ng pulled the truck into the bay back of a cinderblock building and climbed out, dusting his shorts with his small hands. He led Keller to the crest of a hill and gestured almost proudly at the pit of the mine. "Hell," he said.

It might have been hell. It was an open canyon of red mud and white clay so immense that the trees on the far rim were gray with distance. Keller did a professional pan, sweeping the mine east to west so that this vista could be reclaimed from his AV memory. There was so awesomely much of it.

"This was a plain once," Ng said. "A plain covered with jungle. Then the *garimpeiros* came, and the foreigners, and the government to take their twenty-five percent. When they burned off the trees, the ashes fell for miles around."

It was a vista from another century, *formigas* creeping up the inclines like the ants they were named for, deafening with the clangor of hand tools and human voices. This was how the Aztecs must have mined their gold, Keller thought, and he felt a moment of giddy vertigo: an abyss here, too, of time.

Ng occupied a shack in the old town of Pau Seco with a view commanding the mine and the sprawl of the workers' compound. After nightfall the old town came alive. The town of Pau Seco, Ng explained, was a concentration of whorehouses, banks, and bars. Every day one or two of these thousands of *garimpeiros* would come into money; the town existed to extract it from them. Periodically there was the sound of gunfire.

Keller sat out on the wooden vestibule of the shack, drinking cautiously from a bottle of white *cachaca* and listening as Ng explained the trouble they were in.

His English was easy, flat, American in inflection. "I don't know Cruz Wexler." He shrugged. "Cruz Wexler means nothing to me. Two months ago I was approached by a man, he said he was a surveyor working for SUDAM. A Brazilian. He had SUDAM credentials, he had a nice suit. He said there was a buyer interested in acquiring a deep-core stone and was it possible I could set this up?" He stretched out across the three risers that connected his wooden shack to the mud, plucked at a hole in his T-shirt. "Well, it isn't easy. Security is very tight. They named a figure, the figure was attractive, I said I would do what I could."

"It's arranged?" Byron asked hopefully.

"You should have the stone tomorrow. The thing is best done quickly. But you have to understand . . . you came here as couriers, right?"

Byron said, "We take the stone, we carry it out of the country. . . ."

"Nobody told you it might be dangerous?"

"We have documents—"

"Paper." Ng shrugged. "If it was that easy, any *forao* with brains would be walking out of here wealthy." He grinned. "There's not much smuggling because the military is in charge. Mostly, you can do what you want in the old town. But the military is there, and they carry guns and they use them. The official penalty for the crime we're discussing is death. What it means is summary execution. A trial would be"—and the smile widened—"very unusual."

"Son of a *bitch*," Byron said. "It's a *walk*, he says, it's a fucking *vacation*! It's a walk through the fucking *cemetery* is what it is!"

Teresa said quietly, "It's all right."

"He fucked us over!"

"Byron, please—"

"God*damn*," Byron said. But he sat down.

She turned to Ng. "If it's so dangerous, why did you agree to get involved?"

Ng sat back, hugging his knees.

"I'm easily bored," he said.

2. Oh, but I can feel it now, Teresa thought.

In the midst of this brutality it was so close. She felt it like a pain inside her, like the poignancy of old loss, a kind of melancholy.

She lay in the darkness of Ng's small shack, curled on a reed mat at the heart of the world.

Melancholy, she thought, but also—she could begin to admit it—frightening. She was not as naive as Byron seemed sometimes to think, but the mine had taken her by surprise . . . the brutality, the squalor of it, the lives that were lost here. *It was not meant to be this way*, she thought.

She sat up in the darkness. Through the paneless window she could see Pau Seco sprawling at the foot of this moonlit hill. Oil-can fires burned sporadically like stars in the darkness.

She thought of the Exotics, the winged people she had seen so often in her 'lith visions. She was not afraid of them; the impression of their benevolence was strong and vivid. But they were different. There was something essentially unhuman about them, she thought—something more profound than the shape of their bodies.

They would not have created Pau Seco. They would not have expected it to be created.

She lay back in the darkness, weary and confused.

It had not been wholly her own idea to come here. It was an imperative she felt more than understood, a kind of homing instinct. Her own history faded back into darkness, lost in the fires that had swept the Floats fourteen years ago. Her childhood was a mystery. She had come into the Red Cross camps scalded and smoke-blinded and nearly mute. She had been cared for—adopted, though it was never legal—by an extended family of Guatemalan refugees; they fed her, clothed her, and practiced their English on her. They named her Teresa.

She was grateful but not happy. She remembered those days as a haze of pain and loss: the searing conviction that something valuable had been stolen from her. She became attached to a rag doll named Amy; she screamed if the doll was taken away. When Amy fell into a canal and disappeared beneath the oily seawater, she wept for a week. She adjusted to her new life in time, but the nameless pain never went away . . . until she discovered the pills.

One of her Guatemalan family, a hugely fat middle-aged woman named Rosita—whom the others called *tia abuela*—brought the pills home from the public health clinic. Rosita suffered from rheumatoid arthritis and took the pills for, as she put it, "ree-*lif*." They were narcotic/analgesics keyed to the opiate receptors in the brain; Rosita was frankly addicted but, the clinic told her, the pills did not create a tolerance . . . the addiction would not get worse, they said, and that was good, because the arthritis would not get better.

Teresa, alone one afternoon in their antiquated houseboat, stole a pill from Rosita's bottle and hid it under

MEMORY WIRE

her pillow. The act was impetuous—partly curiosity, partly a dim intuition that the pill might work for her the kind of magic it worked for Rosita. In bed that night she swallowed it.

The effect was instantaneous and profound. Inside her a huge and unsuspected tide of fear and guilt rolled back. She closed her eyes and relished the warmth of her bed, smiling for the first time in years.

Tia Rosita was right, she thought. Ree-*lif*.

Rosita collected her prescription twice a month. Twice a month, Teresa took one off the top. Rosita did not seem to notice the thievery, or if she did, she did not suspect Teresa. And Teresa did not dare take more, for fear of drawing attention to herself.

Still, she lived for these moments. The pills seemed to detonate inside her, tiny explosions of purity and peace. Words like *loneliness* and *loss* began to make sense to her; she realized for the first time that they might not be permanent or universal.

When she was sixteen one of the boys she had come to think of as her brother, a rangy twenty-year-old named Ruy, took her out to the empty margin of the tidal dam and showed her a fistful of pink-and-yellow spansules—the same kind Rosita got from the clinic.

She could not help herself. She grabbed. Ruy pulled his hand away, laughing; a cloud of sea gulls whirled up from the concrete pilings. "Right," he said. "I *thought* so."

She stared covetously at his clenched fist. "You can get those?"

"Many as I want."

"Can I buy them?"

"*Acaso.*" He shrugged loftily. Maybe.

"How much?"

"How much you got?"

She had nothing. She had been going to the charity school up in the North Floats, where her English teacher called her "a good pupil" and her art instructor called her "talented." But she didn't care about the school. She could quit, she thought, get a job, get some money . . . *acaso.*

"When you do," Ruy said—walking away, heart-

breakingly, with the pills still imprisoned in his hand—
"then you talk to me."

But Rosita, older and more gnarled but no less vigilant,
wouldn't let her leave school. "What kind of job are you
going to get? Be a whore down by the mainland, like your
sister Livia?" She shook her head. "Public Works is pulling
out of this place, you know. Too many uncertified people.
No documents, no green cards, no property deeds. You're
lucky you have a school. Maybe won't have one much
longer, you think about that?"

But it was Rosita's anger and not any practical con-
sideration that deterred her. She stayed in school, maintained her habit, and ignored Ruy when he taunted her with
his apparently endless supply of drugs. Until, one day, her
art instructor complimented her on a collage she had assembled. She had a real talent, he said. She could go somewhere with it.

It was a strange idea. She enjoyed putting together
collages and sculptures, it was true; sometimes it felt almost
as good as the pills made her feel. It was almost as if
someone else were doing the work with her hands, some
part of her she had lost in the fire, maybe, making its
presence felt. She would abandon herself to the work and
find that hours had passed: it was a good feeling.

She had not thought of making money with it. It looked
like an outside chance. Still, she packed a bag lunch one
Sunday and hiked along the pontoon bridges to the mainland, to the art galleries up the coastal highway. The mainland frightened her. She was not accustomed to the roaring
of trucks and automobiles; in the Floats you saw mostly
motor launches, and those only in the big canals. And there
was the eerie solidity of the ground beneath her feet, rock
and sand and gravel wherever she turned.

She examined the artwork offered for sale in these
landlocked places. Crystal paintings, junk sculptures, polished soapstone. Most of it had come from the Floats and
was considered—she inferred from the way people spoke
—a kind of folk art. Some of the pieces were very good
and some were not, but she realized with a degree of surprise
that her art instructor had been right—there was nothing

here beyond her talents. She lacked the tools to tackle some of these projects, but the work she had done with scrap metal salvaged from the dumpboats was as good as at least half of what she had seen that day. Possibilities here, she thought.

Two weeks later she carried three small pieces across the pontoon and chain-link bridges to a place called Arts by the Sea. She showed them to the owner, a woman only slightly younger than Rosita. The woman was named Mrs. Whitney, and she was skeptical at first, but then—as Teresa unwrapped the oilcloth from her work—impressed. Her eyes widened, then narrowed. "Such mature work!" She added, "For someone your age."

"You'll buy it?" Teresa asked.

"We sell on commission. But I can offer you an advance."

It was, Teresa learned later, a pittance, a token payment; but at the time it was more money than she had seen in one place.

She took it to Ruy and offered him half of it. He gave her enough pills to fill up both her cupped hands.

That night she took two.

Ree-*lif*. It flowed through her like a river. She rationed herself to one a night, to make them last, and worked in her spare time on another sculpture for Mrs. Whitney. Mrs. Whitney paid her almost double for it, and that was good; but Ruy's prices had begun to escalate too. She paid but she hated him for it. Ruy had become suddenly important to her, and she acquired the habit of observing him. He moved down the pontoon alleys swaggering, his bony hips thrust forward. "*Muy macho*," Rosita always said when he struck these poses at home, but out here there was no one to deflate him. He hung around with his similarly hipshot friends by the graffiti-covered tidal dam; she had seen him dealing pills there. One afternoon—nursing her hatred—she cut classes and followed him halfway to the mainland, to a tiny pontoon shack listing in the North Floats, a gasoline pump gushing out bilge into the dirty canal beside it. Ruy went in with his hand on his wallet and came out clutching a fat paper bag.

She summoned up all her courage and, when she was certain Ruy was truly gone, knocked at the door of the shack.

The man who answered was old, thin, hollow-looking. He peered at her a long time—her mouth was too dry to speak—and said at last, "What the fuck do *you* want?"

"Pills," she said, panicking.

"Pills! What makes you think I got pills?"

"Ruy," she said desperately. "Ruy is my brother."

His expression softened. "Well," he said. "Ruy's little sister cutting out the middleman." He nodded. "Ruy'd be pissed off, I bet, if he knew you were here."

"I can pay," she said.

"Tell me what you want."

She described the pink-and-yellow spansules.

"Yeah," he said. "If that's what you want. It's a waste of money, though, you ask my opinion." He rummaged in a drawer in an old desk at the back of his single precariously listing room; she watched from the doorway. "You might like these better."

They were small black-coated pills in a paper envelope, maybe a hundred in all. Teresa regarded them dubiously. "Are they the same?"

"The same only more so. Not just pain pills, hm? Happy pills."

Flustered, she gave him her money. It occurred to her during the long walk back that she might have made a fool's bargain, the pills might be coated sugar. Or worse. That night, in bed, she was not sure whether she should try even one. What if they were toxic? What if she died?

But she had run out of Ruy's spansules and she dared not pilfer more of Rosita's. The need overcame her reluctance; she swallowed a black pill hastily.

Pleasure spread out from the pit of her stomach. It was, gradually and then overwhelmingly, everything she could have wanted: the satisfaction of a successful piece of artwork, the satisfaction that came from being loved, the satisfaction—this perhaps the best of all—that came from forgetting. Afloat on her mattress, rocking in the slow swell, she might have been the only person in the world. She loved the new pills, she thought. They *were* better. Yes. And one was enough. At least at first.

She lived happily with these arrangements for months, selling enough work to Mrs. Whitney to keep her supply up, idling through the days—she had begun to take a pill each morning too—as if they were hours. She felt she could have continued this way indefinitely if it were not for Ruy, who had been cheated out of his immense profit on the cheap pink-and-yellow spansules and who had discovered her arrangement with his supplier. He retaliated by leading Rosita to Teresa's pill box, concealed behind a broken floorboard under the bed. *Tia abuela* Rosita was both angry and hurt, and made a demonstration of washing the pills down the Public Works conduit one by one. Teresa was so shocked to see her store of happiness flushed away that she displayed no emotion, merely packed her things, took what remained of her gallery money, and left.

(Years later she tried to return, with the idea of making some kind of apology to Rosita, achieving some sort of reconciliation . . . but the neighborhood had grown much worse, and her Guatemalan family had gone away. Just packed and left one day, an elderly neighbor told her, nobody knew where or what happened to them—except for that Ruy, of course. *He* had been killed in a knifefight.)

She put together a makeshift studio in the Floats off Long Beach, invested some money in supplies, acquired a new source for the small black pills. She learned that they were laboratory synthetics, synthetic enkephalins, very potent and very addictive. But that didn't matter: she could handle it. She knew what she was doing. She began to meet other Float artists and understood that she was not alone, that many of them depended on chemical pleasures in one form or another. Some of them even used Exotic stones, the oneiroliths from the Brazilian mines. But that was different, she thought; too strange—not the thing she wanted.

She could not say exactly when her habit got out of hand. There was no border she crossed. It didn't interfere with her work; strangely, the opposite was true. It was as if the thing inside her that created art was spurred on by her addiction—the way a dying tree will sometimes produce its most copious fruit.

She did sometimes, in her lucid moments, notice a kind of deterioration. She perceived this as a change, not in herself, but in her environment. Her studio was suddenly smaller: well, yes, she had moved into a cheaper one, saving rent. Her image in the mirror was gaunt: food economies, she thought, making her money go a little further. It proceeded in such gradual increments that nothing seemed to happen—nothing at all—until she was alone in a corner of an ancient bulk-oil terminal with a dirty mattress and a jar of medication. A jar of happiness.

She knew it was killing her. The idea that she was dying eased into her mind so cleverly that it seemed to appear wholly formed and yet familiar. Yes, she thought, I am dying. But maybe dying in a state of grace was better than living in a condition of unrelieved pain. Maybe it was a kind of bill come due at last: maybe, she thought, I should have died in the fire.

But anorexia and malnutrition had made her ill, there was physical pain in her knees and elbows, she was feverish much of the time. For relief she went back to the pink-and-yellow spansules—added them to her now almost exclusively chemical diet—and they helped for a time, but in time the pain reasserted itself. She would have welcomed death—her massively abused body cried out for it—but she could not bring herself to attempt suicide. It was as if she could sneak up on death but must not approach it directly; if she looked death in the face, some force inside her would recognize it, cry out in protest, pull her back from the brink. The frustration left her weeping.

She knew Byron Ostler vaguely: he was one of her dwindling circle of friends, not an artist but a dealer in dreamstones. In constant pain now, frightened of taking too many of the spansules, she reconsidered the idea of using an Exotic stone. It made visions, her artist friends said. Well, she did not want visions. She had had too much of vision. But visions, at least, might force out the demon of pain. It was worth a try.

She was careful to avoid seeing the pity in his face when she approached him. She held out the money in her hand. Only a very little of it remaining now. But he wouldn't take it. Just blinked at her through his moon-shaped lenses, this ragged veteran in his threadbare fatigues, and *gave* her a stone. It was small and faintly blue and oddly shaped; when she took it from him, casually, it made her hand tingle. "Do it here," he said.

"What?"

"As a favor to me," he said. "Do it here."

The visions were intense. She was only tranced out for a couple of hours, Byron said, but it seemed like infinities. She saw, like pieces of a mosaic, the distant world of the winged people. She danced like a whirlwind through history. Strangely, although there was much of misery in what she saw—and grief, and pain—she derived a certain strength from it. From the vigor of it, she thought: this river of life, twining in its endless double helix.

She saw, too—for the first time—the little girl who would occupy so many of her dreams.

The girl wore rags for clothes, athletic shoes bound with twine. "You have to look for me," the girl said solemnly. "You have to find me." And Teresa discovered that the imperative was there inside herself, and maybe had been all along . . . find her, yes.

Byron fired up his motor launch and took her back to the studio down south. Except it was not really a studio. She could see that now. It was a filthy corner of an abandoned warehouse. She looked at her jar of pills, appalled.

"I can bring in a doctor," Byron said.

She shrugged. She was dying, she was resigned to it, she told Byron so . . . but even as she spoke, she felt a new reluctance welling up. "I want to do the 'lith again," she said.

"Then let me bring a doctor. And some food." He looked around. "And maybe clean this place up a little. Christ, it's a pit."

She agreed.

Withdrawal was agony. The doctor Byron brought was a refugee MD who shot her up with vitamin supplements

ROBERT CHARLES WILSON

and charted her neuropeptides on a hand monitor. When the ordeal was finished, Byron coaxed her to eat again.

Health came as a shock. The world took on brighter hues; food tasted better. She began to work again. With some money coming in, she found a place nearer to Byron. She began taking long walks out to the tidal dams to watch the weather sweep in from the sea. She had not stopped wanting the pills—the doctor had said it was a craving she might never lose, burned too deeply now into her neurochemistry—but the dreamstones seemed to take away the edge of the need. She did not understand much of what she saw in her stone trances but she attempted to incorporate it into her work; she did the first of her crystal paintings, a bright Exotic landscape.

She was aware, too, that Byron had fallen in love with her . . . aware that she did not love him.

For a time she tried. She moved in with him; they made love with dedication if not passion. But it was a failed experiment and they both knew it. He wanted her, he said, but he didn't want her as payment.

It made her feel cold. She tried to reassure herself— and maybe stake out some independence—by taking other lovers among the artists she knew, but the effort was finally unsatisfying. Maybe, she thought, she had lost the capacity for love; maybe it had been burned out in her addiction.

Her obsession with the oneiroliths deepened. Byron introduced her to Cruz Wexler, the academic who had written two books about the 'liths and who ran a kind of outlaw academy on his threadbare estate in Carmel. Wexler, a middle-aged man with guileless features and a progressive and untreatable emphysema, was enthusiastic about her artwork; he had agented some of it to his wealthy friends. So she had money again. She refurbished her studio in the Floats; she invested in tools she had never been able to afford.

And when a new unease began to overtake her—a sense that she had gone as far into the 'liths as she could go, and was still lost here, incomplete, on the margin of her own life—it was Cruz Wexler who hinted at the existence of a new *kind* of 'lith, a *deep core* 'lith, a 'lith that might answer her questions.

The eagerness she felt was almost physical. "Can I get one?"

He smiled. "None of us can get one. I've talked to people in the research compounds. The lid is down very tight."

It was a huge disappointment. The stones Byron grew, for all their strange access to the past, had not resolved the mystery of her early childhood. She had occasionally glimpsed the fire—a chaos of smoke and flame—but nothing of herself; she did not know where she was born or when or who her parents were. The memories, Wexler said, were too deeply suppressed. And she had come increasingly to believe that the thing she wanted was hidden in that darkness: a well from which she might draw out a shining key and unlock herself, become a new thing altogether.

A month later Wexler told her he had set up a purchase, not here or in the Orient but in Brazil, Pau Seco, the mine itself. It was an unorthodox and expensive move but it would be worth it, he said: the new stone would yield up answers, secret wisdom—she felt a little of his own flagging enthusiasm—the final gnosis. All he needed was a courier, someone without a criminal record, someone not too closely connected with him.

Byron was appalled when she volunteered. "You don't know anything about it . . . Christ, what were you *thinking* of?"

"You don't understand. I *need* to go." They were walking down a market canal after hours, the boat stalls locked under their awnings, salt glittering along the boardwalk under a string of sodium vapor lights. She took his hands, knowing in that moment that he was authentically frightened for her; that his curious, lopsided love was as alive as it had ever been. "It matters that much. It's not something I can let alone."

"I'll go with you," he said.

She agreed, because he knew the country, because his intuition might have been correct: it might not be as easy as Wexler had promised. And she consented when he chose to bring along the Network Angel, Raymond Keller, also a veteran. But that was all the concession she would make.

And so they had come here.

She was a window away from Pau Seco. She could smell it. She could feel it—the nearness of that ancient artifact, star-stone; its scattered fragments. But the mine was a vast and ugly place, and it had shattered all her certainties. She had risked her life, she thought grimly—and Byron's, and Keller's—because of a voice in her head. Because of a dream.

Because she was lost. Because she had been lost for years . . . lost for most of her life.

She was afraid to go to sleep. Thinking about the tiny black pills, the synthetic enkephalins, had stirred an old longing in her. If I had one now, she thought—it was a dangerous, traitorous thought—I would take it.

She stared through the window at the starless sky, willing the dawn to come.

CHAPTER 9

Stephen Oberg was dismayed when he met the man in charge of the military presence at Pau Seco: a huge back-country Brazilian with dark eyes and an obviously strong sense of territoriality. The man introduced himself as Major Andreazza and offered Oberg a painfully narrow cane-backed chair. His office overlooked the broad canyon of the mine; Andreazza himself occupied a plush swivel chair behind a sumptuous desk. "Thank you," Oberg said.

Andreazza regarded Oberg at great length and said, "You must tell me why you came here."

And so, laboriously, he explained it again. The Pacific Rim powers were very anxious, he said, that the deep-core oneiroliths should not fall into unauthorized hands. To this end security had been tightened up at the research facilities in Virginia, in Kyoto, and in Seoul. However, an informant close to the American cultist Cruz Wexler had tipped off the Agencies to a purchase that had been arranged here, at Pau Seco. Oberg had come to interdict it.

Andreazza turned his chair to face the window. "We put a considerable effort into security ourselves," he said.

"I know." With guns, Oberg thought, intimidation, the making of public examples. There had been hangings at Pau Seco as recently as last year. "I understand," he said. "Still"—treading carefully—"the process isn't air-tight."

Andreazza shrugged. "The *formigas* are frisked every night as they leave. We have informants in the labor compounds. I fail to see what more we can do."

"I'm not here to criticize your efforts, Major. I'm sure they're exemplary. All I want to do is to locate three Americans." He opened his briefcase, withdrew the photographs he had obtained from the SUDAM official, and passed them across Andreazza's desk.

Andreazza gave them a cursory glance. "If they're here," he said, "I don't suppose they look so clean anymore."

"We know they have a contact in the old town," Oberg persisted. "A man who may be sheltering them."

"The mine we control," Andreazza said. "The compounds, yes. But don't overestimate us, Mr. Oberg. There are a quarter of a million peasants who live outside the fence. The old town is an anarchy. Without at least a name, there is a limit to what we can accomplish."

"We have a name," Oberg said.

"Oh?"

"The name is Ng."

"I see," Andreazza said, nodding.

They shared lunch at the military commissary. Oberg was anxious to get on with his work—prickling now with the urgency of it—but Andreazza forced him through the protocols of delay. And the food, of course, was dreadful.

"Oberg," Andreazza said suddenly, "Stephen Oberg . . . did you know there was an Oberg here during the war?

Special Forces, I think. Razed some villages out west of Rio Branco. It was a scandal. Killed a lot of women and children.'' He smiled. ''So they say.''

"I wasn't aware of that," Oberg said coolly.

"Ah," Andreazza said thoughtfully. "Yes."

CHAPTER 10

Roberto Meirelles woke before sunrise on the day of the deal and knew there would be trouble. The question for him had become: to go through with it or not?

He slept on a platform bed in a shack in a valley below the old town of Pau Seco. It was a bad location. Most of the town's sewage flowed past Meirelles's shack in a muddy brown streamlet, down past the ugliest tin habitations and finally into the bush, which the waste matter had made verdant and lush. Everything Meirelles owned was in this shack. He owned two faded khaki T-shirts, two pairs of denim pants, a mattress, a photograph of his wife and child.

And the stone.

This morning—already nervous, but carefully not thinking of the day ahead—he took the oneirolith out from the place he had made for it, a slit in the mattress where he had removed some of the ticking, and regarded it gravely in the dim light of a battery lamp.

You, he thought. You could be my fortune or you could be my death.

He held the oneirolith carefully. Over time he had learned the nuances of the stone. Held gently in the open palm of his hand—as now—it created only the faintest tingle of strangeness, a gentle electricity that seemed to focus a physical sensation behind his eyes. If he clasped it tightly, it would begin to work in earnest. It would make visions; visions of places so impossibly distant Meirelles could not begin to make sense of them; or more often these days, visions of his home.

Meirelles understood that the oneirolith had come from another world, traveled somehow across an unimaginable gulf. And although he had marveled at that once, it no longer seemed strange or remarkable to him. It was a fact, and facts grow smooth with handling. What made the stone remarkable—and precious—to Meirelles was the way it unlocked these memories of his wife and child in Cubatao. With luck, he thought, it could carry him back there—a wealthy man.

He shook his head. Such dreams were premature. Worse, dangerous. He tucked the oneirolith back into the mattress and deferred his decision. As far as it was possible, he worked to make his mind blank.

Outside, the sky was beginning to lighten. Pots and pans rattled, cocks crowed, bony scavenger dogs howled away the night. It was a morning, he told himself sternly, like any other.

He was what the others called a *formiga,* an ant, though he loathed the word himself. Meirelles was a proud man and resented being compared to an insect. Still—joining the surge of humanity down into the overheated canyon of the oneirolith mine, the sun like a blade against the back of his neck—he supposed the comparison was inevitable.

He wore huge canvas bags strapped to his shoulders and waist. The work and the diet of protein stews served in the labor compounds had made him thin but strong. Meirelles was thirty-five years old, and not a young thirty-five, but he had become proud of his body. He had survived the outbreak of Oropouche Virus that had swept Pau Seco a year ago. His body was wiry now—and far healthier, he knew, than it would have been had he stayed in Cubatao.

But the thought was not a pleasant one, and he suppressed it. (His wife and child were still in Cubatao.)

He climbed down the wooden ladders and followed a switchback trail steeply downhill; then rope ladders and another narrow trail to the bottom of this vast open pit. The temperature here was a good ten degrees warmer than at the top, and he had tied a rag around his head to soak up the sweat. Here men were already laboring, *garimpeiros* watching with clipboards from canvas tents or joining in with shovels and picks. The primitiveness of it did not impress him: the factories of the Mogi River Valley had been primitive too.

He set about his work as he did every day. It was impossible to ignore, however, the obvious fact that this was *not* a day like every day. The military police stood in stern phalanxes at the high wire fences that surrounded the mine. Everyone who passed in or out was being frisked. And there were soldiers down here, too, for the first time in Meirelles's memory, moving among the *garimpeiros* and asking questions.

If I had any sense, Meirelles scolded himself, I would leave the stone in the mattress and forget about it, just forget about it. If I had any sense.

Meirelles worked for a man named Claudio, a city man reputed to be a nephew of the Valverde family, a rich man who had taken many valuable stones out of the soil already. Claudio enhanced his profit by hiring workers out of the hopeful masses who thronged the old town, giving them false certification cards and then threatening to expose them to the military police. Meirelles himself was such a person. He earned very little at his work, and what he did earn he sent immediately back to his family in Cubatao; he could eat for free—with his false certification card—in the workers' compounds, and he did not pay rent on his shack.

It was a stern but equitable enough arrangement, Meirelles thought at first: and if Claudio uncovered a valuable oneirolith from the mud, then Meirelles would take his small share and move himself and his family out of the toxic Mogi River Valley. All he wanted was money enough to make a new life.

Time passed, however, and many stones were uncovered, and Meirelles never saw more money than his weekly pittance. One time he screwed up his courage and confronted Claudio in his big tent above the mine, and Claudio appeased him and promised that things would be different in the future. The next day one of Claudio's hired men, a thug, blackened Meirelles's right eye and told him to be grateful for what he had. He had a work permit, didn't he? Well, it could be taken away. He could be turned over to the military police. He should remember that.

He did. He remembered it one day when he drove his shovel into the elastic clay and felt it rebound from something solid there.

The day had nearly ended. Already long shadows were gathering here in the deepest part of the mine. Workers were collecting their tools and readying themselves for the long trek up to the compounds, warm food, a dash through the shower stalls. Feeling suddenly feverish, Meirelles put his hand down into the wet clay and grasped the object he had uncovered. Still bending low, scrubbing the dirt from it, he saw the deep azure glint of the oneirolith's surface. It was a large and perfect stone, undeniably very valuable. He trembled, holding it.

Later he could not say why he chose to steal it. Thievery was difficult and dangerous, and there was no ready market a man like Meirelles could count on. It was undoubtedly an irrational act. Still, he thought of Claudio's bland reassurances and of the man who had blackened his eye. He thought of his wife and child, his daughter Pia coughing in the ugly yellow air of his hometown. A day in the deep angles and convolutes of the oneirolith mine sometimes induced in Meirelles a kind of abstracted dreaminess, as if the alien artifacts beneath the soil were working a subtle influence on him, making the past more real and the present less urgent. And so, with Claudio and his daughter Pia on his mind, dreaming, he thumbed away the excess clay from the oneirolith and used his cotton leggings to wrap the stone and bind it to his ankle. When he stood up, the long hem of his denim pants obscured the bulge.

He had turned and found Claudio himself watching from a few yards away. Meirelles froze. Panic boiled in his stomach; his testicles drew up toward his body. But it was only the routine suspicion Claudio directed toward everybody. "Hurry it up," Claudio said, waving at him with disgust. "Get moving."

At the wire barricade Meirelles had almost passed out with fear. His head was swimming; a cold sweat broke out on his forehead. His teeth began to chatter. He was certain his fear would give him away.

Perversely, it may have saved him. This was at the height of the Oropouche Virus epidemic, and the military guards had become squeamish of the *formigas*, especially if they showed any sign of infection. Meirelles, with his sweaty forehead and his chattering teeth, must have frightened them. He was frisked by a young and pale guard who touched Meirelles's clothing as if he were touching a hot griddle, and then Meirelles was allowed to walk unmolested down the muddy hillside strewn with offal, to his shack, where he secreted the oneirolith inside his mattress.

It became a token of his independence from Claudio, a tangible embodiment of his pride, his hope, his future.

He had been born in the town of Cubatao and was one of the approximately one in five children there who survived to puberty.

Cubatao was an old industrial town. In the twentieth century it had been one of the most toxic places on the face of the earth, factories spewing out sulfur dioxide, carbon monoxide, and polychlorinated biphenyls into the valley air. The toxins denuded the hillsides and killed the children. In the first decade of the next century the factories had been nationalized . . . they were antique, but still, with their low overhead and negligible cleanup costs, very profitable. There were other places in the world said to be worse now. But

the river valley remained very dangerous. The factories—
modified but never modernized—spewed out new poisons:
cyanide and arsenic compounds from the semiconductor
lines, xylene, a substance called TCA.

Meirelles had a factory job running solvents in big rust-
pocked canisters. He worked with a man named Ribeiro, a
patriot who defended the factories whenever Meirelles suggested they might be old-fashioned or dangerous. "The
factories," Ribeiro said sternly, "are necessary for the wealth
of Brazil."

"No, no," Meirelles said. "The dreamstones create
the wealth of Brazil."

"The stones," Ribeiro said, "are sold to foreigners."

"But in exchange for money. And with the money,"
Meirelles persisted, "surely we could modernize the factories?"

"Nonsense! The money services the national debt.
There's nothing left over for the factories."

"Then Brazil *isn't* wealthy."

"Not without the factories!" Ribeiro said proudly. "The
factories are necessary to the wealth of Brazil."

It was a logic he wished he could share. But Meirelles
was married. He had a wife and a daughter. Twice in the
last year Pia had fallen sick with bronchial ailments, and
he knew she might not see her tenth birthday unless he
found some other place to live. Most of the people Meirelles
met were as complacent as Ribeiro—the will of God, they
said—but he prided himself on his thoughtfulness, and
knew it was time to leave.

There was of course no money. He supposed they could
pack up their meager belongings and simply walk away,
but he had heard terrifying stories about the camps for the
homeless outside Rio and São Paulo. No, he thought, they
needed money. And there was only one way Meirelles had
heard of that a poor man could make the kind of money he
needed.

Pau Seco.

It was a legend in the slums. Money in the ground,
they said. Money from outer space. It was there for the
taking. Everyone believed in it, although Meirelles noticed

ROBERT CHARLES WILSON

few believed in it strongly enough to attempt the journey, and those who did never seemed to report back. But then he woke one morning to find Pia down with the croup again, gasping, her face a sickly blue, and that afternoon he spent his last money buying medicine for her and then hiked down the road where a truck might pick him up. Under the circumstances he could not bear to stay.

Over the course of the day Meirelles made several journeys up and down the vertiginous walls of the mine. He was carrying bags of tailings away from the dig to the big wooden machines Claudio kept up top, which would sift the clay for Exotic stones and then dump the residue into a clotted ravine. His legs worked until the muscles knotted against him and he had to stop; his breath hissed in and out. He did not have the lungs of some of the younger men. He was not as efficient a *formiga* as some, and that worried him too: it meant Claudio might decide to get rid of him. Would he simply be fired, or would he be turned over to the military police? He didn't know. There was no one he could ask. People moved in and out of this place like phantoms. Competitiveness was extreme, friendships rare.

Meirelles's only friend in Pau Seco was the man called Ng. If "friend" was the word. Ng was a foreigner and had lived a life very different from Meirelles's. Meirelles had heard Ng was looking for a deep-core oneirolith, and so he had approached the foreigner in a bar in the old town. They didn't talk about the stone. Plainly, it was on both their minds; it was the reason they were together. But it was necessary to prepare the ground, Meirelles thought, and Ng seemed to understand this; they talked about the mine, they talked about the past.

They met several times, and Meirelles came to understand that the small quick-tempered Vietnamese was in some way like himself. Like Meirelles, Ng had cut himself adrift from the familiar world. Ng could have gone home after the war, lived out the life of a career soldier. But he had chosen to stay in Brazil. When Meirelles asked him why,

Ng shrugged: it went beyond words. Meirelles understood.

"You're a smuggler," Meirelles said finally.

Ng blinked his narrow eyes. "Among other things, yes."

"They say you want to buy a stone."

"The right kind of stone."

"They say the money is considerable."

"The money," Ng said, "is considerable."

Meirelles lowered his voice so that it could hardly be heard above the rattle of glasses and the roar of conversation. "How do I know I can trust you?"

"You don't," Ng said flatly. "You trust me or you don't. I can't guarantee anything."

"Ah," Meirelles said.

But in the end he made the deal. And now the appointed day had come around at last and he was lashed with a nervousness that threatened to undo him. There were military police everywhere.

He looked up with dismay when the last whistle sounded. Already the deepest channels of the mine were flooded with shadow. The western wall was dark, the sky an inky blue. Inside the tents of the *garimpeiros* a few lanterns were burning. Meirelles shook his head: the time had eluded him.

Soon, he thought, *you have to decide.*

He trudged up the switchbacks and narrow ladders and was frisked again at the high link fence outside the compounds. His fear, this time, was no defense. A beefy military guard peered deep into Meirelles's eyes and then searched him intimately, his hands probing Meirelles's clothes while the other military men looked on and made ribald comments. "All right," the guard said at last, contemptuously. "Go on."

He went directly to his shack. He walked stiff-legged down the filthy hillside. His hand shook on the sheet of corrugated tin he used for a door.

The stone was still there, inside the mattress.

He took it out and stared at it angrily. It was the stone, he thought, that had put him in this impossible position. He

ROBERT CHARLES WILSON

had planned to meet Ng in a bar in the old town; and if I go, Meirelles thought, will he be there? Or maybe the military police—waiting for him?

He would risk his life for Pia's sake. Gladly. But if the military police took him—what then?

This damn piece of rock, he thought. But then, holding it, he felt some of its strangeness radiate through him. He was momentarily overcome with a memory of Pia running to him outside the door of their two-room house in Cubatao . . . and it occurred to him that the dreamstone had helped to keep him honest these three years in Pau Seco; that another man, or a man without a stone, might have allowed the past to float away from him, might have made a new life for himself and indulged in the luxury of forgetting. Meirelles had not had that privilege.

Abashed, he wrapped the stone in a length of oilcloth and tucked it into his pants.

It was dark outside now. Fires were burning in oil barrels up and down these ragged hills. From the old town the sound of human voices had begun to rise in pitch and tempo.

It was time to go meet Ng.

The bar had no name. None of the bars in the old town of Pau Seco had any names. They were interchangeable, they performed the same function, so there was no reason to call a bar by this name or that. Meirelles recognized the one he wanted because it was at the intersection of the mine road and the dirt path that divided the barrios. He hesitated a final time at the door. His fear now was profound.

As he was walking here, he had passed the hill where Ng had his shack. As his head was turned in that direction, two burly military police had rushed past him; stunned, he watched a half-dozen more making their way up the slope, their high-pressure arclights drilling into the darkness. There was no question where they were headed. They were looking for Ng. They knew his name and knew where he lived.

Ng might know about this or he might not. Either way, Meirelles thought, the Vietnamese might still be inside the bar. Waiting. Ready to deal. Meirelles thought of the money and licked his lips.

But if the police are looking for Ng, he thought, they can't be far from finding him. There were police all over the streets. They might be inside, waiting for the exchange to happen; they might arrest him too. Or Ng might take the stone and refuse to pay. Meirelles was powerless; the stone itself was his only weapon.

He closed his eyes and shouldered through the door, sighing.

But there was only the usual dimness and clangor inside. The stink of *cachaca* and cheap beer made him blink; the pressure of warm bodies forced him up against the wall. He was acutely aware of the oneirolith against his body. In a moment his eyes had adjusted to the flickering lamplight, and he looked for Ng at the corner table where they had met a month ago. Ng was there.

He was there with three others. Ng wore his usual torn T-shirt and ragged denims. The others were dressed similarly, but with dust caps pulled down over their eyes in the style favored by the younger *formigas* who migrated in from the cities. A kind of disguise, Meirelles thought, though not very effective, and in this heat it must be excruciating. Because he saw no sign of the military police, Meirelles worked his way toward the table, wedged his body into a chair and waited for Ng to speak.

"You have it?" Ng said softly.

And Meirelles felt his heart sink. It was obvious from the Vietnamese man's attitude—cavalier, almost amused— that he knew nothing about the police raid on his shack, probably had not guessed that the police were looking especially for him.

Meirelles thought: and if I tell him?

He peered at Ng's companions. Three of them. Two men and a woman. The man on the left was tall, an American probably, with a careful expression and eyes that lingered a heartbeat too long on Meirelles's own. The man on the right was smaller and more obviously nervous, his hair long and dirty white. The woman between them was in a

subdued way beautiful, but very distracted: her hands wres-
tled with themselves, her brow knotted into a frown.

Ng thought, *She's the one who wants the stone.*

"It's here," he said hoarsely, in English. "It's here
. . . I have it."

He saw the subtle light in Ng's dark eyes.

"Give him the money," Ng said.

The white-haired American said, "I don't see the stone."

The woman touched the man's hand: some kind of
subtle communication, perhaps a warning. And the tall
American watched.

The white-haired man sighed, reached into his pocket,
and drew out two slips of paper. One for Ng, one for him.
So flimsy! Meirelles thought. It seemed for a moment a
stupid exchange—the oneirolith, a solid thing, for this note.

He unfolded it and looked at it long enough to establish
that it at least seemed legitimate: a Bradesco bank certificate,
the amount in cruzeiros so large that it made his head swim.
"All right," he heard himself say, "yes."

Ng pocketed his own money and smiled.

Meirelles brought out the oneirolith in its wrapping of
dirty oilcloth. The white-haired American eyed it suspi-
ciously. "How do we know it's what we want?"

But the woman touched his hand again. "It's what we
want."

She feels it, Meirelles thought. She's sensitive to it.
He watched as she reached for the stone, and he felt the
hesitation in her, her respect for it. "Take it," he said.
"Touch it. It won't affect you through the cloth." She didn't
understand his Portuguese but seemed to take solace from
the tone of his voice.

Ng took Meirelles's hand and shook it across the table,
the bargain completed.

Now, Meirelles thought. If he meant to tell them about
the military police, he must say something now. If they left
in ignorance, they might walk back to Ng's home and into
the hands of the police.

And if Ng knows, Meirelles thought . . . will he want
the money back?

He felt the bank certificate in his pocket, a warm pres-

ence. A ticket back to his wife and child. A ticket out of
Pau Seco and a ticket out of Cubatao. A piece of paper
containing a better life.

He drew back his hand as Ng stood up. The Americans
hovered above him.

"Wait," he said.

Ng narrowed his eyes. "What is it?"

Meirelles felt the sweat beading on his forehead. He
looked into the face of the Vietnamese. It was not the sort
of face he was accustomed to. He didn't know how to
read it.

"The police," he said faintly. "You've been betrayed."

Ng regarded him gravely for a long beat. He bent down
with his knuckles on the small wooden table and his gaze
was terrible, riveting. Meirelles could not look away. *Spare
me,* he thought inanely.

But Ng only shook his hand a second time.

"Thank you, Roberto," he said. "Thank you for telling me."

The three Americans followed him out.

CHAPTER 11

1. Ng described a place down the road and told them to wait there. A truck would come, he said.

"It could be a trap," Byron said. "He could be selling us out."

Keller anticipated an angry reaction from the Vietnamese. But Ng only shook his head. "I have my own kind of virtue," he said. "I stay bought."

So they hiked down the road that ran from the mines through the old town, sheltered by their clothes and the night and the press of human bodies around them. They avoided the trash fires and walked with their shoulders bent, purposefully but not too fast, alert for police patrols. Beyond the limits of the town they kept to the shadow of the forest wall. A barrel-ribbed dog paced them for a quarter of a mile, loping on three legs; Byron threw a stone to drive it away.

In time they came to the place Ng had described, an opening in the road where a logging trail joined it from the west. Midnight had come and gone and there was very little traffic. Twice, big antique diesel semis roared by on their way to Pau Seco. Once, ominously, a military transport. But mostly the road was empty, the night noises of the forest ringing in the darkness.

Keller had fallen into a standing doze when a van pulled up at the verge of the road, waking him. The sky was faintly brighter now, and he was able to read the word ELETRONORTE in faint white letters along the rust-scabbed body of the van. The driver waited, his engine idling.

Keller showed himself first, then Byron, and then Teresa. The driver, an Indio with large unblinking eyes, waved them into the back. Keller latched the door behind him and the van jolted forward.

They sat on the empty metal floor with their backs against the bulkhead. Teresa said wearily, "Where's he taking us?"

Byron shrugged. "It doesn't matter. We can't go back through Rio. We should stay away from the big cities altogether."

Teresa held the wrapped oneirolith in her hands, steepled delicately between her fingers. "At least," she said, "we got what we came for."

"You did," Byron said. "And I guess Ray did. Pretty good footage, right, Ray? Damn nice footage."

Keller said nothing. Teresa was leaning against him now, her eyes closing. Keller put his arm out to steady her, and the truck carried them down the night roads, away from Pau Seco.

He drifted on the edge of sleep for a time, conscious of her warmth and of the weight of her against him as the ELETRONORTE van rattled into the dawn. The driver glanced back occasionally but did not speak, the expression on his face faintly puzzled, as if he were trying to make sense of this new and mysterious cargo. At last, when the light fil-

tering back from the cab woke him, Keller managed a smile.
"Thank you for the ride," he said hoarsely.

The driver shook his head. *"Ela e muito gentil."* He
gestured at Teresa. "Pretty girl."

Very pretty, Keller thought innocently.

"Your girl? Your wife?"

"No." Not quite that. But he closed his arm around
her protectively, and she moved against him in her sleep.

"Your girl," the driver said toothily, and turned his
attention back to the road.

And Keller recognized—a moment of insight as pen-
etrating as the sunlight—that it was true, he was falling
in love with her . . . maybe had already fallen in love
with her.

It put him in a bad position.

Adhyasa, Keller thought. He was supposed to be a
machine, and machines are supposed to be indifferent: you
can't suborn a machine. A machine in love might be tempted
to look away.

And yet . . . He sat in the back of the jolting truck
with her body pressed against him and wanted her more
than he had wanted anything for years. The wanting itself
was a new thing, and it ran through him like a tide. A part
of him welcomed it: this thawing of ancient tundra. But he
knew the risks. Stray too far from the Ice Palace and he
would be stripped, vulnerable. Outside the Palace, all manner of things waited.

Old pain. Memories. Things seen.

And yet . . .

"Here," the driver said suddenly. The truck slowed.
Keller bounced back against the metalwork; Teresa moaned
and stirred. *"Avie-se!* Please hurry now."

And then they were alone again, blinking at the sunlight
in a dry junction town called Sinop.

They had bank certificates and cruzeiro notes; enough,
Byron said, to get them out of the country. They should
find a room and in the morning strike out along the eastern
highway to Barreira or maybe Campo Alegre. He knew

people in Belem; from Belem he could arrange a flight out of the country.

They found a cheap room by nightfall. Byron went out with a fistful of coins: he wanted to make some calls, he said, "but not from here." And maybe get drunk. He looked at Keller, at Teresa. Maybe definitely get drunk.

The door sighed closed after him.

Teresa pulled the drapes and switched off the lights. The room was dark as a cavern now, the roar of traffic from the main street loud in the darkness. She climbed onto the cheap sprung mattress where Keller was lying and curled against him. She was wearing the clothes she had worn from Pau Seco, and he could smell the oil from the truck and the pungency of her sweat. After a moment he realized she was shaking.

"Scared?" he said.

She rolled over and nodded into his chest. "We're in over our heads, aren't we? That's what all this means. We're in way over our heads."

It was true, of course. Wexler had promised her an easy trip—"a vacation." But the huge military presence at Pau Seco and the palpable fear in the eyes of Meirelles demonstrated that the project had gone a long way beyond that. Someone had taken an interest in them. The federal agencies, Keller guessed. Wexler must have been harboring an informant at his estate in Carmel. Or Wexler was the informant, or had confessed under interrogation. It didn't matter which. What mattered was that someone had taken an interest in them—someone powerful.

Because he could not think of anything reassuring to say, he soothed her with his hands.

"You're an Angel," she said sleepily.

He nodded in the dark.

"Everything goes into memory?"

"What I see. What I hear."

"Even this?"

He admitted, "Even this."

"Who sees it?"

"Maybe nobody."

"Who turns it into video?"

"I do," Keller said. "I do my own downloading at the Network shops."

"Would you download this?"

This conversation, he thought she meant; or more broadly, what had begun to happen between them. He hesitated. "No," he said finally.

She traced the contour of his skull with her fingers. "You have wires in there."

He nodded.

"They say it affects you."

"It can."

"Does it?"

"Sometimes. Sometimes it's hard to tell. Memory plays tricks." He looked into the darkness. "Just before they installed the harness, back in the military hospital at Santarem, I lifted a text out of the medical library. There was a list of side effects, what could happen if things went wrong. Blindness, amnesia, disturbance of affect—"

"Affect?"

"Emotional affect." He smiled, although of course in the darkness she could not see. "Love, hate."

"You have that?"

"I don't know." The question made him uncomfortable. "Sometimes I wonder."

There was no way to tell her what this really meant. No way to condense the experience. He had emerged from the military hospital into a world of complex uncertainties. It was not the brain the wires had invaded; it was the essence, the *self*. Every perception became suspect, every emotion a potential symptom. So you learn, Keller thought: you practise *wu-nien* very carefully . . . you become, in some fundamental way, a machine.

It was, he wanted to say, a strange combination of clarity and confusion. Like those nights when the fog comes in so thick you might as well be blind, but sound carries with great intimacy over startling distances. You can't see your feet, but a buoy clanging out in the bay comes to you with that high, sad tonality all intact. He was able to register the distant bell-ringing of events, commerce, politics. He was good at it. But the fog concealed love. The fog concealed hate.

"It must be strange." She was calmer now, drifting into sleep, nuzzled against him.

"It is." But he was not certain she heard him. Her breathing grew deeper until she was limp in his arms. "It is." He addressed the dark and silent room. "It is."

They bused into the northern province of Para and stayed a night in Campo Alegre, on the Araguaia River. It was an old cattle town surrounded by corporate ranches; the accommodations were crude, the smell of the slaughterhouse reminded Keller unpleasantly of Cuiaba. They checked into a twentieth-century hotel occupied by the morose agents of foreign meat wholesalers, and surprised the clerk by paying cash. Cash was bad, Byron said, cash was conspicuous; but until they could arrange some black-market credit, cash was also a necessity.

Teresa invested in less obviously American clothes and a canvas bag in which to conceal the oneirolith. Keller had watched the way she carried the stone, the exaggerated care, her obvious desire clashing with her fear. What she wanted from it, he understood, was memory, and that struck him as dangerously naive—the idea that memory would dole out meaning into her life. Memory as buried treasure.

He knew all about memory. Memory, he thought, isn't the treasure; the treasure is forgetting. But where was the stone, the drug or the pill or the powder, with that magic in it?

Teresa stepped into the room's tiny shower stall and left Keller alone with Byron. Byron had been staring out the window, a view of the swollen Araguaia. Now, with the hiss of the shower filling the room, he turned suddenly to Keller and said, "I know what's going on."

Keller stared at him.

"It's hardly a secret," he said. "Christ, Ray. I'm not deaf. I'm not blind." He straightened his shoulders, and the gesture had a pained and immense dignity in it. "It's not hard to understand. And I don't necessarily disapprove. If it's good for her, all right. If you're not using her. But the thing is, I don't want her hurt."

Keller said, "Look, I—"

"You think this is *easy* for me?" He turned away convulsively. "I was like you. You remember? I know how it is. I had good Angel habits. I was dedicated. I did my job. And then I came back from the war, I had my wires stripped. You make these gestures. You think okay, well, that's it, I'm back in the world now. But it's not that easy. You carry a lot around with you. It's not a physical thing. If you really want to be back in the world, you have to reach out for it, take hold of it. You have to care for something." He drew in a deep breath. "I cared for her. It wasn't an infatuation. More than that. More than that. Maybe it was love. Maybe it still is. She was my ticket back into the world, Ray. People find out you were an Angel, you know, they act strange. Like you're some kind of zombie—the walking dead. Maybe I let people think that, or maybe I even encouraged it a little bit. It's not so bad sometimes, being on the outside. But I did not want it to be *true*. You understand? I wouldn't *let* it be true. And she was my way of *proving* it wasn't true. I cared about her enough to save her life; I cared about her enough to come down here with her. I know how she feels about me. The sentiment is not mutual. But that doesn't matter. What matters is that I cared and that I continued to care even when she slept with other men, and that I care now, when she is obviously falling in love with you. Because it's the caring, the caring is what matters." His fists were clenched; he faced the window. "Now," he said, "maybe that's hard for you to grasp. You're still wired, you're still deep in the Ice Palace, even though you probably think you're not. You can look at her from that safe high place, you can allow yourself the luxury of falling a little bit in love. How fucking brave. But my wires are *gone*, Ray. It makes a difference. I'm not a machine anymore. I'm a human being or I'm nothing. A *broken* machine. So I care for her. And if she loves me, that's good, that's best of all, but even if she doesn't, even if it hurts, as long as I care enough to *let* it hurt, then that's good, too, because it means I'm really back from the war, that I'm here in the world, still breathing—'' He rammed his fist against the arm of his chair. ''Still flesh and blood.''

Keller could only stare.

Byron shook his head. ''It's hard talking to you sometimes.''

They heard the shower switch off. Water dripped hollowly in the stall. Teresa was humming some tune in a minor key.

''Don't hurt her,'' Byron said softly. ''That's all I ask.''

2.   And so they came to Belem, an international port at the broad mouth of the Amazon, where Byron knew an expatriate American who might be able to find them passage out of Brazil, and where Keller made love to Teresa for the first time.

They booked a room much like the rooms they had booked at Sinop or Campo Alegre, this one in a corniced brick building overlooking a fish market called the Ver-o-Peso. Byron spent a lot of time at the docks trying to contact his Army buddy, and for several afternoons Keller was alone with her in the room.

They made love with the curtains drawn. A rainfall began and the traffic along the Ver-o-Peso made soft rushing noises. He moved against her silently; she cried out once in the dimness of the room, as if the act had shaken loose some shard of memory inside her.

It was a long time since Keller had made love to a woman he cared about, and he was distantly aware of bonds loosening inside him, a sense of derelict synapses lighting up. He imagined the Angel wiring in his head as a road map, abandoned neural jungles shot through suddenly with ghostly glowing. It was a kind of sin, he thought, but he gave himself over to it helplessly, to loving her and making love to her. He knew that he would not download any of this from his AV memory, and because of that it seemed as if the act had only the most nebulous kind of existence: it existed between them, in his memory and in hers; flesh memory, he thought, volatile and untrustworthy. But he would cherish it. *Adhyasa*, Angel sin, but he would hold it tight inside him.

Afterward they were together in the silence.

The rain had raised the humidity, and her skin felt feverish against him. Her eyes were squeezed shut now. The pressure of the last few days, he thought, the trip from Pau Seco. But not just that. He said, "It's not only the Agencies you're afraid of."

She shook her head.

"The stone?"

"It's strange," she said. "You want something so much for such a long time, and then . . . you're holding it in your hands, and you think, what is this? What does it have to do with me?" She sat up amidst the tangled sheets.

"Maybe," he said, "you don't need it."

Her hair spilled over her shoulders and across Keller's face. "I do, though. I have dreams. . . ." The thought trailed away.

Rain rattled against the casements of the ancient windows. She stood and looked across the room at the bag where the oneirolith was concealed. Keller was suddenly frightened for her. No telling what the stone might contain. "Give it time," he said. "If we get back to the Floats, if everything calms down—"

"No," she said, resolute now in the darkness. "No, Ray. I don't want to wait."

CHAPTER 12

1. The Brazilians held Ng in custody three days before Oberg was informed. He heard about it in an offhand remark from one of Major Andreazza's junior peacekeepers and stormed off to confront Andreazza in his office. "You should have told me," he said.

Andreazza allowed his gaze to wander about the room until it came to rest, laconically, on Oberg. He registered a mild surprise. "Told you about what?"

"About Ng." My Christ, Oberg thought.

"The Vietnamese," Andreazza said, "has been detained."

"I know. I know he's been detained. I want to interrogate him."

"He's being interrogated now, Mr. Oberg."

"Being butchered, you mean? What's the matter, have you beaten him to death already?"

There was a barely perceptible hardening about Andreazza's features; he regarded Oberg icily. "I don't think you're in a position to criticize."

"The thing is," Oberg said, returning the look, "I am."

"I've spoken to SUDAM. And I've spoken to my superiors. As far as any of us are concerned, your role here is strictly advisory. And I would advise you to keep that in mind when you address me . . . assuming you want any cooperation at all."

Oberg fought down a response. What this means, he thought grimly, is that they've fucked up. The stone is gone, the Americans are gone. They had Ng. But Ng was a consolation prize at best.

He experienced a brief flurry of contempt for Andreazza and his soldiers, for the swarming anarchy of Pau Seco. It had astonished him at first, the primitiveness of this place. It was an accident of history, of course, the consequence of a series of diplomatic compromises that had concluded the shooting war in Brazil. But, he thought with some desperation, they don't *know*. They didn't know how important all this had become. SUDAM didn't know and the civilian government didn't know or care, and he wondered whether even the Agencies really understood what their own research had uncovered.

But Oberg knew. He had experienced it. He understood.

The burden of this interdiction had fallen to him. And it was not finished yet. Maybe Andreazza had screwed up. But there was still time.

"I'm sorry," he said carefully. "If I offended you, then I apologize for that. It's just that I would very much like to see this man Ng."

Andreazza allowed himself a narrow smile. "Maybe I can arrange it. If you'd like to wait?"

And so the seconds ticked by. Seconds, Oberg thought, minutes, hours . . . days. While the contagion threatened to spread.

2.   Ng was in a dazed condition when they took him to see the Agency man, Stephen Oberg.

He was dazed because the military interrogators had been at him. They had intercepted him when he tried to run a blockade down one of the logging roads east of Pau Seco, and they had brought him back here, to the cinderblock building that served as a jail. They put him in a cell that was too hot in the daylight and too cold at night, and for two consecutive afternoons they tortured him.

The torture was pedestrian. It was not what they did that frightened him so much as their clumsiness at it. There was a plastic bag they put over his head to suffocate him, and he was worried that they might be too stupid or inexperienced to know when to take it off. Altogether, it was archaic. They played good-guy bad-guy with him. There was a tall *sertao* Indian in a disheveled military uniform who spoke sympathetically to him between torture sessions and promised him leniency—"I won't let these bastards touch you"—but only, of course, if Ng would detail his involvement in the theft of the oneirolith. Ng was careful to seem tempted by this offer, in order to prolong the respite from the pain. But he never confessed.

The next day they tied his wrists and ankles to a two-by-four which they hauled up on a rope to the ceiling beams, and then they struck him with broom handles until he was spinning sickeningly and in great pain. He vomited once, and they beat him harder for it. After a time he passed out. Still he did not confess.

During the coldest passage of the night, when he could not sleep for the pain of his injuries, he wondered why this was. Why *not* confess? It was hardly a matter of principle. It was theft, he thought, not revolution. He was not a partisan, nor was he a martyr. He had no desire to be a martyr.

Still he resisted. In part it was his constitution—literally, the way he was made. He was a creche soldier. His body was good at the chemistry of aggression and not very good at the chemistry of fear. So he was not afraid, and the pain, although it was terrible, was endurable in the absence of fear. Death frightened him—he was at least that human

ROBERT CHARLES WILSON

—but he knew he would be killed whether he confessed or not, and so confession was only useful as a way of abbreviating the pain. He would reach that point, certainly. But not yet.

Too, there was a part of him that didn't belong to the military creches at Danang, a willfulness for which he had often been chastened. It's the risk you take, a Khmer geneticist once told him, with this kind of chemical tampering. Aggression bordered on rebellion. He was headstrong. They had told him so at Danang. They had beaten him for it.

He had performed loyally in the Pacific Rim offensives, and he had killed a lot of *posseiros,* and he could not honestly say it was a moral revulsion that had drawn him away from the military after the war. Maybe that, too, in part. But he guessed his moral sensibilities were as poorly developed as his capacity for fear. What he felt was more personal. Brazil had astonished him. It was huge in every dimension. He had never guessed a single nation could contain so much variety of wealth, poverty, landscape. He sensed a world beyond the narrow margins he had been raised to recognize. He wondered, finally, if there might not be a life for him here, some destiny more subtle than career soldiering in Thailand or the Philippines or in occupied Manchuria. He disappeared during a recreational leave in São Paulo a week after the peace was declared. He became an illegal.

As an illegal he had no rights and was constantly vulnerable to arrest, but he had been able to secure a series of lumbering jobs that led him increasingly closer to the frontier and finally, a few years ago, to Pau Seco. The oneirolith mine fascinated him. The scope of the effort fascinated him, the strangeness of it, the wild contrasts of poverty and fortune. If there was a role for him to play, he thought, it was here.

Well. It was a faulty intuition. Unless, of course, this *was* his role, the unintended role of victim and martyr, and the cautionary role he would play, hanging by the neck on the gallows hill above the old town.

But he did not blame himself and he did not blame the Americans. He had been offered—and briefly possessed—

a startling sum of money. From his new perspective it seemed trivial, but that was death-cell thinking: the money might have bought him a new life, and given the decision to make again, he might make it the same way. He had gambled and lost.

Bad calculation, then. But was that all?

No.

Something else.

In the years since the war he had developed a loathing for the sort of men who controlled Pau Seco, for Andreazza and his brutal soldiers and for the *garimpeiros* like Claudio who exploited their laborers. And in the brief time he knew her, he had developed a guarded sympathy for the American woman, Teresa, who was so startlingly guileless she seemed to exist in another universe. It was a moral sensibility as primitive as his fears but, Ng thought, at least as strong. And maybe, at the base of it, that was why he had frustrated his torturers. He had learned how to hate them.

Oberg was a different case. He already hated Oberg. He had hated him for years.

Ng was aware of the pressure of Oberg's eyes as the guards hustled him into the tiny interrogation room. There were two gray-uniformed peacekeepers in the room as well as the military man Andreazza, but the tension was obvious and direct: it passed between Oberg and Ng.

But I have the advantage, Ng thought. He doesn't know who I am. But I know all about him.

The guards dropped him into a cruelly straight-backed wooden chair. Ng gasped and almost fainted with the pain. There had been blood in his urine this morning, and he was worried that his injuries might be more serious than he had thought.

Maybe these people had already killed him. Maybe he was only waiting to die.

He took deep, ratcheting breaths until his heart was steady and he was able to hold up his head. A swimming blackness obscured his vision. He looked at Oberg and Oberg seemed to be standing at the end of a tunnel now, distant and strange.

Now Oberg was talking.

Oberg said the predictable things. He said he knew all about Ng's connection with Cruz Wexler and the conspiracy to sell the oneirolith. Witnesses, he said, had confirmed the exchange at the bar in the old town. He said he knew the Americans had left Pau Seco and that he wanted Ng to tell him how they had escaped and where they might have gone.

He said all this in a restrained, sweetly reasonable voice that reminded Ng of the whine of the hydraulic pumps deep in the mine. He closed his eyes and envisioned Oberg himself as a machine, a whistling construction of pipes and levers and barbed wire and scalding steam. A machine with claws, he thought giddily; iron claws and searchlight eyes.

A guard butted him awake with his rifle.

Oberg was closer now. Oberg was peering into Ng's face. He was close enough that Ng could smell the American's sanitized breath, hot and perfumed with mint. And Ng understood suddenly—scrutinizing Oberg from the chair, but aloofly, as if from some higher and cleaner place—that Oberg was a lie. His starched collar was a lie; his slick, receding hair was a lie; the restrained tension ticking at the corner of his mouth betrayed a multitude of lies. Oberg was a lie made of flesh.

"I won't hurt you," the American said calmly. "You understand? I'm not here to hurt you."

And that was a lie too.

"I know you," Ng whispered.

"I'm sorry," Oberg said. "I can't hear you."

"*I know you.*"

Oberg frowned.

Ng spoke in spite of himself. A flood of truth into the vacuum of Oberg's lies. "I know who you are." He closed his eyes and hoped the guard wouldn't strike him again. "We marched through Rio Branco," he said breathlessly. "The villages west of Rio Branco. This was in the spring of '37, a little after the April offensive. You were famous. Did you know that? Among the Vietnamese, you were notorious." And Oberg touched him then; Oberg took Ng's long hair in his hand and jerked his head back against the spine of the chair to make him stop. But Ng kept talking. It was as if he had lost the power to control himself. "We did terrible things. We killed people. *Posseiros*. Soldiers mostly. Ragged men, but at least they were armed. It would have been so easy to feel guilt. We were machines, you understand, machines made to kill, but it was possible to feel guilt . . . some of us felt it."

Oberg cracked Ng's head against the back of the chair, and Ng was certain he would pass out. Which made him unhappy, because he was enjoying this in some curious way: it was the only act of revenge available to him. But then Andreazza said in his careful English, "We don't want to kill him quite yet, Mr. Oberg." And the American relaxed his grip slightly.

Ng opened his eyes and looked into Oberg's eyes and understood that the American hated him for what he knew. "We marched out from Rio Branco," he said, "to clean up after you. Clean up the guerillas, they meant. But you had left another kind of mess." The memory was vivid, and Ng, lost in it now, became more solemn. "The bodies were everywhere. Women and children. It disgusted us. Even us. It disgusted even us. And in a strange way it made us feel better. We were machines but we weren't monsters. You proved that to us. You were our consolation. Whatever we had become, there was something worse." He looked at Oberg and, from the depths of his chair, he smiled. "You made us feel human."

Oberg whispered between his teeth; the words were inaudible. Ng felt a brief, untethered burst of happiness. It was a kind of victory. "They've been gone a long time," he said. The Americans, he meant. He felt himself drifting out of awareness, but that was all right now. He had said what he wanted to say. "You won't find them. It's too late to find them."

And closed his eyes. And took deep, painful breaths.

Oberg turned to Andreazza. "Kill him," he said tightly. "Kill the slant-eyed son of a bitch."

"In time," Andreazza said.

3.   The evening before he left Pau Seco, Oberg walked to the gallows hill where the body of Ng had been left to hang overlooking the old town, an object lesson to the illiterate *formigas*.

The day was windy and overcast, and the body turned restlessly on its pivot of rope. The corpse was bloated with death, and Oberg felt only the faintest connection now between this carcass and the man who had faced him in Andreazza's office. Hence only a murmur of satisfaction . . . a shiver of triumph.

The Vietnamese man had lived three more days before he confessed, and the confession he made was useless. Oberg learned the name of the *formiga* who had bartered away the stone—Morelles or Meirelles—but Meirelles had vanished with the money and was beyond punishment now, lost in some smoky industrial barrio. Such men were untraceable. Raymond Keller and Byron Ostler and the American woman Teresa Rafael had ridden an Eletronorte truck as far as Sinop, Ng had said, and presumably then vanished. Toward the east, Oberg suspected; but there was no way to confirm the suspicion unless they attempted to use credit or buy passage out of the country.

Until then it was a question of laborious pursuit, proceeding first to Sinop and then following their trail wherever it led. Tedious and thankless work, but he was braced for it.

The desolate gallows hilltop made him uneasy. He regarded Ng's dead, petulant face, and was possessed by a sudden fear that the eyes might spring open, the mouth unlock; that Ng might tumble free and croak out some new and loathsome accusation.

It was crazy, of course. *What the dead know, they do not speak.* Someone had said that. Someone he did not care to remember.

But the body moved in a river of wind from the Mato Grosso, and Oberg shuddered and turned his back. It was disgusting, he thought. Primitive. They should bury the dead. They should have the decency.

CHAPTER 13

1. Keller went with Byron to a café overlooking the docks along the Amazon, where they had agreed to meet an American who could arrange their passage out of Brazil.

The Amazon here was so broad it might have been the sea. The water was brown and turgid; the ships moored at the dock were ocean ships. Keller ordered *tucupi* and watched an Israeli trawler inch forward from the horizon, its radars and solar panels silhouetted against the margin of the sky. By the time the trawler made port, Byron's contact had arrived: a stubble-haired combat vet with bright, feverish eyes. He shook hands with Keller but flinched when Byron introduced him by name. Denny.

"This was supposed to be private," Denny said.

ROBERT CHARLES WILSON

Byron looked at Keller; Keller nodded, put down money for the *tucupi,* and wandered out along the dock road a little.

He stood against an embankment watching Brazilian stevedores unload a corporate fishing boat, ESPERANCE stenciled in white letters across the gleaming stack flues. *Esperance,* he thought: hope. A commodity they had just about run out of. Teresa had elected to stay at the hotel, pleading a need for privacy; Keller wondered now if they should have left her.

She was tempted by the dreamstone. They had been in Belem a week, and he had watched the dance she did with it, a nervous pirouette of attraction and fear. Better, of course, to leave it alone until they reached some safer venue. But she was drawn to it. She said so. Fear and hunger. Fear and *esperance.*

Too, he was worried about the time they were wasting. They were fugitives, and it was too easy to forget or ignore that. The longer they stayed in one place, the more vulnerable they became. Worse, their prospects were not improving. Twice now Byron had attempted to buy them onto a clandestine flight out of the country. Twice the deal had fallen through. Denny was a long shot, friend of a friend, reputedly a smuggler of some kind . . . but in Belem that was hardly a distinction. The port city was swarming with transients and foreigners, and Keller consoled himself that it was probably the best place to be, under the circumstances. Here, anyway, three indigent Americans were not conspicuous.

But he was aware of the forces that had been mustered against them, and he was far enough now from the consolations of *wu-nien* that he worried especially about Teresa.

He looked at the café and saw Byron waving him back. Denny had left. The negotiations had been brief.

Keller hiked wearily up the cobbled street. "Did he deal?"

Byron shook his head. "He'll call us."

They walked in silence back to the hotel off the Vero-Peso. Byron knocked at the door—there was no answer—then plugged his key into the lock. The mechanism clattered, the door eased open. Byron hesitated in the doorway. Keller, anxious now, pushed past him.

Teresa lay curled on the floor, the dreamstone clutched in both hands.

2.   She was embedded in the dream now.

It was all around her and more vivid than it had ever been. It surrounded her like an ocean, and at the same time she contained it: an embrace of knowledge. She knew more than she had ever known.

A surfeit of questions. An excess of answers.

She was curious about the blue-winged people. In so many ways they seemed so familiar—so human. She was able to take in their history at a glance now, to *remember* it, and the similarities, she thought, were awesome. Like human beings, they had evolved from arboreal creatures sometime in the ancient past. They possessed opposable thumbs, a large cranial capacity, a vast array of cultures and languages. They had mastered human technologies: flint knives, fire, agriculture, iron. She knew all this instantly and without effort.

So human, she thought. And yet . . .

Their history was curiously placid. There were wars, but fewer and briefer than human wars had been. Their religions were more often ecstatic than militant. They were pantheists and nature worshippers. They were quick to develop written language, and quickly fostered an almost universal literacy. They had been using crude printing presses as early as their Bronze Age.

They possessed a genius for information technology which had led them from books to binary circuits to molecular memories and beyond that into storage-retrieval mechanisms so subtle and immediate she could not begin to comprehend them. She understood that the oneiroliths were the end product of this process, its final and most absolute incarnation.

The stones were more than they seemed. They existed in a complex hidden topology, each linked to each, each in some sense a reflection of each, each with a special affinity for the geometry of sapient awareness . . . and their function was almost ludicrously simple.

They remembered.

They contained the past, or were a kind of passport to it: the distinction had been lost. They were both history book and time machine, limited only by a kind of proximity effect. The Pau Seco stone contained most of the history of the Exotics and much of the modern history of the Earth. Beyond those margins—as if that weren't enough—she was unable to see.

The oldest memories were dim. She saw the blue people most vividly as they had been at their apex: a world made so strange that it defied her understanding. They had expanded to the limits of their planetary system, colonized the cold ring of dust and stone that marked its farthest outpost, constructed there the fragile, huge interstellar vehicles that went winging out like butterflies between the stars. The pilots of these vessels were immortal, binary intelligences undisturbed by the passage of vast spans of time but recognizably modeled after the winged people, and in some sense descended from them. The butterfly ships in their diaspora mapped more barren worlds than Teresa cared to think about. One of them had angled past the Earth when the Chou Dynasty was succeeding the Shang and the Assyrians were marching into Babylon. (A few neolithic American tribes actually saw the craft in its looping polar orbit: a star of many colors. The observant Babylonians were preoccupied; the Chinese were in the wrong place.) It was a divided and primitive world—*still is,* Teresa thought distantly—but the winged people had deemed it at least potentially worthy of their gift (it *was* a gift), which they directed, perhaps wisely, into the then-uninhabited and unnamed depths of the Mato Grosso. A garden for the tree of knowledge.

And winged away once more, and passed out of Teresa's knowing.

She had seen much of this before, but scrambled and chaotic; it had never made sense to her except as visionary flashes, the fractured output of the cruder dreamstones. She was astonished now at the scope of it. The stones, she understood, were magnets of consciousness. They absorbed and recorded the flickering traces of experience . . . at a distance, without contact, automatically, through some mechanism beyond her grasp. Lives, she thought: they stored and recorded the passing of lives.

And so the human past was here too. A Babel of languages and customs and battles, sanguinary births and premature deaths. She could have descended at will into any part of it (the thought was dizzying), lived a moment with Hammurabi or Aristotle or any of the peasant millions who had marched into nameless oblivion. But not now, she thought. Later. Enough to know that they were preserved here, that in some important sense they had *not* died. She preferred for the moment to hover above it all, to take in the shape of it entirely and at once, humanity like one creature, a single voice, a river.

She contemplated it for what seemed an endless time; and would have gone on, enraptured, but for the voice that called her away.

I'm here, it said . . . faint and faraway, but terribly persistent. *I've always been here.*

It drew her down. She gasped, frightened now.

She gasped. Keller bent over her, worried.

"Don't touch her," Byron warned.

But she was trembling, wrapped around the dreamstone and clutching it to herself. She was in some kind of pain, he thought. Or dreaming some unbearable dream.

"Let her work it out," Byron said. "There's nothing you can do for her."

"It's hurting her."

"She'll come out of it."

"How do you know?" He recognized that he was close to panic. *Wu-nien,* he thought. But the instinct had deserted him. "It's not the same. It's a new kind of stone."

"It's her decision."

She shuddered against the floor, eyes squeezed shut. She looked lost, Keller thought: fallen into some chasm of herself. He wanted to shake her.

Byron put a hand on him, restraining him. But the phone rang suddenly. "Let it happen," Byron said, and turned away. The phone's CRT had burned out years ago; Byron gazed into a carbonized blankness.

Keller turned back to Teresa, took a blanket from the bed and spread it over her. She opened her mouth and made a brief, anguished cry.

Memory, Keller thought helplessly.

He knew what it meant. He could have told her.

She saw the little girl.

She saw the little girl living in a float shack somewhere out by the far margins of the tidal dams, out of sight of the mainland. She knew a few things about the little girl now. Things she had not known before.

The little girl was a good little girl. The little girl was obedient. The little girl lived with her mother and spoke good and careful English, not the Hispanic patois of her playmates. The little girl had learned to read at a Public Works school operating out of an abandoned grain storehouse which stood on concrete stilts above the floating ghetto. The little girl was cheerful and blithely unaware of her condition of poverty, except when the government checks failed to clear, or the time when the bank machines closed down after the riots. Then she was hungry. And frightened, and irritable. But food came eventually, and she learned in time to endure even these brief bouts of hunger: she was confident that they would end.

She took pride in her goodness in a way that sometimes offended her friends, and she grew increasingly circumspect. But she knew, without actually thinking the words, that this was not a priggish or gloating kind of goodness; that the skills her mother encouraged in her were in fact survival skills, and survival was by no means assured. She had witnessed the attrition among her friends. Many of her friends had died of diseases or had been remanded to orphanages or had simply moved away, a fate she associated with death because she could not comprehend the notion of a larger world. She accepted these truths with a resignation accessible only to the very young, and acquiesced to her mother's regimen of education and careful virtue. She was a *good* little girl.

For many of the same reasons it did not seem strange that she did not have a father. She had had one once. Her mother told her so. Her father had been a wise and brave man who had died attempting to bring them over the border from the Republic of Mexico when she was just a baby. They had been respectable people in Mexico. Her father had been a lawyer. In the Aguilar purges of the '30s, any member of the bar was considered an enemy. And so they had to escape, but Aguilar was a staunch friend of the United States and the border had been closed even to respectable lawyers and their families. They made a border run with thirty other ragged men and women, running a gauntlet of desert and barbed wire and infrared detectors and satellite surveillance and the broad concrete no-man's-land that separated the sovereign nations. The little girl had no memory of this, but the story had been told to her many times: it was a kind of legend, a brave and daunting mythology. Many of the refugees had been cut down by automated gunfire. Her father had been one of these. Her mother took up the child and pressed on, too frightened even for grief. (The grief, it was implied, had come later.) Many more of their group had been arrested and deported; a few had escaped into the Hispanic ghetto sprawls that crowded against the border fences. The little girl and her mother had been among this lucky minority.

They were not wealthy enough to start a new life as Americans—they could not afford permanent black-market documentation—but there was enough money to buy passage into the Floats, where the rules were suspended and they could have, at least, this compromised shadow existence; never legal, but no longer vulnerable to the caprices of the Aguilar regime.

She could not remember her father except through these stories, and so his absence never seemed strange to her, until the day her mother brought a new man home.

She was ten, and she was outraged. She saw the guilt in her mother's eyes and was both angry and frightened by it. She was too young to understand the adult clash of loyalties, the fear of age and the fear of death. She was only old enough to feel betrayed. She did not deserve this. She was a *good* girl.

She hated the man instantly. His name was Carlos and he worked at the loading dock where the girl's mother did occasional day labor. Meeting her, Carlos bent down, put his immense hand on her shoulder, and told her he had met her mother at work. "She's a good worker," Carlos said. He straightened, grinned obscenely, swatted the girl's mother across the bottom. "Eh? She does what she's told."

The girl was appalled by this sudden vision of her mother as a separate entity, a grown-up woman with a hidden life of her own. She did not say anything, only stood with her face carefully blank and one hand bracing herself against the kitchen table. Inside, she was writhing. Everything seemed suddenly tawdry. She was conscious of the peeling tile under her feet, the shabbiness of the float shanty they inhabited. Beans were cooking on the stovetop; a smoky, foul aroma filled the tiny room. And Carlos continued to grin down at her, the broad pores of his face radiating sweat and insincerity. His teeth were chipped and vulpine; his breath smelled like spoiled food.

He was not a lawyer.

He moved in. She was not consulted about it. He moved in and filled the shack with his noxious presence. He took up more space, the little girl thought, than any ordinary man. He bumped into things. He drank—though not, at first, excessively. His huge hands moved over the girl's mother with an aggressive intimacy which was received without resistance or encouragement. The walls dividing the two rooms were thin enough that there was no mystery about what happened during the night: it was sex, the little girl thought, a messiness of grunting and moaning, unspeakable. When it happened, she would hide her face and cover her ears. In the mornings Carlos would grin at her and whisper: "How did you sleep, little one? Too noisy for you?" And laugh a secret, terrible laugh at the back of his throat.

One day when Carlos was at work, the little girl dared to ask her mother why she had allowed him to move in.

The contempt in her voice was impossible to conceal, and her mother slapped her for it. The girl gaped and raised one hand to her wounded face. Her cheek was on fire.

The girl's mother flushed. "We're not in a position to choose," she said fiercely. "Look at me! Am I young? Am I pretty? Look! Am I rich?"

And the girl observed for the first time that her mother was none of these things.

"He brings money in. Maybe you don't know what that means. You don't look at your plate when you eat. Maybe you should. There's meat there. Meat! And green vegetables. You have clothes. You don't go hungry."

So we are poor, the girl thought. Carlos was the curse of their poverty.

These things astonished and frightened her.

She might have adjusted, even so. Except that now Carlos himself began to change. Bad as he was to begin with, he grew worse. His drinking intensified. The girl's mother confided that Carlos was having trouble on the job, fighting with the foreman. Some nights the grunting and moaning in the next room would end in muffled curses. Carlos would not make jokes the next morning, merely glower at his breakfast. His casual intimacy with the girl's mother became more aggressive; he tossed her back and forth in his arms in a way that made the girl think of a woman being mauled by a bear. Increasingly that was what Carlos seemed to her to be: a large and powerful animal fuming in a cage. But the cage was insubstantial; the cage, its restraint, could vanish at any moment. She didn't like to think about that.

He began to touch her more often.

She accepted this at first the way her mother accepted it, with passive resignation. She was aware of her mother watching closely when Carlos coaxed her into his lap. Carlos had hands like hairless animals, hands like moles. They moved with a blind volition of their own. They touched and stroked her. Usually when she had endured this for a time, Carlos would stand up abruptly, scowl at her as if she had done something wrong, take the girl's mother off into the bedroom.

ROBERT CHARLES WILSON

Her mother apologized one day. They were alone. The float shack rose in a gentle swell; rain beat against the roof and the bilge pumps rattled under the floor. "I'm sorry," her mother said. "What's happening . . . I didn't expect it."

The girl felt an anger well up in her, huge and unexpected. "Then make him leave!" She astonished herself with tears. "Tell him to go away!"

Her mother hugged and soothed her. "It's not that easy. I wish it were. I'm sorry. I'm sorry. It's hard to be alone. You don't understand that. It's been difficult. Difficult to be alone. I thought he would help, you know. I really thought he would." She stroked the girl's hair. "I thought he might learn to love us."

That night, when Carlos began to touch her, her mother told the little girl to go to her room. She listened through the door as the two adults spoke and then shouted. There was a scuffling, the girl's mother cried out, a door slammed. The little girl waited but there was no more sound. She was afraid to go out. She slept finally, trembling in her sleep.

In the morning Carlos scowled at her and left the shack wordlessly. The girl's mother had a blackened bruise across her cheek. She touched it periodically and with an expression of wonder, as if it had appeared there by magic. Her face, with the bruise, looked terribly old. The girl gazed at it in confusion. When had those lines grown out from her mother's eyes? That webbing of brittle skin beneath her jaw?

Now it was the girl who wanted to apologize. But the room was full of awesome silences, and she was not sure how to begin. When she did, it was a disaster.

"Mama," she said, "I'm sorry if—"

"Sorry!" Her mother turned on her. Grease spilled from the stove in a sizzling puddle. "You're *sorry*! My God! If it weren't for you—"

Her hand leapt to her mouth. But of course it was too late. The words had escaped. The girl held them in her mind. The words were like hot coals: impossible to touch, but intensely interesting. She was both stricken and curiously pleased. Pleased, because she understood things at last. How simple it was! It explained everything. It explained the foul looks Carlos had given her. It explained the bruise on her mother's cheek. *She had caused it.* She was at the center of this tempest. She had tempted Carlos somehow—seduced him. She had not been conscious of it. It was not something she had *set out* to do. But she had tempted him, and Carlos had enacted his anger and frustration the only way he could—with the girl's mother. In bed. And with his fists.

She told herself that this was an adult thought and that she should be proud of herself: she was not being childish anymore.

The good little girl understood that she was not such a good little girl after all.

Byron leaned into the camera angle of the telephone, absorbed. Keller could only stare at Teresa. He had never seen her like this. Her eyes were moving wildly under the lids; tears streaked her face.

It was obscene. He couldn't let it go on. He must not let this happen to her.

You see somebody hurting, Keller thought wildly, the thing to do is *help*. He had learned that. A long time ago.

Byron turned away from the phone and said, "Hey, no—Ray—"

But he was already reaching for her.

The fire began at an oil terminal by the sea wall.

Later, people would say it had been inevitable. The Floats possessed only the most rudimentary public facilities. There had been no zoning laws, no building codes, no safety commissions. It was a community made of wood and paper. Some places, oil runoff had filled the water beneath the factories and the balsas. The fire began as a trivial industrial accident involving an acetylene torch; it quickly became something else.

The little girl was home that day. Carlos was at work; her mother was patching the kitchen wall with plaster. The little girl climbed out onto the flat tin roof of the shanty float—it was a sunny morning—and was surprised to see a line of smoke rising from somewhere north along the sea wall, punctuating the seamless blue arc of the sky. The smoke seemed to be drifting straight up; in fact the wind was carrying it almost directly toward her.

She was fascinated by this.

Humming to herself, lulled by the wash of the sunlight, she watched for a time. The line of smoke slowly broadened and became a kind of wall, a clouded turmoil sheeting the sky, and when she stood on tiptoes she imagined she could see the flames at the base of it, still far away, licking up from the float shacks miles down the placid canal.

Shortly before noon a fine rain of ashes began to fall.

The girl's mother called and, when she didn't answer, came up the ladder to the roof. "My God, girl! I thought you were lost! I thought—"

"Look." The little girl pointed. "Fire."

Her mother stood for a moment with her mottled housedress billowing in a wind that had grown stronger and tindery dry. Then she crossed herself wordlessly and clasped her broad brown hand on the girl's arm. Her voice when she spoke was toneless. "Come help me."

As they were descending, a County of Los Angeles helicopter clattered overhead toward the fire, then veered and hovered a moment.

The girl felt her own first tingle of fear.

Her mother was muttering to herself. She began moving in large purposeful strides across the peeling tile, stacking things on a bedsheet in the middle of the room: clothes, welfare documents, canned food. Dazed now, the girl peered out the shack's single window. The snow of ash had grown much denser. There were people on the pontoon walkways in knots, and they gazed up apprehensively at the pall of smoke. The sky had grown dark with it.

Her mother pulled her away. "We can't wait any longer." Her voice was distracted and she swiveled her head nervously. The girl understood—another adult intuition—that this was how her mother must have looked crossing the border from Mexico: this animal fear in her. "I would wait for him, you understand? For Carlos. But there isn't time."

She folded the sheet with their meager possessions in it and carried the bundle out to their tiny single-engine motor launch. It was hardly more than a canoe with an engine bolted to it, and it wallowed under the load. Their shack backed onto a small tributary feeding one of the larger canals, but the ordinarily quiet water was already crowded with boats. In some of them the people were weeping. The girl wondered what catastrophe this was that had overtaken her life. The ashes came down like snow around her.

Her mother led her back into the shack one more time. "You look around," she said. "Anything you need or can carry, you take it. One minute! Then help me with the rest of the food."

The girl picked up an old flea-market doll, the first toy she had owned. She didn't care much about it now. But it seemed like the kind of thing she ought to take. She tucked it under her arm, satisfied.

It was then that Carlos came home.

He pushed through the door laughing a screaming, drunken laugh. Instinctively the girl slipped into the gap between the kitchen door and the wall. The smell of new plaster was suddenly pungent in her nostrils. She squeezed her eyes shut. She covered her ears.

She heard it all anyway.

Carlos had left work early. The whole morning shift had been dismissed because of the fire. They assumed it was a joke at first; they went to a bar by the tidal dams and began to drink. But then the fire spread until most of the industrial buildings were burning, and it was obvious then that something terrible had happened and was continuing to happen. One by one the men joined the growing exodus toward the south. Carlos had battled through the crowds with a bottle in his hand. The bottle was still in his hand now, but empty.

He was very drunk and very frightened. The girl's mother tried to soothe him but the fear was in her voice, and Carlos must have recognized it. "We're leaving," she told him. "We can follow the canals to the mainland. There's time. There's still time."

"The canals are full," Carlos said. "Nothing's moving. The canals are fucking *burning*. Is that what you want?"

"We can walk, then—"

"Walk! Have you seen it out there?" He waved his bottle recklessly. "The fire's coming too fast. There's nothing we can do—nothing!"

And he was probably right, the girl thought dizzily. She could hear the screams coming from the pontoon bridges only yards away.

"Then why come back here?" the girl's mother said. "Why torture us?" Fear and a kind of petulant outrage mingled in her voice. "To hell with you! I'm leaving! *We're* leaving!"

But Carlos said they would die together because they were a family and because he was afraid to die alone. Then the fighting began. The girl listened, paralyzed. There was a terrible dull thudding noise, the sound of fists on flesh. She couldn't help herself: she stepped out from behind the door.

Her mother was moaning; her face was bruised. Carlos had pushed her against the kitchen table and hiked her dress above her thighs. The fire burning so close, and all he could think to do was rape her. It made the girl angry, and for a moment she forgot her fear. "Stop it!" she cried.

Carlos looked around.

The alcohol and the fear had done some terrible thing to him. His face was livid, choked with blood. His eyes were all whites. Seeing him, the girl experienced a kind of awe at what he had become. "You," he said. And went to her.

His hands mauled her. His hands tore at her clothes. She experienced a sudden lightheadedness that seemed to lift her out of her body; she floated aloof from herself and was able to see Carlos, the window, the ash-laden sky, all with a strange and curious impassivity. His hands were to blame, she thought. It was his hands she hated. Carlos was probably innocent. Her mother had said as much. My fault, she thought. She had seduced him. Worse, somehow she had seduced his hands.

She could not clearly see her mother, who lay stunned

across the peeling tiles. She did not see, therefore, when her mother roused from her stupor and blinked at the act that was proceeding before her, stumbled in horror to the wooden cabinets by the sink and drew out a knife from the cutlery drawer. The girl was not aware of anything much until Carlos gasped and stiffened above her and then rolled away. His blood, mysteriously, was on her dress. Carlos lay noisily dying, his hands closing on air. The girl's mother looked down at her with eyes gone as wide as an animal's. "God help us," she whispered. "Come on now."

They ran to the motor launch, but the press of boats in the tiny canal had beaten it against its moorings until it listed into the water and capsized. They gazed at it only a moment. The fire was close enough to smell. It was a sour, rubbery smell. It was acrid and hurt the girl's nose. Smoke eddied down the canal among the boats and beneath the pontoon bridges crowded with refugees. People were everywhere, fleeing. They had not yet panicked, but she could tell panic was only moments away. And then they would begin to push and run, the girl thought, and what then? What then?

Her mother tugged her forward. They had nothing to carry. Their possessions were all lost. Carlos was lost. Carlos, if he had not already died, would surely perish in the fire. A secret part of her exulted in that, and another part of her recorded the exultation: she had been the occasion of his death and, worse, his death had pleased her.

They traveled a half mile to the south and east with the fire on their heels—a burning as vast as the girl had ever seen, and the fire 'copters helpless in the face of it—before the crowd began to panic. The girl's mother lifted her up and carried her for a time, but she was heavy and her mother was no longer a young or healthy woman. They toppled together against a mesh-wire restraining fence. More bodies fell against them until the fence gave way at last and dropped them into a waste canal. The girl sank deep into the foul water, and she might have died there—*wanted* to die there. But it was as if she had become two people. Her body strove for the surface. Her legs pumped, her lungs gasped for air, she splashed until she saw the flames licking up behind her. She dog-paddled down the mesh- and concrete-lined canal until she could scramble up a pontoon and rest there, gasping.

She looked for her mother, but her mother was gone. Her mother and Carlos. Both gone.

It was, of course, her fault.

The fire too. She might have willed it into being. She had wished for it often enough, she realized now: an apocalypse to devour Carlos and erase her untimely adulthood. And wishes count. "Be careful what you wish for," her mother used to say. "You might get it."

The heat was agonizing on her face, the massed screaming of hundreds of voices awesome. The little girl realized that she was talking to herself. *"If wishes were horses."* Under her breath, low and staccato, as she joined the fleeing mob. *"Then beggars would ride."*

Knees jostled her. Once, a woman tugged at her hair in an effort to climb around her. But she moved steadily and without panic. If wishes were horses, then beggars would ride. If wishes were horses . . . If wishes . . .

She walked herself into unconsciousness in the guilty knowledge that she should have died in the fire. In some real sense she did die then. The thing she had been was dead. *Be* dead, she thought; be dead with Carlos; be dead with Mama. She willed herself to die. And died, though her body sustained her through the crush of frightened adults. The hours that followed were obscure and anarchic, but it was enough to know that she had awakened, her face singed hairless and her lungs thick with fluid, a fever raging in her—but alive—in a Red Cross camp on the mainland. She was a new creature now, blank and anesthetized, without history, nameless, with only a single certainty: that she was not a good girl and never would be.

All this Teresa had seen.

But the girl wasn't gone. The girl was the girl in her dreams, and she stood now in her twine shoes and with her large eyes, not a memory but someone tangibly real, a separate entity. They stood in limbo, and she understood that this was a place inside herself, a place the dreamstone had brought her, the place the little girl lived. And if the girl is here, Teresa thought, and if she can speak, doesn't that mean she's alive somehow still? Alive *inside me*?

"You know who I am," the little girl said solemnly.

She did, of course. The girl was herself. But more than that. A kind of ghost. A ghost of what she had been, a ghost of what she had never become.

It was possible to see all this, to understand it; it was possible, she thought, even to forgive. The girl had done nothing wrong. But the vision had been vivid and shocking, and the idea of stepping back inside that abandoned shell, of becoming, in some sense, this ragged girl again—

"But you have to," the girl said. "Seeing isn't enough."

No. It was impossible. Too many layers of scar, a life built on that denial. To *own* all that torment, to own her mother and Carlos and the fire . . . it was terrifying.

Fire and guilt had made her what she was. She was Teresa; she could not put aside Teresa.

The girl stepped closer. Not really a little girl anymore, Teresa thought: more like a reflection in a mirror, but tousled and frightened. "I didn't die. I walked you through the fire. I walked you to the mainland. You tried to kill me. You tried to kill me with the pills. But you can't do it that way."

Go away, she thought dazedly.

"I've been hidden too long," the girl said.

Teresa said desperately, "It wasn't your fault. I know that now. I—"

But the girl shook her head. "It's not enough!"

A swirl of panic. "What, then?"

"Take me back." The girl advanced. "Touch me." She held out her small hands. *"Be me."*

Teresa struggled to frame an answer, but could not: she was lifted roughly, shocked by a sudden and terrible light, surrounded at once by gunfire and smoke and the plangent stink of fear.

CHAPTER 14

Keller put his hands on her shoulders. Her eyes blinked suddenly and unseeingly open; the dreamstone was still clasped tight in her hands.

The contact between them was electric and strange, vastly more powerful than it had been that moment in the church in Cuiaba. He was lost in it.

He smelled the hot, granular earth of a manioc field in Rondonia, and knew the memory would be a bad one.

Until the moment of the ambush, Keller had every reason to believe this patrol would turn out okay.

Everybody said so. Meg said so. Their CO said the *posseiros* were hanging fire against the possibility of a dry-season offensive in the populated west. Covert sensors along guerilla supply trails had registered diminished activity for more than a month. Keller's platoon had walked patrol into five government-held strategic villages in this ravaged farm country, and the only sign of enemy action had been a single undetonated flail trap loaded with monomolecular wire: the trigger had rusted open. They disarmed it and marched on.

Keller felt the obvious sense of relief, but also, curiously, a muted disappointment. Not that he was anxious to see combat. He wasn't naive and he wasn't stupid. He had seen the wounded ferried in to the base hospital at Cuiaba; he understood about pain and death. Nor was he, in the cute Psych Corps phrase, "hypermotivated"—he was here strictly because his lottery number had come up.

But he could not help thinking of what Megan had told him that night in his bunk. "Out there, Ray, it's easy to do things you're not proud of."

It was more than anyone else had said to him. "Out there," she had said. Like it was the name of a place. Out there. A mystery. No one talked about it, but it was at the center of all their lives. They were trained for it, they dreamed about it; Keller was reminded a dozen times daily that he was, by this final criterion, a virgin. And so he asked himself all the dumb and obvious and impermissible questions. Will I be brave? Will it hurt? Will I die?

But the end of the patrol had almost come, and Keller had begun to believe the questions would not be answered this time out. And he was occupied with this curious mixture of gratitude and disappointment when the dread thing actually became real—when the ambush came down around him.

They were crossing a manioc field toward the margin of the contested highway, BR-364. They were in loose formation. A nineteen-year-old named Hooper was walking point. Hooper was weighed down with sensory extenders and a heads-up helmet display that made him look like a cockroach (Byron had said this) on its hind legs. Hooper should have warned them. But Hooper was goofing off. In the glare of the first explosion Keller saw Hooper diddling his arm controls—maybe trying to focus in on some suspicious image but more likely just playing with the display, turning the sky purple or some shit like that. They warned you about that in basic. Don't play games. It was elementary. Keller's first reaction to the attack therefore was this burst of petulance toward Hooper. Hooper! he thought. Hooper, you asshole!

The shock wave knocked him down.

The next moments were timeless. By dint of luck he had fallen into a bomb crater as wide as his body. It afforded a little protection against the wire barrage flailing out from tree cover. Keller rolled on his belly in time to see Logan, a black Spec/4, take a wire. Keller was shocked into dispassion. It was as if Logan had walked into a hail of razor blades. He was blood all over, toppling like a tree. He was too cut up to make any noise. He just fell.

My Christ, Keller thought.

His rifle was compressed in the mud beneath him. He drew it out now, trying not to panic, wanting the protection of it, but there was nothing obvious to shoot at: only the stand of distant trees, the empty ribbon of highway, the still air edging toward dusk. In this momentary lull Keller was able to hear the CO shouting incoherent orders somewhere off to the left, this escalating into a scream. He belly-crawled forward until he was able to scan a section of the field. Everybody down, whole or cut. Hooper down. The CO down and bleeding. Yards away, in the meager cover of a stump, the radioman made a staccato call for aid and air cover. With a dizzying combination of reluctance and urgency, Keller forced himself to look for Meg.

His eyes lingered a second on Byron Ostler, the platoon Angel, who was down and whole and scanning the scene methodically. Watching, Keller felt a microsecond of envy. He was deep in it, Keller thought: lost in some neurological subroutine, miles beyond fear. Angel Zen. The thinking part of him had closed up like a nut. It must be sweet.

All this in an eyeblink.

And then he found Meg. She had been walking to his left and a couple of yards to his rear. He had to crane his head to find her. When he did, he wished he hadn't.

She had been hit.

The horror of it was giddy, skull-cracking. Keller blanked

on it—was not sure for a second what he was looking at.

She had taken a wire in the legs, and her legs below the knees were a hideous red confetti. She couldn't walk. She couldn't stand. She was exposed, out there on the furrowed blankness of the manioc field. And she was alive.

She was gesturing to him. Her hand was out. *Ray,* she seemed to be saying. She wanted him to pull her into the crater with him, somewhere where she might be safe—might live until a medevac unit arrived. He blinked, watching. She stretched her bloody hand toward him, and the look in her eyes now was fervent, terrifying. He scuffled forward and reached for her. When someone hurts, he thought, you help. It was as simple as that.

But then a second barrage began, the eerie high keening of the wire weapons followed seconds later by the concussion of cluster bombs, and Keller froze. The terror that overtook him was a new thing. He imagined it was a mirror of the fear in Meg's own eyes. He heard screams above the din of the barrage and knew immediately that this was how his own screams would sound, imagined the terror liberated from his throat in one of those long animal howlings, the last constraints of sanity unbuckled in the onrush of pain and death. He felt the burr of shrapnel in the air above him, and pulled back his hand.

I'll die, he thought. There was a cool and relentless logic in it. If I lift myself up there and grab hold of her, I'll die. All of this was calculable: impact, detonation, velocity, speed, weight; God, he guessed, was a kind of mathematician, handing down these neat calculations.

It might have been only a moment's doubt. Later he would tell himself he *had* meant to help her, that he was only shocked by the concussions, trapped in a second's indecision. . . .

But she died while he hesitated. A wire barrage found her, the monofilaments flaying into her midriff. The impact took her, and she moved in the familiar ballistic, lifted and carried back. He saw her dogtags whirl in an arc through the boiling air, severed from their chain. She tumbled into the high weeds limply.

The motion was simple but profound. It meant, Keller

thought, that she had entered into the mathematics of inanimate things.

He understood about death. People die all the time. People die especially in combat: it's the nature of the thing. It's bad, he thought, but it happens.

But he had loved her.

But the people you love die too. The comprehension of death had come early to him. He had seen his mother stretched out in a mortuary box when he was only seven years old, and understood that—although she appeared to be lost in some especially deep and troubled sleep—the fact was that she would not wake up. The breath would not sigh in and out again, the eyes would not blink open ever. That was death, substantial, right in front of him.

When his father died some years later, Keller was old enough to take a job, keep up the apartment over the bodywork shop. He preserved everything meticulously in its place. Hanging onto the illusion of normalcy. It was another way of hiding the eyes, subverting this juggernaut of grief; it was a habit, and he had acquired it early.

And so after Meg's death and his own mute complicity in it, he came to understand Byron, the Angel, the Eye. "You saw," Keller accused him in a drunken moment days later.

But Byron shook his head. "The machine sees, Ray. I don't see a fucking thing."

My God, Keller thought. It must be heaven.

He thought later of trying to get access to the recordings, assess his own guilt, look at the thing—somehow—objectively. He put through two formal written requests, but both were denied; the recordings had passed into the archival limbo of Intelligence Evaluation, far beyond the grasp of mortals like himself.

He volunteered for Angel basic. He learned *wu-nien*. He was earnest about it; he took his wires seriously. In the end he was assigned to a patrol boat policing the quiescent waters of the Rio Negro, and he served out his time without seeing another shot fired.

It didn't matter. He was a good and thorough Angel now. What was once a habit had become a way of life.

All this with great clarity, compressed into a moment. Her hand opened.

The dreamstone dropped to the carpet of the hotel room in Belem.

Keller rolled away from her, blinking and gasping.

But he had come here for this. It was clear to him now. This resurrection: it had been in his mind since the day Byron said the word "Brazil." He had been thinking of Megan Lindsey. He had never stopped thinking of her.

Teresa sat up now, pained and terrified. Byron swiveled his chair away from the phone.

I came here for Meg, Keller thought. As if there were answers here. (There were not.) As if the placid mud out along BR-364 might yield some epiphany after all these years. As if she could come out of the ground and forgive him.

Stupid, inarticulate, idiot thoughts.

Teresa was looking at him now. She mouthed the words: *I'm sorry!*

Keller looked away.

"That was Denny," Byron said.

They stared at him.

"On the phone," Byron said. "He made the arrangements. He found us a flight out of here. He says—Jesus Christ, what *happened* to you people?"

CHAPTER 15

They had been here, Oberg thought.

The hotel room in Belem was empty now. The windows were open, the yellowed curtains thrown back. Oberg had intimidated the local police, who had intimidated the American expatriate community, and the process had led him here: to an empty room. But not long empty.

Time had been his only real enemy. It was a long journey along the bus lanes from Pau Seco to this noisy Amazon fish town. But they had been here. He could tell.

He made himself silent, concentrated his awareness.

It was something more subtle than a scent. It existed under the reek of the Ver-o-Peso and the ancient dusts of the hotel. It was the trace, Oberg thought, of the oneirolith itself, an alienness lingering in the air. Spoor of other worlds.

He knew, too, where they had gone.

A loose cannon, the Brazilian Chief of Station had called him. Maybe, Oberg thought. Maybe that's what I am: a loose cannon. But not entirely without direction.

Chief of Station in the American embassy in Brasilia was a ponderously fat Harvard poli-sci graduate named Wyskopf. Oberg had contacted him on his first day in Belem, by phone, more than a week over schedule. It made Wyskopf angry; Wyskopf ordered him in.

"I'm not finished here," Oberg had said into the eye of the telephone. "I'm very close."

He could have said something placating, but he had come a long way from Pau Seco and he was too weary to deal with Wyskopf diplomatically. The point of a job, he thought, is to do it. It should have been elementary.

Wyskopf had sighed. He communicated his immense patience down a thousand miles of optical wire. "We work for the same people," he said. "I'm on your side, all right? But look at it from a broader point of view. We can't devote an infinite amount of resources to this effort."

"You want to abandon it?"

"Not that exactly," Wyskopf said, and Oberg understood suddenly—it startled him—that they *did* want to abandon it, that Wyskopf was looking for some painless way to tell him so. My God, he thought, they still don't understand!

"You're making a mistake," Oberg said.

"You don't tell me that. You don't tell me my job." Silence for a beat, the sigh again. "It isn't up to me. I got a call. You're ordered in. That's it."

Oberg squeezed his eyes shut. Three days on the road and he had not slept much. He felt a kind of dizzy aloofness. All of this was talk; none of it mattered. Wyskopf's ignorance offended him, and he told Wyskopf so.

"I have your psych profile," Wyskopf said. "I could have predicted this. You're obsessive and you have an a-voidance complex you could drive a truck through. I have a raft of complaints on my desk: SUDAM and the military and a half-dozen civil officials. It was a bad decision to send you down here, and anybody asks me, that's what

I'll tell them. The last thing this office needs is some fucking loose cannon rolling around." He leaned into the camera. "Refuse my direct order to come in. Do me that favor."

"You don't understand. The stone—"

"The stone is gone! It's time to admit that, don't you think? The consensus is that nobody on the black market will want it anyway: as a drug, it's terrible. It's a horror drug. Leave it alone. Leave it alone and there's a good chance it'll disappear out in the Floats somewhere. Meantime we tighten security at Pau Seco and the research facilities. Sooner or later there's a leak, it's inevitable, but by then we have the advantage in basic research."

"It's not just that. It—"

"I don't want to discuss it. This is policy. You understand, Mr. Oberg? You are ordered in from the field. I want you in this office tomorrow morning, and I want you contrite."

He was stunned. "I can't do that."

"You're refusing?" A certain relish now in Wyskopf's voice.

"Yes," Oberg said, "all right, fuck it, I'm refusing. But you don't understand. You—"

"Shit on that," Wyskopf said.

The screen went blank.

None of them understood.

He went to a bar, sated himself with a meal of *feijoada*, drank and played wordless pool with three grinning fishermen. He made money and then, still drinking, lost it. Walking down a narrow night street, alone, he thought: I am a soldier and a veteran and a patriot, and I have been closer to this thing than any careerist in any of the federal agencies.

He had been touched by it. Literally.

He had come out of the war twice-decorated and with a thoughtful respect for the horrors of combat. He had seen terrible things, participated in terrible things . . . but that was the nature of war, and it was not something you could enter into halfway. War was a state of mind, war was all or nothing. It was what they told him in basic. Oberg had been part of a segregated battalion of what the psych people called Latent Aggressives, highly motivated men inured to violence. He hadn't volunteered for it. His EEG had volunteered him; his genetic map had volunteered him. He had all the earmarks, they said: spike discharge in the cerebellum, periodic episodes of depersonalization, a stunted endorphin system, a history of petty violence. His CO, a rural Georgian named Toller, explained that they were unique because they had all been born without their "bump of sympathy." And grinned, saying it. *God made us what we are.* And it was true, wasn't it? Trite but undeniable.

They called themselves God's Own. The baseline troops called them Babykillers.

They were terror troops. They penetrated the guerilla-held outlands in a series of punitive raids against *posseiró* villages, destroying crops, burning buildings, racking down the guerillas' political and economic base. It was bloody and vile work. They all agreed about that. But it was uniquely their work. *God made us what we are.*

He rose in the ranks. He acquired a certain notoriety.

He did not care to remember much of what happened during those years. What really mattered was that the war had given him an identity, a sense of self. He had been drafted out of a foster home in rural southern Texas, where his life had been a haze of fast violence and routine indignities. He was incredulous when a Juvenile Offenses worker told him he would love the Army. But he did. It was a fact. The Army had groomed and educated and disciplined him. The Army had analyzed and decoded him; the Army made him useful. And if the Army required him to practice his vices in the hinterland of this terrible country, then that was the least of what he owed them.

He assumed, when he was discharged, that the violent part of his life had also ended. He took civilian work with the Agencies on the recommendation of an Army buddy. He was a good field man, despite what Wyskopf had said. His life was stable—had been stable. And if he had not acquired a wife or family or the accouterments of a statistically normal existence, perhaps it was because he could not shake the image of himself as a Latent Aggressive, God's Own, one of the blank-eyed minority born without a bump of sympathy. But he did not think about it often.

He had harbored a deep suspicion of the oneiroliths even before he was assigned to the Virginia facility. In part it was his instinctive fear and hostility for the foreign, the Other. But it was also a deeper revulsion. He disliked occupying a room where one of the stones had been. He was sensitive to the aura of them. It made his hair prickle, his stomach churn. He was conscious of the tremendous value of the oneiroliths, of the data being downloaded from them: but it represented a gift of unknown provenance, and gifts made him wonder about motives. Lots of abstract knowledge, but nothing about the Exotics themselves, who they were, where they had come from or why. And this strange interaction with the subjects from Vacaville. It was like all those antique movies. Body snatchers from outer space. Oberg took the idea seriously, though he knew the research people would laugh at him; the research people had no perspective. It was his business to be suspicious. He represented the federal agencies; he represented the less overt but no less solemn suspicions of his employers. For twenty years the world had been lulled into a blithe familiarity with these artifacts, while Oberg cultivated a professional paranoia.

But he had only been convinced of the essential evil of the stones with the arrival of the more potent deep-core oneiroliths from Brazil. He had seen their influence on hardened criminals like Tavitch . . . and he had felt it himself.

The contact was brief but unavoidable. He lived in the research compound and several times a day shuttled from his cell-like room to the communal toilets one locked door away from the inmates' wing. He was making this pilgrimage one winter day, a cold front out of Canada seeping through the inadequate insulation and into the hallway of the cheap concrete buildings, when the wire-mesh security door burst open and the convict Tavitch came bulling through.

Tavitch was clearly insane. His eyes rolled, spittle flew from his open mouth. He stared back at the open door, ahead at Oberg. A pair of orderlies tumbled through behind him. They stood on two sides of Tavitch, panting; neither seemed to want to move. "You were supposed to lock the goddamned door!" one said. The other remained silent, eyes on Tavitch.

Tavitch, the murderer. Tavitch, who claimed to see into the past. Oberg felt his hackles rise. He was trapped in this tableau.

Tavitch stared at him. Their eyes met, and Oberg was appalled by the look of recognition Tavitch gave him. "Christ," he said quietly.

Tavitch's fist was clenched.

"Take him," the second orderly said, but Tavitch ran forward then, directly at Oberg. Oberg's instinct was to flinch away, but he was conscious of the orderlies watching him, and he threw a body check into Tavitch instead. They toppled onto the cold tile floor together.

The contact was momentary. A second, maybe less. But it was enough.

Horrified, Oberg felt the strangeness of the dreamstone pulsing through him.

He opened his eyes and saw a village deep in the hinterland. Some Indio village. Men in bowl haircuts and ragged T-shirts, women with their pendulous breasts exposed. Some deep river village, he thought dazedly, maybe refuge for a few *sertao* revolutionaries or an East Bloc weapons cache, more likely not: but there was a thread-rifle in his hand and the assault was on, he was in the midst of it, firing into their bodies, into their eyes like the startled eyes of deer caught in headlights, and he was getting into it, rolling with it; it was singing in him, the high eroticism of this mass kill. *God's Own*. But suddenly it was not good at all. By some terrible miracle he was sharing their terror and their pain, these Indios he was killing, scything wire into his own body somehow, burning his own village. The pain and outrage boiled up in him unstoppably, and it was more than wounding: it opened a hole in him through which any horror might at any minute rush.

He gasped as the orderlies pulled Tavitch away and

the corridor fell into focus around him. A nightmare, he thought desperately. But Tavitch stared down at him with a terrible, knowing leer.

"You and I," Tavitch said. "You and I."

Oberg threw up in the hallway.

He was methodical about his divorce from the Agencies. He drew a large sum of money from an Agency account in Belem before they cancelled his credit. And he had money of his own riding in hidden accounts Stateside.

He didn't hold a grudge against Wyskopf or the people Wyskopf represented. Their naiveté was inevitable; he associated it with their "bump of sympathy." They took his concern with the oneirolith for an obsession, but it was not that. The connection was more subtle. Oberg was a Latent Aggressive, God's Own, less than entirely human. Like the stone itself, he was a step outside nature. His understanding was therefore more subtle, more complete.

He knew a little about these people now. Teresa Rafael, Byron Ostler, Raymond Keller. He knew what they looked like. He knew where they had been. Most important, he knew where they were going.

He caught a morning flight. It was pleasant to see the Amazon falling behind him, the angles of it hidden by cloud, to rise effortlessly into the sunlight, spiraling east and then north, cut loose from history, cut loose from the Agencies, a loose cannon, purified in his purpose, aimed, he thought, and fired.

PART 2

WHISPERS
FROM
THE
ANCIENT
WORLD

CHAPTER 16

1. It would not have been safe to take her back to the studio by the tidal dams, so Byron located a tiny balsa deep in the Floats and put the last of his Brazilian money on the rent.

He liked the location. There was only the distant rise of the San Gabriels to remind him that the continent existed, salt breezes and morning fog to remind him of the sea. Otherwise it might have been some indefinite confluence of wood and water, paper houses rising on pontoon foundations, bobbing walkways, Chinese lanterns, eggbeater windmills ticking against the sky. A market canal ran in from the east, so there were fresh eggs and vegetables. A mixed population, with maybe a plurality of Latinos and East Indians. Some decent jobs available at the wharves beyond

the tidal dam, not too much violence. A good place, Byron
thought.

He liked it more than he should have. It soothed him,
and that was dangerous. He had to think about the future
now . . . for Teresa's sake as much as his own.

She wasn't safe here. The terrifying thing was, she
might not be safe anywhere.

Thinking of her, he followed the boardwalk along the
margins of this canal, a right-of-way between the old float
shanties standing like stilted birds above the water. He thought
about Teresa.

She betrayed very little. It was wounding, the way she
hid herself from him. Since her stone trance in Belem, she
had been withdrawn, subtly lifeless, would turn away when
he touched her. Her eyes were often on Keller, but Keller
was equally distant: as if some weird electricity had put an
opposite spin on the two of them. Something had passed
between them, he thought, that time in the hotel room on
the Ver-o-Peso. Some intimacy too awful to sustain.

The pain of it was obvious.

And yet she clung to the oneirolith. She had smuggled
it back in her hand luggage, and she kept it concealed now
in a Salvation Army dresser at the back of the balsa. Token
of something. Her past, her future.

He had grown to hate it.

He hated it for the sadness it had created in her, and
he hated it as a token of his own past. There were times
when his life had seemed to him like one prolonged act of
sleepwalking. Drafted out of a career college in the midwest,
he had volunteered for Angel duty. The Psych Corps said
he had "an aptitude for the work." And maybe that was
true, maybe he did. Maybe that was why, when his duty
tour ended, he chose to have his socket pulled. A feeling
that it was in some way too easy, that he could have continued to stumble through life in a pleasant fog of *wu-
nien*—like Keller—or worse, ended up with a joychip plugged
into his socket. He and a couple of war buddies had come
to the Floats under the tutelage of a former CO named
Trujillo, who wanted help setting up a drug lab. Byron

pulled out at the last minute: he could not picture himself synthesizing enkephalins and rogue adenosines for a population of degraded addicts. He was attracted to the dreamstones, however, because they seemed comparatively wholesome, and because they were popular with the artists beginning to make their presence felt in the Floats. He contacted Cruz Wexler, who set him up in business. It was simple and lucrative work but in time it began to press his conscience. He acquired a respect for the strangeness of the 'liths. They possessed a healing power, possibly a darker power as well. He came to question the wisdom of selling them as one more feelgood drug to the moneyed mainlanders who came down to the tamer Float clubs every Saturday night. Buy a dreamstone from the Angel vet: it was daring, it was fashionable. He overheard his name in conversations. "Probably had his balls shot off in the war," one of his clients said. And the dreadful thing, he realized, was that it might be true, his life in the Floats might be one more variation on the theme of *wu-nien,* a kind of castration. In some important way he had been neutered.

Teresa was his road back into the world.

He had not consciously chosen her for the role, nor was it entirely coincidence. Some mingling of the two. She showed up at his door, because she needed him; he fell in love with her, because he needed to fall in love.

There had never been any question of indifference. Some telegraphy in the shape of her face or the color of her eyes had communicated her necessity to him. She was emaciated and ill; he was a demobbed Angel, a parody of a combat vet. It should have been comical. But he cared for her.

But she was dying.

The stone saved her life, and that was good; it did not occur to him until much later to wonder whether he had merely postponed the inevitable. She really did want to die. He learned that about her. She was punishing herself for some sin she could not even consciously remember, some buried enormity lost in the trauma of the fire. But there were other forces in her, too, and he was certain he had kindled one of them: a spark of resistance, her rebellious desire to live. It was as if there were two Teresas woven between and around each other, each working to deceive and subvert the other: death tricked into life, life into death.

In all this the oneirolith remained a mystery, a conduit between these fractions of herself, necessary but dangerous. He had been afraid of the deep-core stone because it threatened to upset a delicate balance, and that was what it had seemed to do: the spark in her was all but extinguished now.

And so there was nothing to do but find this place for her to hide, a pontoon shack in the Floats where she would be safe, at least, from the Agencies. She might pull out of it. He told himself so.

But what angered him—and it was a deep and profound anger he wasn't certain he could control any longer—was Keller's coolness toward her.

Keller, whom she loved. Keller, who could have saved her.

Keller wanted to go back to the mainland.

He met Keller at a market stall and they walked out along the tidal dam in an awkward silence. "I'm finished here," Keller said at last. "That must be obvious now."

"She needs you," Byron said simply.

He followed Keller's gaze out beyond the boardwalk, past the featureless wall of the dam. Out there on the clean horizon a Thai tanker seemed to sit motionless. Gulls whirled overhead. "There's nothing I can do for her."

"You owe it to her to try."

He shook his head. "I don't owe her anything."

There was some secret knowledge moving behind his eyes. Byron felt angry, excluded, helpless. He recognized Keller's aloofness for what it was: the Ice Palace, Angel instincts, a cold and willful vacancy of the soul. Keller said, "I have a job to do."

"Fuck your job." They walked a few paces with this envelope of anger around them, not speaking. "You go back there," he said finally, "it could be dangerous. The Agencies could find you."

"I download, I put everything through an image processer, I destroy the original memory trace. Even if they find me, there's nothing that constitutes evidence. Nothing they can use against her.''

"You care about her that much?"

The question seemed to trouble Keller; he didn't answer.

"If you cared," Byron said, "you would stay."

"I can't."

"So what then? A new name? Another job somewhere?"

He shrugged.

"You tell her," Byron said wearily. "Leave me out of it. You tell her you're leaving."

Keller said, "I will."

2.   She was at the back of the float shack watching TV.

Keller looked over her shoulder. It was some Scandinavian love serial, satellite programming syndicated through Network. But she wasn't really watching. Her eyes were averted. She glanced up at him and they were alone for a moment in the silence of the small room, the floor lifting and falling in the swell. "You're leaving," she said.

It startled him. But she would have guessed. It was hardly surprising. The evidence of small silences, looks avoided, hands untouched. He made himself aloof: an act of will. "I have work to do," he said.

She smiled faintly. "Downloading memories?"

He nodded.

"And then," she said, "they're video. Right? You don't have to live with them anymore." She stood up, ran a hand through her hair. "Will you come back?"

He was torn by the question. The odds were that he would not. A part of him wanted desperately never to come back, never to see her again. But he was not entirely free from *adhyasa,* powerful and traitorous impulses. "I don't know."

She nodded, as if to say: all right, yes, thank you at least for being honest. She held out her hand and he took it. But when he moved to turn away, she held him there. Her gaze was intense and her hand tightened painfully. "It doesn't matter," she said fiercely. "Anything that happened, it doesn't matter to me. What happened with Meg —it doesn't matter."

He pulled away. For a moment he wanted to believe her, accept what she was offering him. But it was not in her power to forgive.

She knew. And that was unbearable.

"It doesn't matter." She followed him to the door. "Remember that, Ray. Do that for me, please. Please just remember."

3.   He rode a boat taxi down the market canal to the big chain-link fences that marked the mainland, and by the time he had located his car—parked this last month in a security garage—night had fallen. The urban access routes were crowded; the car audio pumped out dizzying rondos of pulse music, muscular and grim. The city was a river of light and concrete rolling from the Mexican border up into the dry conduit suburbs, from the ocean to the desert; and after Brazil, he thought, it should have been daunting. But it was not. It intoxicated him.

In these night canyons he was one among many, finally anonymous; here he might lose his guilt, his memories, his history, himself.

CHAPTER 17

1.   A Thai taxiboat driver led Oberg to the empty studio by the tidal dam.

It was an impressive balsa. Oberg looked up at it from the tiny canal dock abutting the pontoon walkway and said, "She lives here?"

"Did," the driver said laconically. "Maybe still does. Though I haven't seen her lately." He waited, pointedly. Oberg pressed a few faded cash notes into his hand; he nodded and sent his boat whirring away.

Alone, Oberg climbed a mossy concrete stairway to the boardwalk and casually forced the door.

There was dust inside.

He had expected as much. They would not have come back here. They were wiser than that. It had been too easy tracing her: she had dozens of contacts among mainland art dealers and in the galleries up the coastal highway. She had been, by every account, a woman of predictable habits.

So she had not come back here, and he had anticipated that, but he remained convinced of two things: that she had gone to ground somewhere in the Floats, and that—it was pretty much inevitable—he would find her.

What he wanted here, in this closed green bamboo retreat she had once inhabited, was as much mystical as practical: a sense of her presence, a token of her life.

The still air stirred around him. Quietly now, he moved up the stairs.

He had taught himself about the Floats.

It was not a single community. The plural noun was necessary. Years ago, in a decade-long infusion of state and federal funding, the tidal dams had been erected off the California coast. It was a feat of engineering as ambitious as the building of the Great Wall, and it represented the pressing need for energy resources rolling over a host of practical and ecological objections. After years of cost overruns and the extinction of a half-dozen minor marine species, the project went successfully on-line; even today it supplied most of the electrical power soaked up by the urban sprawl. Inevitably, not enough; but there were the Baja and Sonora photic generators shouldering the overload, technologies the Exotic stones had made practical.

More important from Oberg's perspective was the demimonde that had grown up in the shadow of the dam. The becalmed and enclosed coastal waters were initially a kind of industrial free zone. There were massive landfill projects off Long Beach, deepwater shipping bays abutting the Harbor Dam. Inevitably, a population moved in to feed the market for semiskilled labor. Just as inevitably, many of these were semilegals with dubious documentation. The first crude boat slums were erected in the lee of the factories, but the population grew even when the new industries faltered in the face of competing Exotic technologies. Squatters occupied the shells of abandoned warehouses.

The unemployment riots of the '30s had established

MEMORY WIRE

for the first time a perimeter of autonomy, a border beyond which the civic and harbor police refused to venture. The County of Los Angeles withdrew its official jurisdiction in a series of negotiated settlements with strike leaders. It was a precedent. Even after the fire that swept the floating ghettos in the late '30s, the only government agency with real power in the Floats was the Public Works Department.

And so the Floats had grown into a refuge for anyone who fell through the cracks of the mainland world: artists, criminals, addicts, the black market; undocumented immigrants and the chronically poor. Within its vast acreage of pontoon bridges, balsas, and canals, there were a dozen autonomous communities. Slums spilled out from the urban mainland, dangerous places in which, Oberg understood, any life was negotiable. Elsewhere, and particularly here in the more spacious north, real communities had been created. There was money, employment, a limited commerce with the outside world. People moved back and forth. A place to live, Oberg thought. Especially, he thought, a place to hide.

But no place could hide her for long. He understood, climbing the stairs, that his separation from the Agencies had been both necessary and inevitable. He was no longer bound by Agency protocols. He could move in this twilight place, away from the mainland. He was a loose cannon. He could roll where he liked.

The thought made him smile. *See me roll.*

He moved lightly over the wooden floor of the room that had been her studio.

It was a spacious room set around with windows. Parallel angles of sunlight divided the floor. He opened drawers, peered behind mirrors. He did all this methodically and in a state of finely tuned concentration. He was not sure what he was looking for: only that he would know it when he saw it.

He saw it, at last, nestled at the back of a dresser drawer behind a pastel cotton shirt. It was a tiny plastic vial about the size of a film canister, unlabeled. In the opaque hollow of it, something rattled.

He pried up the lid with his thumbnail.

The odor was faint, pungent, attractive. He rolled out a tiny black pill onto his palm. The pill was resinous with age; there was only one.

It was something she had saved, he thought. A kind of insurance; or a proof of something, an object lesson.

He touched his finger to the oil at the bottom of the vial and raised it to his tongue.

Bitter, astringent taste. But the faintest sense of well-being swept through his body.

Enkephalins, he thought. In potent concentration.

He tumbled the pill back into its container, snapped shut the lid.

For the second time, he smiled to himself.

2. Her dreams were worse after Keller left.

The little girl again, of course. But the tone of the dream had changed. She had learned too much from the Pau Seco stone. The little girl appeared against a terrifying montage of the fire: flame, smoke, and frightened faces. Her eyes were wide and soot-streaked, and she was alone, cut off from the mainland, afraid for her life.

"I need you," the girl said. "I saved you once! It's only fair! You can't let me die here!"

But in the dreams she could only turn away.

The dreams left her sweating. She woke up alone at the back of this new balsa deep in the Floats, lost a moment in the darkness, the unfamiliar spaces. Byron slept in the front room, which doubled as kitchen; she slept in the back. Stirring, she felt as hollow as a bottle tossed up from the sea. The floor rose in a momentary swell, as if a hand had lifted the boat. She closed her eyes resolutely and prayed that she would not dream again.

Morning came hours later, a lightening at the room's single high window.

She sat up, wrapped a robe around herself, drew a deep breath. Since Belem she had felt mostly numb. Numb and rootless and empty. The way Keller felt, maybe. Angel fugue. Except she was not an Angel. Only herself, moving through this fog. Periodically she would ask herself how she felt, how she *really* felt, but it was like tonguing an abscessed tooth: the pain overwhelmed the curiosity.

She moved to the kitchen and fried an egg for Byron over the old electric grill. It was the last of their food.

Byron was wearing khaki fatigue pants and his moth-eaten combat jacket. She looked at him but could find nothing to say. She had not talked to him much—really talked—since Belem. Some barrier of guilt or shame had come down between them. She hadn't even hinted at what she had seen in her 'lith trance, the complexities of time and history, the world's or hers. When he finished eating, he stood up and hooked his eyeglasses back of his ears. He was going out, he said.

"Where to?"

"Making contacts," he said vaguely. "We need cash if we're going to stay here. There are people who owe me."

"You have to go?"

He nodded.

"Well," she said. "Be careful."

He shrugged.

Being alone was the worst thing.

It surprised her, how much she hated it. Better to have things to do. Keeping busy helped.

Byron had left her grocery money. So she would shop, she thought, wander out along the market canal to the big stalls by the tidal dam. That would be good. She tucked the cash into her shirt pocket and buttoned it. Check the cooler, she thought. Cheap rental cooler, came with this cheap pontoon shack. There was a bottle of fresh water, a loaf of stale bread. They needed, let's see, fruit, vegetables, maybe even a little meat. Something to keep body and soul together.

She had skipped her own breakfast.

The market canal, then. But first she stepped back into the small room she had made her own, regarded the tousled bed and, more carefully, the antique Salvation Army dresser. Idly, she pulled open the top drawer.

The Brazilian stone was inside.

It looked small and unprepossessing in a nest of her clothes. Ordinary . . . until you looked closely at it, allowed its angles to seduce the eye, stared until you couldn't stop staring. A part of her was tempted to pick it up.

A part was not. She slammed shut the drawer.

She had regained a sense of its alienness. It was the stone, she thought, that had driven Keller away. In that moment in the hotel room in Belem, she had seen into the heart of him, the terrible guilt he had hoarded all these years. The dying woman in Rondonia: Meg, her name was. His hesitation. Worse, the caustic sense of his own cowardice.

She understood, of course. It was not a difficult sin to forgive.

But he could not bear that she had *seen*.

And there was the rest of it. The little girl, the fire, the terrible man Carlos. She had lost so much: not just Ray but a sense of purpose, her intimacy with the stones, the idea of a future. . . .

She put it out of her mind. She would think about it later. She left the float, double-locked the door, joined the crowds on the pontoon walkway beside the big canal. The sun was bright and she held up her face to it, eyes squeezed shut. She wished she could see the ocean.

Walking felt so good that she forgot about the shopping. She walked past the big stalls with their colorful awnings, past the market boats moored against the boardwalk, turning instinctively toward the sea.

The walkway looped north and parallel to the seawall. She climbed a set of chain-link risers until she was level with the broad concrete lip of the dam. Public Works property, isolated in its churning moat of floodwater, huge turbines down there somewhere. To the south she could see a line of abandoned factories and warehouses, waste stacks starkly black against the cloudless sky. To the east, across the tangle of the Floats, a hint of the mainland; the razorback San Gabriels. North, more boat shanties . . . the tidal dam tapering landward. And to the west there was the sea.

Gulls circled overhead and dive-bombed a refuse boat.

The wind smelled of salt and sea wrack. She should have brought a sweater.

Keller was gone, of course. The scary thing was that she both knew it and understood it. Because of what she had seen, he could not bear her presence. It was logical and inevitable.

But she felt the loss more deeply than she could have anticipated.

Funny how things changed. For a while she had known what she wanted. She had wanted the mystery of the dreamstone; she had wanted a door into her past. But it was like that proverb about answered prayers. She understood more about the Exotics, probably, than anyone outside the federal research programs: their origins, their history. They were vivid in her mind even yet. But there was still something fundamentally alien about them, some profound dissonance between their world and hers. She felt it, a stab of poignancy inside her, a silence where there might have been voices.

The mystery of her own past was just as obdurate. She was the little girl, of course: the little girl was Teresa. Teresa before the fire. She knew that now. But knowing was not enough. Memory was the memory of old pain. What she wanted, she realized, was healing. But the 'lith couldn't do that. The stone only remembered. Healing, it seemed to imply, was up to her: some act of reconciliation she could not begin to imagine.

Maybe there was no such thing. Maybe the past was always and only the past. Taunting, fixed, unassailable. You couldn't talk to the past.

She walked north through unfamiliar floats. She was not sure where she was going. She just walked—"following her feet," Rosita used to say. Her feet carried her down pontoon bridges, past crowded market stalls. She paid no attention to the Spanish and English voices swirling around her. She thought a little about wanting and getting. The paradox of it. Wanting the dreamstone, she had found Keller. Now she wanted Keller . . . but the stone had driven him away.

The past had driven him away.

"I'm sorry, Ray."

She was embarrassed to realize she had said it out loud. But only the gulls overheard.

But now she had come to a place that triggered her memory. She suppressed the sense of familiarity, but her heart beat harder. She had come here for some reason. This was the place her feet had led her. Wise feet. But it was best not to think too hard about it.

The float shack had not changed much. The same dangerous-seeming list, the same bilge pump gushing oily water into a waste canal. She descended an ancient flight of chain-link stairs to the door and knocked, breathless.

The old, hollow man was older, hollower. She was surprised that he recognized her. His eyes narrowed in stale amusement from the dark frame of his doorway. "You," he said.

He still kept the pills at the back.

CHAPTER 18

1.   There was still the possibility of selling the stone.
Byron was in no position to grow copies; he dared not risk
even a visit to his basement lab in the Floats. They had only
the single 'lith, and he was not sure how Teresa would feel
about him selling it . . . but that was a problem he could
deal with later. Right now they needed money.

He hired a canalboat and cruised until he found a func-
tioning Public Works phone booth. The call code he thumbed
in was private, but he was not surprised when it failed to
enter. There was an ominous pause, then a Bell/Calstate
symbol in crude pixels and the scrolling message: THE NUM-
BER YOU HAVE ENTERED IS OUT OF SERVICE. PLEASE HOLD
AND YOUR CALL WILL BE REROUTED.

To the Agencies, Byron thought grimly. He hammered

the ESCAPE key and climbed back into his rented barque. Within minutes he was lost in traffic.

At a second booth deep in the factory district, he placed another call, strictly inside the Floats exchange: a friend, a local artist named Montoya. Cruz Wexler's estate in Carmel was off the optic lines, Byron said, and did Montoya have any idea why?

Montoya became wide-eyed. "It was maybe a stupid idea to call him. You just back in town? The Agencies raided Wexler weeks ago. The building is closed up and his files are in custody."

Byron considered. It must have happened shortly after they left for Brazil. Not, he thought, coincidence.

"They even raided some places in the Floats," Montoya said. "Very rough time. Some good people were up in Carmel when the hammer came down." He shook his head.

"They took Wexler?"

Montoya's eyes narrowed; he licked his lips. "It's not that I don't trust you, right? But could be somebody asked you to ask."

Byron took hold of the camera lens, forced it left and right on its rusted pivot. "Do you *see* anybody?"

"Ask Cat," Montoya said, and cleared the monitor.

"Cat" Katsuma was a petite second-generation Floater who did crystal paintings for the mainland galleries. She had known Byron and Teresa for years; she expressed her pleasure at seeing him again. "I heard bad rumors," she said. "I'm glad you're okay."

"Reasonably okay," Byron said. "Tell me about Wexler."

"You really need to talk to him?"

"It would clear some things up." Though the prospect of money had retreated.

"Well. Meet me this afternoon, then," and she named a café by the sea wall south of the factories.

He figured Wexler owed him—minimum—an explanation.

Running south in the rental barque, he totaled up everything he knew about Cruz Wexler.

Much of it was public knowledge. Wexler was, or had been, a celebrity. During the war years crystal 'liths had begun to circulate in the drug underground; they enjoyed a kind of vogue during which public curiosity had peaked. Wexler held a Ph.D. in Chaotic Dynamics but had been cashiered when he began publishing articles in which he described the dreamstones as "psychic manna from an older and saner civilization." He lost his tenure but gained a following. He had been prominent in bohemian circles for a few years, had once owned property in the Floats. But the notoriety subsided and Wexler had pretty much retired to his estate in Carmel these days, fighting a progressive emphysema and playing wise man to the stubbornly faithful. He still had a following among the Float artists who drew their inspiration from the stones. Periodically they would make the migration to Carmel, bask in his presumed enlightenment. Byron figured it was pretty much all bullshit. But it was Wexler who had underwritten his lab, and it was Wexler—if anyone—who could make sense of the Pau Seco debacle.

He moored his boat at a by-the-hour dock behind the ruin of a cracking plant and walked to the café Cat had specified. It was a dicey neighborhood. Not terrible, but you got a certain influx from the slums farther south. Inside the chain-link perimeter he recognized Cat sitting at a high table overlooking the canal. A man was with her. The man had a Navy cap pulled down over his ears and a few days growth of beard, but it was Wexler; he was not hard to recognize. Byron, nervous and focused now, ordered a beer and carried it to the table.

"Byron," Cat said warmly.

But he was staring at Wexler. Wexler said nothing, only returned the look. His eyes were steady and blue. Still a charismatic figure. People didn't believe he could lie with eyes like that.

His breath rasped in, rasped out.

Cat stood up, sighing. "I'll talk to you later, then." She touched Byron's shoulder, leaned over him. "Go easy

ROBERT CHARLES WILSON

on him, all right? I've been bunking him in my float. He's got nowhere to go and his lungs are pretty bad."

When she was out of earshot, Byron said tonelessly, "I have every reason to believe you fucked us over."

Wexler nodded. "I can see how you might feel that way."

"A walk, you said. A vacation."

"Unforeseen circumstances," Wexler said. "Is Teresa all right?"

"More or less." He resented the question.

"You have the stone?"

No, Byron thought. You are not entitled to that datum. Not yet. He smiled. "Worry about it," he said.

Wexler sat back and sipped his coffee. "I'm not here," he said at last—meaning the Floats, Byron took it—"by choice. You might have noticed."

"Cat said you got burned."

"They came in force. I was not expecting it."

"But you weren't home? That's a pretty good coincidence."

"I didn't expect any of this. Or I would not have sent you people south. May I explain, or would you prefer to break my nose?"

Byron realized his fists were clenched. More bullshit, he thought bleakly. But he might as well listen. And he realized then that he had come here not for money or satisfaction, but for Teresa's sake. Her unhappiness was patent and frightening and connected very closely with the stone. If anybody understood it, Wexler might.

A gull circled overhead, screeching. Byron tossed a crumb from the table and watched the bird chase it down to the dark canal water. "I'm listening," he said.

The Agencies came and closed the estate, Wexler said. It was a radical sweep. They had always ignored him before. The dreamstones were technically contraband, but it was a law not much enforced; the scale of the crime was minuscule, and intensive enforcement would not have been cost-effective. "The new 'liths changed their mind," Wexler said. "The deep-core 'liths."

"You *knew*," Byron said.

"I was warned," he admitted. "I have my own contacts. Obviously."

"Some good people were there."

"There was no time to get them out. They've been in custody, but my understanding is that they'll be released soon." He sipped his coffee, labored for breath. "You have to understand about the stones."

Wexler had a contact in the government research facility in Virginia, a highly-placed member of the research team who had been feeding him news about the deep-core oneiroliths. "And it was heady information. You have to understand that. It was everything we wanted. Everything that came before, impressive as it was, was blurred or obscure by comparison. For years we'd been decoding data in which every third bit had been erased by time. Reconstructing it, really. Even so, we learned a great deal. But never anything substantial about the Exotics themselves. As if they were holding themselves aloof, standing out of reach."

But now, Wexler said, the data came in torrents. Too, the Virginia team had begun serious work with what they called "the human interface"—mostly convicts recruited out of Vacaville. This was not hard data; it was "of dubious provenance" and sometimes contradictory. But much of it correlated with the new translations from the big mainframes. A preliminary understanding of the Exotics began to emerge.

"The question had always been, why do we have these artifacts? Why were they buried in the Mato Grosso? Were they a gift, an accident? The great mystery."

Byron said, "Is there an answer?"

"Hints," Wexler said. He leaned forward now. His own fascination was obvious and undimmed. "We deciphered a little of their history. The history, especially, of their information technology."

"I don't understand," Byron said.

"Well . . ." Wexler paused to catch his breath. "First there are the stories around the fire. Neolithic data storage. The past is recorded, but it's not very efficient. Errors creep in. Then the written word. The beginning of real history—

a better grip on the past. Compared to oral history it's a fairly dense medium, fairly incorruptible. Then the printed word, the book. Better yet. Photography, audiotape, videotape . . . and suddenly the past is very much with us. We have digital technology, we have molecular memory. We have people like you.'' He looked a moment at Byron's faded Angel tattoo. ''Walking data storage. The Exotics were like us in this respect, but more focused . . . you might say obsessed. The idea of the loss of the past terrified them. They had a profound, ontological fear of forgetting. Without memory, no meaning; without meaning—chaos.'' He sat back. ''The oneiroliths are the logical product of that obsession: complexly folded in spacetime, linked somehow directly into sapient consciousness. You could say that they contain a sort of recording of experience itself, an archive of every human life since they arrived on this planet. Better perhaps to say that they allow us access to the *experience* of the past—the only kind of time machine we are ever likely to have.''

Well, Byron thought. He had seen Teresa do her trick with the old people who visited her float: pulling the past out of a stone. Strange but not world-shaking. He told Wexler so.

''But it begs the question,'' Wexler said. ''Our best estimate now is that the Exotics encountered our planet some thousand years before the birth of Christ. It fascinated them. It must have. They would have asked themselves the questions we've been asking about them: how are these creatures like us? How are they not?''

He sipped his coffee, momentarily breathless. Byron waited.

''My guess,'' Wexler said, ''is that they considered us defective. Suppose we traveled to another world and encountered a race of myopics. That's how it must have seemed to them. Here we are, obviously sapient, tool-using, clever individuals. Our bodies are not unlike theirs; we have opposable thumbs, as they do. The distinguishing feature is . . .'' He tapped his forehead. *''Memory.''* He smiled faintly. ''The best evidence now suggests that the Exotics possessed what we would call eidetic memory. A human mind can't do this; the few cases of human mnemonism on record have been deeply disturbed individuals. It's the way we're wired. We have to assume the Exotics could forget, in the sense that the past was not always vividly in their mind—no living creature could cope with that. But there was no fully experienced moment that could not be recalled at will . . . or could be willfully or permanently suppressed. Presumably, this is what fueled their obsession with information technology. For them, the idea of *forgetting* was indistinguishable from the idea of death. To pass out of memory was to pass out of the world. To conserve memory was to confer immortality.''

Byron walked with Wexler out along the seawall for a distance.

It was more private out here. The ocean seemed to lend a credibility to all this talk of time, immortality, memory.

Byron believed most of it. The talk had ignited an old enthusiasm in Wexler's lined face, too immediate to be faked. None of this addressed the problem of betrayal, money, Teresa. But he was content, for now, to let the man talk.

"I wanted one of these new stones, of course. It seemed to me we could do so much with it. They used human subjects in Virginia, but usually the criminally insane, and they were reacting badly to the experience—hypermnesia, specifically of repressed material. Whereas in Carmel the response was almost always positive . . . at least with the traditional 'liths. Why not these new ones? It would be bigger, stronger, better. Real contact this time. Contact with an alien sapience: I cannot communicate how intoxicating that idea was. Not the exchange of mathematics, but *real* contact—spiritual contact."

Byron said coolly, "Spiritual?"

The faint smile again. "I used to be freer with words like that. But yes, spiritual. It was what we wanted. The authentic touch. Across that chasm." He waved his hand at the sky. "But of course everything was locked up very tight. The Agencies were scared of this whole thing. For the last thirty years national governments have been presiding over some fairly tumultuous social changes. A direct product of the oneiroliths. Fortunes made and unmade. That kind of instability is frightening. The idea of *accelerated* change—well, it made them nervous.''

"So you set up the buy at Pau Seco."

"I really believed it would be safe. I spent a considerable amount of money on it. I bought cooperation at the highest levels of the SUDAM bureaucracy. There was a risk involved, of course. I told Teresa so when she volunteered. But even if there had been legal trouble, I might have bought you out of that too . . . the Valverde regime is extremely pliable.''

"It was worse than that," Byron said.

Wexler averted his eyes. "So I understand. My contact in Virginia was compromised. And then the estate at Carmel was compromised. And so the house of cards came tumbling down. I have no influence over the Agencies . . . I didn't know they would be involved." He looked at Byron. "You managed to get away with the stone?''

"Yes." No point in hiding it now.

"You have it still?"

He nodded.

"Has Teresa used it?"

"Yes."

"Her reaction was not positive?"

"No," Byron said.

Wexler nodded, registering the information. He looked back at the sea. The sea was wide and deep, Byron thought, and it went on forever. Like the sky. Like the stars.

"I don't think they wholly understood us," Wexler said. "The Exotics, I mean. They gave us the stones, and they were a gift, hidden until we could usefully decode and reproduce them. Binary code propagating across axes of symmetry. Microvoltages trickling down folded spacetime. But with this other aspect . . .'' He smiled again—sadly now, Byron thought. " 'Spiritual.' I think they simply wanted to make us whole . . . to cure what they saw as our tragic failure. Failure of memory. Which is failure of conscience. They were surprised, I would guess, by our capacity for aggression. For ruthlessness, for inflicting pain. Conscience is memory . . . and the stones would restore it.''

"But it doesn't work that way."

"I think because we are divided against ourselves in a way they could not imagine. We suppress memories; the memories lead a life of their own. We create images of ourselves and the images spring to life. We have names for them. The conscious and unconscious mind. Id and ego. And so on. Always, the crucial act is the act of forgetting. To be forced to confront the past, really confront it . . .'' He shook his head. "It would take a great strength."

"I'm worried about her," Byron said.

Wexler said quietly, "I can't help you."

The sun was low in the sky when they turned away from the ocean.

"If you had the stone," Byron said, "if you had it now, what would you do with it?"

Wexler moved like an old man. In this light, he was not inspiring. He walked with his legs bowed, his head down. "I don't know," he said.

"Would you touch it?"

"I don't know . . . I don't think so."

"Why not?"

He was a long time answering. His lips were pursed, his gaze abstracted. "Maybe," he said, "there are things I would like not to remember."

"Like what?"

Silence.

Byron said, "You were the only one who knew. You were the one who sent us to Pau Seco, and you were the one who made the arrangements. Nobody else knew."

His voice was faint now, tremulous. He said, "Suppose I lied. Suppose I *was* arrested in the sweep. Suppose I was interrogated by the Agencies." He closed his eyes. "Suppose I was afraid, and suppose that—because I was afraid—I confessed, I told them about the arrangements I'd made in Brazil. And suppose, because I told them, they let me go." His smile now was bleak and humorless. "Wouldn't that be something I might like to forget?"

ROBERT CHARLES WILSON

* * *

By the time they reached the café, night had fallen, the air was cool, and most of the tables were empty. Wexler ordered a drink; Byron said he had to get going.

"I can tell you one thing that might be useful," Wexler said.

Byron waited. The beaten look on Wexler's face had begun to make him nervous.

"I still talk to people at the Virginia facility," he said. "There are a few untapped bit streams, if you know where to find them. The news now is that the Agencies have cooled off a good deal. The stone left Pau Seco, and they are not interested in tracing it. They decided it doesn't have a big future on the black market—and from what you say, that is probably true. The issue is dead, except that they'll install a military force at Pau Seco to oversee the Brazilians.

"But you may have a problem yet. There was a man at the Virginia facility, an Agency man, a latent sociopath from the war years. His name is Stephen Oberg. He was in charge of the Pau Seco interdiction. Word is that he has an obsessive personal fear of the oneiroliths . . . and that he went rogue after the stone left Brazil." Wexler peered at him, wheezing faintly. "He may still be on your case."

"Oberg," Byron said. The name was faintly familiar. It called up some sinister echo.

Wexler sat down among the shadows. He pulled his collar up, as if against a chill only he could feel. "Rumor has it," Wexler said, "the man is quite insane."

2.   Byron navigated his rental barque home through the night canals now, past neon-lit dance shacks and constellations of paper lanterns.

He was mindful of the Angel tattoo on his arm: Wexler had mentioned it. He had spent so much time, he thought, trying to erase it. Not the symbol but the thing, the fact, what he had become in the war.

What he had told Keller back in Belem was true. He did not want to be a machine; he understood that he had become a machine; he understood that the road back into the world was treacherous and painful. Teresa was his road. All he had ever wanted was a life with her. That would be enough. But if not that, then at least the scars of humanity: the pain of a commitment he could not revoke.

The question he entertained now, for the first time, was: *when is it enough?*

How much pain is proof? How much is too much?

I could disappear, he thought. I could buy documents and disappear into the mainland. Leave the Floats, leave the dream trade, leave no trail for this Oberg to follow. Make some new life and disappear into it, maybe find a woman who might love me, he thought, and make babies with her. The old tattoo had pretty much faded. A sleeve was enough to cover it.

It was an intoxicating thought, but also dangerous. He forced it away as he docked the boat. Too much unfinished business. She needed him yet. There was still the possibility he could do something for her.

The balsa was dark inside. Pushing through the door, he heard a moan from the back bedroom.

He flicked a wall switch; an antique incandescent bulb radiated sterile and sudden light. "Teresa?" But she only moaned again. The sound might have signified pain or pleasure.

He pushed through a rag curtain into the back room.

She was alone on the bed, blinking at the light. Her pupils were massively dilated.

Byron picked up the small wide-necked bottle from the floor beside the bed. It was three-quarters full of tiny black pills. Enkephalins, he thought. Concentrated, potent. "My Christ," he whispered.

Her moan was abstracted pleasure. She was obviously ashamed—in some corner of her mind—that he had found her this way. She averted her face. But the shame could not override the flush of chemical well-being. There were pinpricks of sweat on her forehead.

Hardly aware of himself, he sat on the bed and cradled her head against him.

She rolled away. "I'm sorry," she said. Her voice was faint, hollow, oceans distant. "I'm sorry. I'm sorry."

But there was nothing to say. Nothing worth saying.

He held her, and the boat rose in the swell.

CHAPTER 19

Keller contacted Vasquez, the Network producer, and negotiated an infusion of credit into one of his phantom accounts. Vasquez also supplied some temporary documentation and access to the downloading facilities in the Network technical compound. "But make it quick," Vasquez urged. "I'm under a certain amount of time pressure. Is it good footage?"

Keller recalled Pau Seco, the mine and the old town, the bars and brothels. He nodded.

"Good," Vasquez told him. "You have an appointment with Leiberman."

Leiberman, the Network neurosurgeon, plucked out Keller's memory chip and closed the socket wound with adhesives. In a month there would be no visible scar. "Once again," Leiberman said loftily, "you are merely human." He handed Keller the memory in a tiny transparent pillbox, as prosaic in its bed of cotton as a pulled tooth.

Keller went directly to the Network compound, displayed his new ID to the machine at the gate and claimed an editing booth. The technical compound sprawled over a vast expanse of desert west of Barstow, bunkers and Quonsets and a string of satellite bowls solemnly regarding the southern sky. There was a floating staff of Network engineers, but most of the people here were independent contractors—by his ID Keller was one of these—sharing time on the Network mainframes.

The booth was private, a small room crowded with monitors and mixers. Keller plugged his memory into a machine socket, named it and gave it an access code. He pulled the keyboard into his lap and put his feet up on the mixer.

TIME, he tapped.

Forty-one days, the monitor said, *twenty-eight minutes, fifteen seconds* since the memory was activated. He registered a faint surprise: it had seemed like more.

He instructed the edit program to install index marks at every twenty-four hour point—day marks—and then divide them into hours. "Laying ordinance," it was called. He installed special index points at Day Seven (ARRIVAL, RIO), Day Fifteen (ARRIVAL, PAU SECO), and Day Twenty-five (ARRIVAL, BELEM). Further index points could be installed as necessary; these were the basics, a kind of crude map. Now he could call up a day or an hour and retrieve it at once, enter it into the mainframe memory as part of the ROM package he would eventually hand Vasquez.

Protection first, however. He called up the IDENTITY PROTECT subroutine, then scanned through DAY TWO until he arrived at a full-body image of Byron Ostler.

The central thirty-inch monitor showed Byron in front of his huge, ramshackle balsa deep in the Floats. Keller stilled the image, zoomed on the face, keyed ALTER. The face was replaced abruptly with its own ghost image in topographic lines against limbo, glowing amber.

Keller used a light pencil to push the lines around.

Cheekbones up, a narrower chin. He rotated the image and similarly altered the profile. He called up flesh again and there was Byron standing by his float once more, but it was not Byron any longer; the face was not even faintly familiar. It was some older, heavyset, hawkish man. A generic face, neither good nor evil. RETAIN, Keller typed. The authentic image would never appear in the finished edits.

Next he called up Teresa.

This was more painful. The sight of her stirred old feelings in him, a longing he labored to suppress. She moved across the monitor, regarding him.

I can't see making this trip with somebody I don't trust . . . intuition is all I have right now, you understand?

Her voice filled the booth. A sixteen-bit recreation of the trace he had laid down on this chip. She peered out from the monitor into, it seemed, his eyes. Convulsively, he called up ALTER.

She became a matrix of lines, an artifact of geography. Better that way.

Sweating now, he changed the lines with his light pencil. Moving with professional instinct, he flattened the mouth, rounded the nose, shortened the hair. He worked by rote, eyes narrowed. *Wu-nien*. It was a question of not caring.

He performed similar alterations on Ng and Meireilles, who might still be vulnerable—he was conscientious about protecting his sources—then paged ahead to the most significant footage, the footage Vasquez wanted, the Pau Seco footage.

DAY SIXTEEN. The frame shook as he stepped out of Ng's Truck. HOLD FRAME & PAN, he typed, and played it back. Now the motion was smooth, effortless. The image flickered as he blinked away dust. Keller keyed out HOLD & CORRECT; the dropouts vanished. Beginning to look like video now. The perspective moved up to the lip of the mine, peered into its depths, began a slow pan. AUDIO, he typed.

The sound came up instantly. Clatter of ancient tools. Human voices ringing off distant cliffs. Abyss of time. *Formigas* moving in insect lines up those clay steppes and rope ladders: it might have been yesterday or today or tomorrow. Keller reached for a fader, but his hand struck the volume slide instead. The clangor of voices and tools was suddenly deafening, a roaring in the booth. He blinked at the monitor and for one giddy instant believed he had actually entered the past, transported himself somehow back to Pau Seco, that he might turn and find Teresa beside him.

He slapped the ENTER key.

The playback ceased. The booth filled up with silence.

When he could not bear the work any longer, he signed out and drove west. He had used a portion of the advance from Vasquez to rent a hotel room, but he didn't head directly back. He drove west along a high, fast traffic artery until he hit the coastline, and then he turned north. On his left the Floats sprawled out to the distant gray line of the tidal dam. He drove through colonies and outposts of the cityplex, malltowns and industrial parks. He had gone miles before he understood where he was going.

Bad idea, he thought. It was a bad impulse that had brought him here: Angel sin. But he pulled off the highway when he spotted the sign.

ARTS BY THE SEA. She had mentioned the name once, long ago.

It was not the newest or the best of these businesses. Bamboo walls sunk in a cracked concrete foundation, roof of chalky-red Spanish tile. The door rang a bell when he opened it. Inside, a buckled wooden floor supported shelves and display cases of thick protective glass gone gray with time.

The items on display were, in Keller's judgment, fairly prosaic Float work. Soapstone carvings, junk collages, a few high-priced crystal paintings under glass. He gazed a while at a stylized trance landscape, bread-loaf hills rolling under an azure sky, treehouses like pagodas clustered in the foreground. Some real place, Keller thought, some Exotic venue wrenched out of time. He was staring at it when the proprietor pushed through a curtain from the rear of the store.

She was a chunky gray-haired woman in layered pastel skirts, and she regarded Keller across a chasm of suspicion. "Is there something you were especially interested in?"

"A certain artist," he said. "I understand you sold some of her work. Her name is Teresa . . . Teresa Rafael."

She looked at him more carefully now, his face and his clothes. "No," she said finally. "We have nothing."

Keller extracted the Pacific Credit gold card Vasquez had obtained for him. In fact his account was strictly limited, but the card itself was impressive. He slid it across the counter; the woman ran her finger over the embedded microchip. "She hasn't displayed here for years. Her work has appreciated in value. You understand? She has a reputation now. A following."

"I understand."

The woman licked her lips. "In the back," she said.

Keller followed her through the curtain. There were a dozen pieces in this smaller room—all "appreciated," Keller assumed: it was a commonplace practice for street dealers to hold back the work of a promising newcomer. But he recognized instantly which of it was Teresa's. "These," the woman said loftily, "are early pieces."

She must have been a girl when she did this, Keller thought. He was impressed. Some of the work was awkward; none of it was naive. A few pieces displayed the obvious skill and muted passion that had made her successful. Mostly they were junk sculptures, assembled out of pipe and copper wire and mechanical oddments scavenged from the old Float factories gutted in the fire; but she had polished and shaped the material until it seemed nearly alive, more liquid than solid.

"You're familiar with the work?"

"No . . . not really."

Under the woman's alarmed stare he picked up a small piece of sculpture and examined it. The metallic tangle resolved into the image of a face. No—two faces. He rotated the piece in his hand.

A woman's face, gaunt but curiously childlike in its sadness.

And a child's face, with an adult's expression of fierce resolve.

The proprietor took it from him. Keller was startled; he restrained an impulse to take it back. She named a sum,

ROBERT CHARLES WILSON

and it was approximately the money Vasquez had entered into Keller's account, minus living expenses. A huge amount. But he agreed without haggling.

He drove home with the piece beside him in the car, confused and faintly shocked at himself. He was like a sleepwalker, acting out some dream. He knew only that he wanted something from this knot of metal, something tangible; a piece of her, he thought, a relic, or that forbidden and finally dangerous thing—a memory.

In the morning he went back to the Network technical compound and called up yesterday's work on the monitor.

The sight of it shocked him. He sat back in the cloistered silence of the editing booth and stared.

He had altered Teresa's features to protect her anonymity. Standard procedure, and he had worked by rote. Successfully. It didn't look like Teresa anymore.

But the face he had given her was Megan Lindsey's.

CHAPTER 20

Stephen Oberg had stepped outside the bounds of propriety often since the debacle at Pau Seco, but he did not feel authentically like an outlaw until the day he rented a cheap balsa in the Floats.

It was an outlaw place; he was an outlaw in it. The faces he saw along the market canals were furtive, obscure, hidden. He imagined he looked the same. A shadow-thing now, outside the bright thoroughfares of law and custom. The only light here was the beacon of his own intense desire; the abyss of the ocean was unnervingly close.

It worried him a little. The night he moved into the balsa, he rolled out his mattress over the stained wooden floor and wondered whether he might have gone too far. He had always depended on an external structure for discipline, for rules. The Army, in an important way, had made him what he was. They had named him. Potent magic. He was a Latent Aggressive. And it was not a pathology but a talent, a useful quirk of character. He could be depended upon for certain acts. He was conscienceless but loyal: it was a loyalty that had never faltered.

Until now. Now he was an outlaw, a loose cannon. He had assumed a task and made it his own, and he could not see beyond it. Without him, the deep-core stone from the Pau Seco mine might be casually reproduced, might spread—and surely that was what its unknowable creators had intended—among the furtive and marginal people of the Floats. And he could not allow that.

Because he *understood*, and he was persuaded that he was the only one who understood. He understood the nature of the stone: its alienness, its powers of memory. He had touched Tavitch, and through Tavitch, the stone. And the stone had touched him.

It was a bad and dangerous thing, a kind of weapon. It eroded the marrow of the soul. It must not be allowed to exist.

He believed this as fiercely as he had believed anything in his life.

The force of his belief was its own justification. It comforted him.

It was a fire to warm him, out here in this wilderness.

In the morning he placed a call to an Agency bureaucrat back east, a man named Tate. Tate, seeing Oberg's face in the monitor, did an elaborate double-take. "You!" he said.

Oberg smiled. "Me."

"One minute."

Oberg waited while Tate called up a security program, shunting his terminal out of the routine record-and-monitor loops. Tate, a pockmarked man of Oberg's age, looked harried when he reappeared. "That was a stupid thing to do!"

"I need your help."

"You're hardly entitled to it. Everybody knows you went rogue back in Brazil. Fucking bad form, Steve."

MEMORY WIRE

"This isn't an official call."

"We're not friends."

"We're old friends," Oberg said.

"The hell we are."

But it was true. If not friends, then at least something like it: comrades, colleagues. Tate had been a point man for Oberg's platoon.

It was not something that drew them together; they had seen each other only a handful of times since the war. But they had parallel careers; and there was that unspoken bond, Oberg thought, the tug of old loyalties. He said, "I want whatever you have on the three Americans. I assume you processed the files from SUDAM. There must have been something."

"That has nothing to do with me."

"You have clearances."

"I'm not your dog. I don't fetch when you say fetch." He looked pained. "This is not your business anymore."

"As a favor," Oberg said.

"As far as I know," Tate said, "there's nothing substantive. A couple of Floaters, no extant ID except what they bought. You know all this."

"There's the third man."

"Keller. Well, we have the name. But this all went into limbo when you turned up AWOL. Are you listening? Steve: nobody *cares*."

"Check it out for me," Oberg said. "Please."

"Give me a number where you are. I'll call you back."

"I'll call you," Oberg said, and cleared the monitor.

For a couple of days he explored the neighborhood.

It was a seedy area south of the factory district, close to the urban mainland. Most of the people here worked mainland jobs during the day. At night the boardwalks lit up with paper lanterns; the bars and dance shacks opened for business. Commerce came the opposite way after dark —venturesome mainlanders shopping for the illicit pleasures of the Floats. These were more legendary than real, Oberg understood. But there were certain things for sale.

Drugs, for instance. Well, drugs were everywhere. It

was a truism that the economy could not function—or at least compete—without the vast array of stimulants, IQ enhancers, and complex neuropeptides for sale on the street or by prescription. Oberg had done time with the DEA and understood that it was a traffic no one really cared to interdict. Most of the field agents he knew were either neurochemically enhanced or skimming money from the trade. Or both. It was called free enterprise.

But the Floats made dealing a little looser. No government functionaries to take a percentage, although he understood the Filipino and East Indian mobs would sometimes muscle in. Generally, though, it was a loose friends-of-friends distribution network . . . and that worked in his favor.

For three nights he frequented a bar called Neptune's, which catered almost exclusively to mainlanders. He watched the canal traffic, the waitresses, the tidal flow of alcohol over the bar. In particular he watched a lanky, pale teenager who occupied a rear booth—same booth all three nights—and who would periodically step out with one or two customers, through a back door onto a catwalk overlooking a waste canal. The boy was not a hooker; there were others, more sophisticated, handling that trade. But he fit the mainlander's image of a drug pusher, and Oberg guessed that was an advantage here; it was like a sign, an advertisement. The teenager kept his hands in his oversized jacket, and when he brought them out, Oberg imagined, they would be holding pills, powders, blotters.

His fourth night in the Floats he approached the boy.

"I would like to buy drugs," he said softly.

The teenager looked at him, amused. "You would like *what*?"

Oberg showed him the vial he had taken from Teresa's studio. He shook out the resinous black pill into the palm of his hand and held it so the boy could see it.

The boy laughed and looked away. "Shit," he said.

"I'm serious," Oberg said.

"I bet you are." The teenager tapped his hand nervously against the tabletop.

Probably he was doing some CNS stimulant himself, Oberg thought, pumping chemical energy out of his neurons. Crash every morning, up every night. It was pathetic, and he resented the boy's condescension. "I can pay," Oberg said.

The boy took a second look. "You prepared to buy in quantity? I don't sell candy."

"Whatever you want."

"Well."

The boy led him outside.

The walkway was narrow and dark. Presumably, it was useful for dumping trash. It overlooked a waste canal, dark water drawn down open conduits to the sea. There was a single sodium-vapor lamp overhead and nothing beyond the canal but the blank stucco wall of an empty warehouse. The sound of music trickled out from the bar through this single door, closed now. The sound was anemic and far-seeming.

The boy dug into the deep recesses of his jacket and brought out a sweaty handful of pills. They glistened in the harsh light. They were small and black. "This is all I have," the boy was saying, bored with the transaction already, "but you come back Tuesday, I might—hey!"

Oberg swept his fist out and knocked the boy's hand away. The pills flew up in an arc, twinkled a moment, dropped inaudibly into the canal.

The boy stared, a little awed. "Son of a *bitch*!" No one had ever done this to him, Oberg thought. Oberg could have been anyone, a mob enforcer, a new competitor. But the boy had only dealt with mainlanders. He was surprised and confused.

Oberg waited.

The boy's eyes narrowed. "You can fucking throw them away if you want to," he said finally, "but you pay for 'em either way. So pony up, asshole." He took a knife from under his belt.

Oberg had anticipated it. He leaned inside the boy's reach, bent the arm, extracted the knife. He held it against the boy's throat.

He felt a pleasure in this that he had not felt for years.

He understood it was something he enjoyed, the rush of it, something he had missed all this time. An old and profound pleasure. But it was not a thought worth dwelling on.

Loose cannon, he thought giddily.

The boy was wide-eyed and pale.

"Tell me where you got them," Oberg said.

The boy said, faintly, "Fuck you!"

Oberg let the blade draw out a line of blood. The blood was bright and oily in the stark light. He felt the boy twisting against his restraint. "Tell me," he said.

It took time, but in the end he extracted four names and four approximate canal addresses. It would be useful, an approach to the woman, especially if Tate failed to produce any useful information. The boy relaxed, sensing that Oberg had what he wanted: the ordeal was over.

And it was. But not the way the boy expected. Oberg drew the knife deeply across the boy's throat and in a single motion levered the body over the railing and down into the waste canal. There was a momentary thrashing, a choking sound, silence immediately after.

It felt good. It was deeply gratifying.

He used a handkerchief to clean the blade of the knife, and threw the handkerchief after the body.

The knife he took home.

The past is dead and gone, he thought. That was the way it should be.

He had trouble sleeping sometimes. Tonight, for instance. In part it was the adrenaline that had rivered through him at the death of the boy. In part, a more obscure stimulation.

In his worst dreams he was back in Brazil, back in the war, running what his orders called "punitive raids" on farms and villages where guerillas had been harbored. In the dreams he killed people but they would not stay safely dead: they rose and pointed accusing fingers at him; they protested their innocence. He killed them once, twice, three times. They rose up sullenly and said his name.

In Virginia he had touched Tavitch when Tavitch was touching the stone; and Tavitch had looked into his eyes

and had seen these same dreams. But they were not dreams.
That was the terrifying thing. Somehow, through Tavitch,
through the Pau Seco stone, it had actually happened.
The dead had risen stubbornly; the dead had pronounced
his name.

He lay in the darkness and was haunted by the memory.
It was unnatural; it was alien, an alien ruse, a mind trick.
The past was gone, the dead were dead and did not speak,
and everybody dies; one day Oberg would be dead and
silent, too, and that was as it should be: the broad and
welcoming ocean of oblivion. It made life bearable. It was
sacred. It should not be tampered with.

With this new thought he achieved ease and finally a
sleep as calm as that vast and silent ocean; he did not dream;
he woke strengthened in his resolve.

In the morning he made a second call to Tate.

"Keller is an Angel," Tate said. "He's working for
an independent producer name of Vasquez. He's in L.A.
now, probably downloading at the Network compounds."
He regarded Oberg guiltily. "I assume this is what you
wanted."

"Yes," Oberg said.

"You're crazy, Steve, you know that? You're fucking
nuts."

It might be true. It didn't matter.

The monitor blanked, and Oberg stared a long moment
at his own reflection in it.

CHAPTER 21

1. Byron knew he was losing her. The knowledge was unavoidable.

He didn't talk about the pills. They didn't talk much at all. Talk was superfluous; worse, it might have required lies. He was watching when she tossed her pill bottle into a waste canal, and the act kindled a flare of hope in him. Later he found the pills themselves hoarded in a corner of her dresser; it was only the bottle she had discarded. It was a gesture he had been meant to see.

He understood that this was the old Teresa, the Teresa he had found on his doorstep years ago, dying and frightened of dying and wanting to die. The part of her that needed to survive had been silenced—silenced, he guessed, that day in the hotel room off the Ver-o-Peso—and he was helpless to call it back. He could not touch her that way, because she did not love him.

He was not accustomed to thinking about these things so bluntly, but the facts were as obvious as they were painful.

He ate dinner with her. There was bread in ragged loaves from the bakery stall, a cut of real beef. The meal represented very nearly the last of their money. Teresa ate mechanically; when she was finished she said she was going for a walk. "I'll go with you," Byron volunteered. But she shook her head. She wanted to be alone.

Alone with her pills, he thought. Alone to watch the Floats light up, alone to watch the waves roll in. She closed the door behind her, and he was left by himself in the float shack with the ticking of the bilge pump and the moan of the floorboards moving in the swell.

He thought of Keller.

Keller on the mainland. Keller drifting back into his Network career, surrendering to the momentum of it.

Keller, whom she loved.

Keller, who might have helped her.

The thought was galling, but he could not resist it.

He used to feel sorry for Keller. Keller was the thing Byron might have been; victim of, Christ, a catalogue of things: his childhood, the army, his own cowardice. Forgivable sins, Teresa said one time. But now Keller had walked out, and that was inexcusable.

And here was the irony. Teresa was hurting . . . and the only thing I can do for her, Byron thought bitterly, is to call up Keller and beg him to come back.

Beg him to take her away from me.

It was galling. But he thought about the Angel tattoo on his arm and what it meant, and he was on the verge of doing it—getting a message to Keller through Keller's Network producer, Vasquez—when there was a knock at the door.

He opened it cautiously.

Cruz Wexler stood outside. In the dusk he might have

been a thousand years old. He labored at the salt air as if he could not draw nourishment from it.

"I want to talk to her," he said.

2.   Teresa found him waiting when she came in from the boardwalk. Her reaction was an instinctive and immediate happiness: he was a link to a better time in her life.

She hugged him and sat down across from him, and only then realized how much these past weeks had aged him. He had been fading for years up in Carmel, of course, gone from celebrity to local eccentric, and she understood that the part of him that was showman and con-artist— maybe a large part of him—had resented this decline. But she had always believed he was sincere about the oneiroliths, sincere in the conviction that they belonged to the world, not just a coterie of government scientists. He was always talking about what he called the gnosis, the Mystery, a kind of conquering wisdom: his optimism had been as vast as it was naive. These last days must have shocked him.

They talked into the night. She had taken a pill while she was out walking, but only one, and the effect was a mild buoyancy which disguised her fatigue. (But she wouldn't think about that.) Byron excused himself and took his bed-roll into the back room. Then Wexler asked her about Brazil, and she found herself telling him about it—the story spilling out of her. She told him about Ray. Maybe because of the pill, she was able to say things that surprised her. She talked about the new oneirolith, its potency, the terrible memories it had provoked in her and in Ray. The wedge of knowing it had driven between them. She expressed her pain and surprise, was astonished when a tear trailed down her cheek: strange. She wasn't sad. She felt all right.

Wexler nodded thoughtfully. His beard had grown out into gray stubble and his breathing was noisy and forceful, as if breathing were not automatic but a task he had to consider and perform. His eyes were full of gentle concern.

He talked about the Exotics.

He had spent his life in this kind of speculation. She understood that it was his nature, that he asked the questions no one else wanted to ask. Everybody was deriving technical data from the 'liths but nobody asked the profounder questions: maybe, he said, because they were afraid to. But Wexler had seen the trance landscapes, had glimpsed the whirlpool of history.

"If someone asked me now," he said, "my guess would be that it was planned. All of it. There's one kind of stone, very common, with its binary microvoltages: basically, it talks to machines. It says something altogether different to people like us. There are visions, a sense of significance, a sense of *imminence*. And then this rarer stone. It has even more to say. But at a price."

She shook her head. "I don't understand."

"Neither do I. Truly. But I can guess. It depends, doesn't it, on what the Exotics thought of us—the kind of creatures they took us to be. And I think, to them, we were broken things. Fractured. Divided." He paused for breath. "Divided against *ourselves*. Not only collectively but individually. The mind against itself. I think it surprised them."

She said, "They were different?"

"Whole, in some important way, where we're broken. But you must have felt it."

She had. The memory was warm but somehow chastening, a kind of rebuke. The pill wearing off, she thought. She felt the gritty flush of sobriety.

"They anticipated us," Wexler was saying. "They understood that we were good with tools. They guessed, I think, what we might do with our technology."

She shook her head, confused still.

"Well," he said, "what *have* we done? We can manipulate the mind itself. But we don't heal it. We don't make it whole. Instead we fracture it. We divide it. We have creche soldiers, we have battalions of neurotics. We train our psychoses as if they were dogs, to do tricks for us. We make ourselves over to suit our function."

"Like Ray," Teresa said.

"Like Ray. Like everybody else. And it's bad, it's dangerous. It makes us conscienceless; in some important way I think it makes us soulless."

But he had said much of this before. She remembered

ROBERT CHARLES WILSON

him at his estate in Carmel, a rambling Spanish-style ranch house he had bought with the money from his early successes, maintained—but shabbily—with the money funneled back through 'lith chemists like Byron, lecturing to a crowd of equally shabby Float artists. He had talked as grandly about the traditions of Paracelsus, the Gnostics, cryptic wisdom. Grandiose nonsense. And it had come down to this: a sick old man in a decaying float shack. It depressed her.

He must have seen her skepticism. He ducked his head; he put his hands on the table. Old hands. The skin was pale and papery, the nails gnawed short. "I'm sorry," he said. "I get carried away."

"I couldn't bear it," she confessed. "The stone. The Pau Seco stone. It was what I wanted. It really was. The memory. *Myself*. But . . . I couldn't bear it."

"I wonder if that's true."

She glared. "You weren't there."

"Obviously. But I think it's what they demand of us." He said gently, "It makes sense."

She felt offended, obscurely threatened.

"It's the part of themselves they withheld," he said. "The part of themselves they wouldn't give to the machines. A wealth of real knowledge. Time and history. But only between mind and mind, you understand? A *whole* mind."

"I don't want it that badly."

"Maybe," he said softly, "you *need* it."

She stood up. Her head had begun to ache. He had come here and confused her, and that was bad. "You do it," she said petulantly. "You be the one."

His voice was faint. "It frightens me," he said. A confession. "Distressing. After all this time. The gnosis. The real thing. But it frightens me." He smiled hollowly. "Not only that. I think it demands a kind of innocence. Which I do not possess."

"You think I do? You think *I* do?" Mysteriously, she was shouting. The words erupted from her, sourceless. "I'm not innocent!" She was panicking. She needed a pill. Quiescence. Peace. Her body cried out for it. "I'm *not* good!"

She ran for the door.

MEMORY WIRE

* * *

Byron had been listening from the other room.

Wexler stood up when the chemist emerged. "I'm sorry," he said immediately. "I thought—"

"It's the way she's been," Byron said.

"I meant to help."

"I understand."

"Well . . . I should leave."

Byron said, "You meant all that? What you told her?"

Wexler nodded.

"We can't help her."

"Apparently not."

"But Ray could?"

The old man shrugged. "Maybe."

Wexler allowed Byron to roll out a mattress for him in the corner of the float. Too late to go back to Cat's; his breath was troubling him. So he accepted the offer. Three people in this two-room shack.

He was awake when Teresa came home. She moved through the darkened room with the elevated grace of her enkephalin high. She had been an addict, and she was spiraling back into her addiction now with terrifying speed.

He had sent her perhaps blithely to Pau Seco. But in fact he had anticipated none of this . . . suspected, at least, that if a crisis came it would be a domestic crisis and she would be safer out of it. The arrangements had been meticulous, and he had put a vast amount of money into it, confident that he was guaranteeing her safety.

What he had not counted on was his own weakness.

So he owed her whatever help he could give. And so he had come here.

But the help she needed—as Byron had pointed out—was not within his power.

He slept and dreamed of a terrible and oppressive future, half men like Oberg riding out to the stars in warships, chitinous bodies of metal welded to flesh, protein circuits spiked into their nervous systems. It was not so much dream as prophecy, and he woke from it with a sense of imminence, a sense that this conflict—between Oberg and Teresa, between Teresa and her fears—would one day be played out on a much larger stage. That what they did here prefigured an enormity.

It was an oppressive idea. It was more than he wanted to believe.

He woke with morning light harsh in his eyes.

Terrible, he thought, to be so old and so frightened.

Teresa was cooking up breakfast; he resolved not to mention their conversation of the night before. He moved around her cautiously. Her attention was focused on the food.

It was for him, she said. She wasn't hungry.

He said, "Byron's gone?"

"Gone to the mainland." She regarded him across the table. "I think he's gone to look for Ray."

CHAPTER 22

1. Keller was alone in the booth when Byron found him.

The lights were dim and the monitors running, images cascading across the tiny enclosed space: the Mato Grosso from the window of a bus, Pau Seco, the Ver-o-Peso. The audio was faintly audible on all these sources—ghost whispers from an ancient world. Keller said, "I'm surprised you found me."

"I talked to Vasquez. He gave me a Network pass."

Keller worked while Byron talked. His fingers moved deftly over the mixing board. He felt quite firmly embedded in his Angel training now, gliding over this memory landscape around him, an archeologist among the ruins of his own experience. On a dozen monitors the altered Teresa gazed palely across the docks at Belem, at a Japanese tanker moving with silent grace toward its harbor. All events converging, Keller thought; all of us moving toward harbor.

He had been drinking a little.

Byron talked in a soft, persuasive voice about the Floats, about the shack he had rented there, about Cruz Wexler (who was impoverished and alone now)—finally, about Teresa. "You know," Byron said, "she's not really here. You edited her and you ran your programs on her and you filed her and now you think that's her—this picture you made. But it's not. I know how that works. It's easy, and it feels good. But she's not here." He waved dismissively at the monitors. "She's out in the Floats, Ray. She's flesh and blood out there. And I think she would like to see you again." He hesitated, then—firmly—"She needs to see you again."

Keller turned away from the board. "You don't understand."

"No. I don't. Definitely not. But I will tell you what I do understand. I understand that she is in a desperate situation, and that I can't help her, and that she is wanting you so bad it hurts."

"I can't help her either."

"Maybe you're wrong."

Keller said faintly—it made him unhappy to admit it —"We were together. Back in that hotel room with the stone. Together in a way you can't imagine. She saw things—"

"You think . . ." Pure outrage in his voice. "You think that *matters*?"

There was silence for a moment. On the walls luminescent numbers counted down seconds to the minute, minutes to the hour. Past time, Keller thought, spooling away.

He had been awake last night, staring at the sculpture he'd bought at the gallery up the coast, the twin faces of it, woman and child verso. It fascinated him and it made him uneasy. She needed help. Well, obviously she needed help. Maybe she had always needed help.

I would go, Keller thought bleakly, but there are things I cannot face. Her fears and his had been connected somehow. The stone had connected them. She could not face the child in the sculpture; he could not face her.

He could not imagine this changing.

But . . . *if someone is hurting, you help*.

Wu-nien, he thought desperately. The Ice Palace. He longed for it; lately it had been elusive.

Byron said slowly, as if the words had been drawn from some kiln inside him, "She's on the pills again. She's doing enkephalins, Ray. It's a bad downhill road, and it will end with her dying unless we do something." He looked at Keller; Keller was startled by the fierce, obvious pain in his expression. "Unless you do something."

But that was impossible.

She couldn't die.

She was here. She was all around him. She was video now. She was substantial.

She had only begun to exist.

Byron stood up.

He disliked this place where Keller was. It was a bad place, an Angel place, and it reminded him too much of the socket he used to wear. He had spent the war years in the same kind of wire daze Keller had entered now, the gauzy and pleasant territory of not-caring, which people like Keller rendered as "objectivity." He understood the attraction, but it was the same attraction Teresa must feel for the pills: a surrender. He hated it especially because he wanted it. After all these years, he still had the taste for it.

But he had proved something today. It was maybe a hollow consolation, but he felt as if he had erased the Angel tattoo on his arm: if he looked for it, it would be gone. He had pleaded with Keller—who had become Teresa's lover —to go back to her, and surely that was the last labor that was required of him . . . this pain, surely, was sufficient. He had done that for her, and there was no more he could do. He had earned his way into the world.

But she would die anyway, and that was the terrible thing, the irreducible thing, maybe the thing he wanted so desperately to hide from: you do everything you can, and sometimes the bad thing still happens.

"Listen," Keller said suddenly, "you don't have to leave. You—"

But it was pointless. They didn't connect. Byron felt an abstracted pity for Keller, gaunt in his plush chair, hands poised over the faders. "It's okay," he said wearily. "Do what you need to do."

Out in the world, the sun was terribly bright.

2.   Keller was alone then.

Memories cascaded around him in cool crystalline light. Voices whispered.

One time, talking about Byron, Teresa had said, "He is the best of us." Keller hadn't understood. Now he felt a flicker of comprehension. But it was the kind of goodness he did not wholly understand, troubling and absolute. The old phrase echoed through him: *When someone is hurting, you help.* If it had been a video memory, he could have excised it, looped it out of existence; but it persisted, and it frightened him.

After a time he left the editing booth.

His hotel room faced one of the old suburban arteries, traffic noises all night and running water between ten and ten. He poured a drink, took a long shower, regarded himself in the mirror. His reflection—he considered it objectively —looked strung-out and haggard. His cheeks were sunken, his stubble unshaven. Who was this man? He looked like some wirehead. Some faded combat veteran dying in the Floats.

He closed his eyes.

In the night, drinking again, he called up Lee Anne, with whom he had once had a contract for affection: he recalled, with some fondness, the scent of her perfume. She appeared in the monitor as perfect as ever, stark in white makeup and her lips a piquant red. She peered at him coolly from the crystal display. Keller forced a smile. "We had a contract once," he said. "You remember? We—"

But she shook her head. "I don't know you," she said. The monitor went blank.

* * *

In the morning he was back in the booth.

It was almost unbearable. He winced away from the image of Pau Seco, the open oneirolith mine like a wound in the earth. It was all too vivid. He could smell the squalor of the old town, the dust, the stale heat. It was terrifying: it seemed about to rise from the monitors and surround him.

If someone is hurting, you help.

She was hurting, Byron had said. Keller circled the knowledge but dared not approach it. She was hurting. She was wounded. But the resonance was too terrible to acknowledge.

He hurried through the last of the editing. The print he delivered to Vasquez would be coldly objective, panoramic, a glimpse into the mechanics of the dreamstone trade, Pau Seco, SUDAM, the *garimpeiros* and the *formigas,* this last and strangest frontier. The rest—the merely personal —would be erased. Erased, it would in some important sense cease to exist. Erased, it would become bearable.

His hand was poised over an EDIT command when the door opened.

He swiveled on his chair, thinking it might be Byron again. He saw instead a carefully dressed man with receding hair and a generic smile. Some Network executive maybe. But the man stepped closer, and suddenly Keller could smell his mint-scented breath and feel a hint of his terrible and enormous hostility. The man was smiling even as his hands balled into fists. "My name is Oberg," he said.

CHAPTER 23

Killing Keller would have been redundant, though in some fashion satisfying, and Oberg was practicing his best professional manners. A death in the Network compound would have alarmed too many people. So he had come prepared.

He struck Keller once; Keller fell to the floor, dazed. Quickly, Oberg bound Keller's hands with tape and ran a strip of the same metallic tape across his mouth. Keller's eyes were closed. The Angel blinded, he thought; the Angel silenced. He worked methodically now. He rolled Keller over and put a foot across the small part of his back, to immobilize him. From his hip pocket Oberg withdrew a miniature scalpel and a tiny pronged microchip.

He had purchased these things from a black-market neurotechnician working out of the Floats. The chip was a joywire chip, slightly modified. Attached to the socket behind Keller's neck, it would pulse a voltage down Keller's neural wiring, stimulating the reward centers in Keller's brain. But Oberg had instructed the neurotechnician to substitute a more powerful voltage source.

"It's insane," the neurotech had told him. "You'd burn a man out. It would not be pleasure, it would be pain—immeasurable! And disorientation. And the victim —I can only say victim—would burn out in a matter of hours. Days, at most. He would proceed almost instantly to the last stages of wire psychosis. It would be murder."

So of course Oberg had to pay extra.

He used the scalpel to pare away flesh from Keller's socket. The socket had been opened recently, so this was relatively simple. He used a handkerchief to sponge away the blood. The socket gleamed beneath the derma, an oily coppery color. Keller had flinched from the pain of the cutting but was not yet fully awake. Oberg installed the joywire chip hastily but did not activate it.

He left Keller bound and turned to the memory editor.

It took him a few minutes to sort out Keller's ordinances, isolate a moment of time. He hoped that what he wanted had not been erased. But it was the most recent layer of memory, intact, unedited. He accelerated the sampling rate and watched the monitor in front of him.

Time ran like water. Days flickered past. He would still the motion periodically, recognizing the docks at Belem, the air terminal, a flight to some tiny landing strip in Costa Rica; an ancient American jetliner arriving at the L.A. Harbor terminal. Faces and somatypes had been altered throughout, but he was able to identify Byron Ostler and Teresa Rafael by their repeated appearance in the trace. This was critical now: a shack in the Floats somewhere, cheap furniture and grimy windows; the place, Oberg assumed, where they had gone to ground. He followed the recording back to the mainland and then forward again, slowly, establishing the route. Somewhere in the North Floats. No real addresses amidst this twining of boat shanties and canals, but the route was simple enough to memorize. He did so.

He looked back at Keller.

Keller was awake now, watching him with wide, frightened eyes.

Oberg turned to the keyboard and called up a global delete. The machine paused and then inquired whether he was certain he wanted to empty all the contents of this file. He tapped an affirmation and watched as the monitors cycled through a kind of apocalypse: Cuiaba vanished, the Amazon lost in dead pixels, Pau Seco gone, Belem gone, all disappeared into chaos, signals become noise, Keller's memory trace evaporating into the air as if it had never existed.

Oberg smiled.

Keller was pale, blinking.

Oberg had parked his car directly outside the editing booth, and it was simple to maneuver Keller to his feet and outside without being seen. There was a guard on the road at the entrance gate but he did not glance up as Oberg passed. And they were away free.

He drove a mile down a firebreak road into the hills. When he could safely do so, Oberg pulled up on the shoulder and opened the door on Keller's side. They had reached a wasteland of rusting oil derricks; the road beside the car was littered with bottle glass and aluminum cans glistening in the sunlight. Keller was staring at him now, waiting, strangely calm.

Oberg reached behind Keller's head in a gesture that was almost tender and used the pressure of his thumbnail to activate the joychip.

Keller's face contorted with sudden pain.

Oberg used his feet to shove Keller out of the car.

Keller fell among the weeds and high grass, hidden, dying.

Oberg closed the door, wiped his bloody thumb against his handkerchief, and began the long drive toward the sea.

CHAPTER 24

Teresa was watching the sun go down when she resorted to the pills again.

She had climbed to the top of this raggedy float shack with the pills in her pocket, not intending to swallow any —the desire was never that explicit—but just holding them in reserve, savoring their reassuring closeness. She wore a sweater. Coming on winter now. The nights were early and cool. She sprawled across the tin roof with her back against a heat exchanger, feeling the thrum of the bilge pumps and watching the western sky fade to red.

She took out a handful of pills and regarded them.

They were small, black, unmarked, faintly resinous. Faintly sordid. They had been cooked, she thought, in some

Float laboratory, formed in a primitive pill press, sold furtively to addicts . . . to her.

But she needed them. It was not a question of self-indulgence. It was as if her traumatic 'lith trance in the Vero-Peso had opened old wounds: she needed the anesthesia. She had dreamed about the little girl, increasingly felt her as a tangible presence, scolding and demanding. Now, for instance. Now the little girl wanted her to throw the pills away. Her voice was a real voice, faint but distinct.

I saved your life.

But that was crazy.

In the fire. You would have died. You wanted to die. I saved your life.

Mysteriously, she had become two people.

I saved your life. You took the pills. I made the sculptures. You sold them. . . .

No, Teresa thought.

She took several of the pills into her mouth and swallowed them dry, choking a little. Too many, maybe. But they made the voice fade away.

The euphoria began as a sense of lightness spreading from her stomach. It was inside her, until it reached her head, and then she was inside it; the euphoria contained her perfectly. The sky was dark now, the wind from the tidal dam chilling, but she didn't care. She wrapped the sweater over her shoulders and leaned back, breathing in a deep, steady rhythm. All over the Floats lanterns were flickering on. A fog rolled down the canals.

She was oblivious when she heard Byron's voice as he entered the float, and Cruz Wexler's following, their conversation—they must not have known she was up here—like a tired duet between broken instruments. It was funny, she thought, how sad they sounded. How hopeless and resigned. She closed her eyes and listened to the sound of their voices, the last night cries of nesting gulls. There were high lunar tides out beyond the dams, fresh water from the spillways creating a gentle, pulsing swell. The shack rocked under her. She sighed, alone in this luminous darkness. All voices stilled, she thought. What a blessing silence was.

But then—moved by some muted note of alarm deep within her—she sat up and saw the lone man approaching down a boardwalk from the east.

It was later than she had realized, most of these balsas dark now, only a dim glow from the dance shacks out along the seawall. The man walked methodically and with an air of intense, frightening vigilance. He came alongside the shanty float. He stopped. Teresa, on the flat tin roof, ducked out of his line of vision.

Death at the door, she thought.

It was a strange idea but she considered it calmly. Death had always been at the door. Since the fire, so many years ago. She had been courting him. Seducing him. What was remarkable was that he had taken so long to get here.

She listened to him knock.

CHAPTER 25

Keller lay for a time on the verge of the road by the ancient oilfield.

The sun raked over his closed eyes; he saw starbursts. The gravel under him felt as acute as knives and razors. When an airliner passed overhead, the roar was a demented music.

He wanted to move but could not.

He was lucid for moments at a time, but even his lucidity was painful: an acute, exaggerated sobriety in which the world invaded his senses.

He understood what was happening to him. Oberg had plugged something into his socket, something like a joychip but more intense, something that was sending him rapidly into burn-out. It was clever. A clever kind of murder. If no one found him, he would die; dead, he would look like any other burn-out case. If he were discovered here before he died, he would be mistaken for terminal and remanded to a death ward. No culpability, no obvious crime.

The prospect was so daunting that it overwhelmed him. The voltage pulsing down his wires acted as an amplifier, stimulating the flow of acetylcholenes, flooding him with dopamine. Everything was painful. Breathing was painful. He felt the air searing in and out of him like fire. The slightest motion, a twitch, was agonizing. He opened his eyes once, and the sun was like a lance; he screamed.

He moved in and out of delirium. Delirious, he believed he was back in Brazil, in the war, in the manioc field in Rondonia. The voltage down his wires sluiced out these buried memories. He convulsed, and in one of his convulsions broke the metallic tape Oberg had used to bind his hands. Blood ringed his wrists. It was painful, but no more painful than any other sensation. He rolled away from the margin of the road and felt himself tumbling downward.

When he opened his eyes again, the sky was dark. A ghastly yellow illumination flooded out from the sodium vapor lamps planted along the firebreak. He had rolled down an embankment into a stand of weeds; his wrists were gashed, his face abraded.

The pain was agonizing but briefly—for the moment —bearable. Moaning, he sat up.

He knew this interlude of sanity would not last long. He reached behind his head and touched the raw wound Oberg had left there, felt the spindly angle of the joychip. But not a joychip. It was eroding him, he thought, eating him from the inside. The idea frightened him and threatened to draw him back down into a blind panic. The joychip was slippery with blood and he could not grasp it or withdraw it; it was embedded too deeply in the socket. Just touching it sent spears of pain through him.

He closed his eyes, opened them. Gritty rasp of eyelids over cornea. The hammering of his own heart was deafening. He was in the midst of a wasteland: the insect shapes of oil derricks stilled for decades, their corrosion like scroll-

ROBERT CHARLES WILSON

work in the bleak light. He tried to stand up and fell back, shrieking. The earth spun dizzyingly beneath him.

He was not sure how much time he had. There was no knowing how potent Oberg's burn-out chip might be. It would kill him, he thought, but even before it killed him it would begin to destroy neural tissue. He had seen joywire addicts rescued too late from their addiction, left in a state of hopeless dementia. It could be beginning already. Might already have begun. He was trembling. . . .

But that was a bad thought and he suppressed it. Oberg had seen the memory trace; Oberg knew the way to Teresa. Cling to that, he thought. Oberg would kill her. It was a fact. Oberg might be there already.

He was the only one who knew. He was the only one who could help.

When someone is hurting, you help.

But he felt himself slipping down into delirium again.

Frantically, he scrabbled in the dirt and weeds around him. He knew what he wanted. There were shards of glass here, broken bottles, but they were all rounded and sun-faded. They wouldn't do. Sobbing, he groped through the dark. Surely, he thought, surely somewhere in all this trash—

—and he touched something then, his hand encountered a brittle edge—

—but the pain and the delirium carried him back into darkness. He rolled on the ground, stricken.

It might have lasted forever.

He was back in Rondonia forever, and Megan Lindsey was extending her hand to him forever, calling out to him, fear and pain and a terrible grieving disappointment etched on her features . . . an eternity, until he understood that it was not Megan's face but Teresa's.

But that was impossible. He had edited Megan out of his memory: she could not touch him. And he had edited Teresa. Angel training. *Wu-nien.* They were looped out, excised, extinct.

But then, he thought giddily, it would happen again. That was the curse. As Megan had died, Teresa would die.

Teresa was not Megan but she was like Megan; he was in love with her, and he was letting her die. Dying here, he was allowing Oberg to kill her. And that was a fact, and he could not erase or edit it; it was written on some larger, indelible scroll.

She could be dying now.

The thought shocked him back to awareness.

He couldn't tell how much time had passed. There were a few dim stars; there was a trail of light, miles across this wasteland, a traffic artery. His limbs jerked spasmodically and he knew that he might not have another lucid moment: Oberg's joychip might already have damaged him beyond repair. But it didn't matter. Teresa mattered.

He understood that, suddenly and with a bright, calm clarity. Strange, he thought: burned into innocence. It had all fallen away, his Angel training, *wu-nien*, all the architecture of his life, all seared away, and yet this luminous thing was left: his love for her. Burning, he understood and admitted it.

He groped in the weeds for the blade he had located moments or hours before. He found it when it sliced into the flesh of his thumb: an agonizing, amplified pain. Moaning, he picked it up and regarded it. It was an aluminum lid peeled off somebody's lunch months or years ago, foggy with oxides but not hopelessly rusted. It flashed in the bitter sodium-vapor light. He was not certain he could do what he needed to do with it. The pain . . .

But there was no avoiding it.

He lifted the wedge of aluminum behind him and sliced it down spastically against the socket at the base of his neck.

The pain rang through him like a bell. His hand shook, which complicated things. After the second attempt he came close to passing out. His head was like a dry gourd, drained of everything but pain. He thought of flesh severed and bleeding, neural wires severed where they joined the spine, pain distilled and purified down screaming basal ganglia. It was impossible, he thought; even for her, even for Teresa, whom he loved; even for her, it was impossible . . . but the third gouging attempt succeeded and he felt the socket fall away like an abscessed tooth.

ROBERT CHARLES WILSON

* * *

He felt a shuddering sense of relief. Relief and a huge, encompassing weariness. He wanted to sleep. He was exhausted. Had to sleep.

But he couldn't sleep. Not yet.

Sighing, unsteady, trembling and bloody, he moved up the embankment toward the road.

CHAPTER 26

Dazed, obeying some impulse, Teresa moved down from the roof of the float shack into the back room, through the door into the kitchen.

The man in the kitchen had a gun.

Byron and Wexler sat at the table, motionless. Wexler was staring at the gunman, his eyes wide, skin pale, lungs laboring at the still air. Byron turned slowly to look at her. He was warning her with his eyes—don't do anything, don't move—but there was a limpness, a hopelessness in the motion which made her feel afraid.

The enkephalins were powerful, but she had taken them hours ago; her heart was beating hard now, her fingertips tingled. Stress hormones rivered down her bloodstream.

She had become, she thought distantly, a kind of chemical battlefield.

She looked at the man with the gun. He stood in the doorway with the door ajar behind him. He was a man of maybe Byron's age, receding hairline and a pursed, narrow mouth. His eyes were fixed, unblinking, remote. He was calm in a situation that should have made any normal person anxious, and that was worrisome: there was no judging what this man might do.

Death, she thought. Death in these drab clothes on her doorstep.

The man looked at her and said, "I want the oneirolith."

She answered without thinking. "I don't have it. It's gone." A lie.

Strange, that she should lie.

The man—who could only be the rogue Agency man, Oberg, the one Wexler had talked about—moved the gun fractionally so that it was pointed now at Byron. "Bring the stone or I'll kill both these men."

"It's in the back room." No hesitation this time, because she understood he was telling the truth.

"Get it," he said. "Leave the door open."

She stumbled once against the doorframe, then moved in dreamy, slow steps to the old Salvation Army dresser.

Watching from his chair at the table, Cruz Wexler gasped for breath.

He could only stare at Oberg. Oberg with the gun, Oberg who had found them somehow. The gun was aimed only a degree away from him, and it was too easy to imagine a bullet erupting from the muzzle, tearing into him, the damage it would do.

But he was dying in any case. His emphysema was advanced and he impoverished; his money was tied up in Agency liens and he could not afford new lungs or long-term treatment. Why should it matter how he died, if the dying was inevitable?

But of course it did matter. It mattered very much.

He had spent the last decades of his life pursuing mysteries. Wisdom, gnosis, the Philosopher's Stone. It had been a game and a profitable business, but he had been sincere too. The oneiroliths had always inspired this feeling in him, of trembling on the brink of a revelation.

But death—this final mystery and most absolute gnosis—it frightened him terribly.

He watched Oberg watching Teresa. "Now bring it here," Oberg said. The stone, he meant. That mystery abandoned too: Oberg feared it and would destroy it.

But there was a motion in the darkness, in the doorway beyond Oberg, a flicker of movement . . . seeing it, Wexler felt his heart hammer suddenly against his ribs.

Pick it up.

Teresa stared down at the Pau Seco artifact in its oilcloth binding, shadowed in the depths of the wooden drawer.

Pick it up. Touch it.

It was the old and new voice inside her, the voice the enkephalins should have quieted. The voice of the little girl who had died in the fire fourteen years ago, unaccountably alive inside her. Almost dead now for real, Teresa thought, but drawn out once more by this crisis: *Pick it up, hold it, touch it.*

The dreamstone. This well of memories.

She glanced back at the gunman, Oberg. He made an impatient hurry-up gesture.

She reached into the drawer. For one timeless moment she envisioned a scenario in which she would give the stone to Oberg, Oberg would take it, would leave them alive, and she would be better without it, after all, free from the yoke of remembering, free to inhabit the opaque but comfortable womb of her enkephalin addiction: she dreamed it would happen, that Oberg would allow them to live.

Knowing at the same time it was impossible. Oberg was Death; he looked like Death and he smelled like Death. He would kill the three of them. It was inevitable.

Pick it up. The voice was more insistent now, a clamoring.

Well, Teresa thought. It was the girl who wanted to live. Who cared. Not me. Never me.

Picking it up, she held it at first by its binding; but the ancient oilcloth unraveled and the naked stone fell back into the drawer. She reached for it instinctively.

The power of it throbbed in her arm as she turned.

CHAPTER 27

Keller had tied a handkerchief around his throat to conceal the bleeding, but by the time he reached the Floats the handkerchief itself was sodden with blood.

He was conscious of the time that had passed. He had walked for what seemed like miles along the verge of the road, across the oil barrens to a tiny Hispanic neighborhood, an all-night bodega from which he could phone for a taxi. He was filthy, his clothes were torn, he was bleeding: he had to offer up credit and ID before the cabbie agreed to open his door. Climbing out, he left bloodstains on the seat.

In the Floats he had lost himself twice—wandering too far down a darkened canal, past the yellow lights of empty cafés and market boats creaking in the midnight swell—crazed with fatigue and with this unrelenting sense of urgency. A cold salt wind sluiced through his clothes. Lost, he had to retrace his steps until he recognized a pontoon walkway or canal intersection and could correct himself, march on, while the stars wheeled overhead like the advancing hands of a clock. Time, he thought. But maybe time enough still to save her.

Then, at last, he identified the feeder canal that ran past the float shack Byron had rented. It was an old, narrow commercial right-of-way; fenced water, shanties pressing up against it, defined with chain-link and barbed wire fences and salt-emblazoned concrete risers. A boardwalk followed the canal along the mainland side, giving access to a row of shanties of which Byron's was one: one of the few still showing lights at this hour. Everything dark, everything quiet. Rooftop windmills moaned in the fitful breeze from the tidal dam.

Fatigued beyond words, but careful now, Keller moved silently down the boardwalk.

The door was ajar.

He worked to steady his breathing. He was no longer in the state of heightened sensitivity Oberg's counterfeit joychip had created, but he was in great pain. The wound he had hacked into his neck and shoulders was deep and had bled profusely. It was possible he could pass out at any moment . . . but only a little longer now, he told himself. Only a little longer.

Oberg was inside the door.

He shuddered, recognizing the angle of Oberg's body, seeing the gun in Oberg's hand. Here—from this edge of the boardwalk, a low wire fence behind him and the bulk of a concrete pillar—he was able to see Oberg and, beyond Oberg, the small table at which Byron and Cruz Wexler sat motionless. He couldn't see Teresa. But, he thought dizzily, that doesn't mean she's dead. She might still be alive.

It was necessary to believe that.

He realized with a dawning incredulity that he had no weapon, no means of threatening Oberg. Not even a pocket knife. He was helpless here. He had come all this way, but too late. It was almost funny. He was tempted to laugh.

Instead he calculated the angle of that half-open door, the chance that he might manage to throw himself into it, topple Oberg, make it possible for Byron or Wexler to do something. Small, pathetic hope. But, hoping, he drew a deep breath and stepped forward.

But a dew had condensed on the mossy, ancient wood of the boardwalk, and he was massively fatigued; his foot slipped forward, his knee buckled.

He caught himself crouching, eyes on the doorway, but the slap of his palms on the wet wood was explosive in the night, and he watched helplessly as Oberg turned, the gun pivoting in his hand.

Wexler stood up as Oberg wheeled around.

He surprised himself. He had not contemplated this. There was no heroism in him, only this crippling fear. And yet here he was in motion. His body rebelling against his helplessness.

Standing, he did not hesitate. He upturned the flimsy wooden table and was aware of it tumbling forward. Byron looked at him, agape. A pain stabbed through his chest; his body screamed out for air. But he was able, for the moment, to ignore it.

He moved toward Oberg.

Oberg recoiled from the door. His impassiveness had failed him; he seemed startled and, briefly, frightened. The angle of the gun dropped. He blinked as the table thundered against the floor.

Wexler was moving now with some speed. His momentum carried him toward Oberg. He had forgotten everything but this mad rush forward, arms open in embrace. He was dimly aware of Byron coming to his feet, of Teresa's movement in the back room, but these were distractions: his attention was devoted entirely to Oberg.

Oberg backed against the wall. Something changed in his face then: a settling, a hardening. He brought up the pistol in a swift motion.

Too late, Wexler thought. One of us is too late.

The gunshot was explosive in this tiny space.

The pain and the impact pushed him backward.

ROBERT CHARLES WILSON

* * *

Keller burst through the door—*if someone is hurting, you help*—but was brought up short by the sight of Wexler bloody on the floor. He looked at Oberg, and Oberg was smiling absentmindedly; the gun was aimed at Keller.

"Christ," Byron said. "Oh, Christ."

Keller slumped against the wall. The world had come down to this man, this gun, and there was no way around it now, no exit from it. He closed his eyes briefly.

When he opened them again he saw Teresa: she was moving toward Oberg, and the stone was in her hand.

CHAPTER 28

Lost between worlds, between the drone of the enkephalins and the electricity of the dreamstone, Teresa opened her eyes.

She saw Byron's float shack. She recalled a similar shack, a long time ago. The man in the next room was named Oberg. The man in the next room might have been named Carlos.

She held the stone in her hand.

And if I look in the mirror, she thought giddily, I'll see the shoes bound with dirty twine, the old denim open at the knees. It was the thing she had resisted, the thing she had feared, the vision that had haunted her since that day in the hotel room off the Ver-o-Peso.

She would fall into the mirror, tumble into history, turn back into herself.

The voice of the girl was inside her now, louder and more insistent than it had ever been. The voice was warning her that she would die, that the man with the gun would kill her, that she had to do something, do something *now*.

It was the voice that had sustained her through the fire, buoyed her up when she wanted to die, when she knew she *deserved* to die.

But death was not so tractable. Death had finally come to finish what he had begun. It was only an appointment she had missed a long time ago. She had been expecting it and maybe even—it was possible to admit this now—maybe even *wanting* it, wanting it for years. Searching for it in pill bottles, the peace of it, an end at last to this quarreling with herself. . . .

No, the voice said.

And for a moment the memory overtook her. She felt the smoke stealing her breath, the heat of the fire behind her. Carlos was dead and Mama was dead and she should have died too: because she was not a good girl and never would be. It was the bedrock on which she had built herself, this guilt.

Be me, the voice insisted. *Take me back*.

No, Teresa thought. . . .

But then there was the splintering of wood in the kitchen, the table split and broken, Cruz Wexler throwing himself forward . . . and then the gunshot, Wexler bleeding on the floor . . . and the door opened, and it was Ray, he had come back, some miracle had brought him back, and her heart hammered, seeing him . . . but he was bloody and exhausted and Oberg had turned the gun on him now. . . .

And so she relented: all right, *yes*, she thought, and in a motion that was not physical she embraced the little girl, gave herself wholeheartedly to the stone, felt time run back until she was young and whole and wanting desperately to live, for Ray to live, running toward Oberg (or Carlos) now, twine-bound sneakers on her feet and denim out at the knee, allowed at last to hate him, hating him with everything that was in her, screaming out to him this ancient, buried truth, that she was *not* bad, she was *not* bad, she was *not*.

CHAPTER 29

1.   Seeing Teresa running from the back room—knowing that Oberg would kill her if he managed to swivel the gun—Keller summoned the last of his strength and leaped sideways.

He heard the crack of gunfire following him. He fell against the wall in an awkward crouch, unhurt but briefly helpless. Surely the next bullet would come soon. He lifted his face toward Oberg, exhausted beyond fear.

He saw Teresa stumble into the Agency man.

She moved oddly. Her eyes were wide; her face seemed curiously transformed. Like a child's face, Keller thought.

The Pau Seco stone was in her left hand. With her right she touched Oberg.

She fell against him.

Oberg's eyes were fixed on Keller, and in that moment Keller felt some of the horror that erupted from him. It was wounding, awesome. . . .

"The gun," Byron said, stumbling out of his chair. "Christ's sake, Ray, get the gun!"

2.   Oberg was taken by surprise.

He was leveling his weapon at Keller—who had hacked away his neural socket somehow, somehow tracked him here—when the woman rushed him from the back room.

He had sensed her approach and his arm was cocked to shove her away. It should not have been a problem. But the stone—

She touched him with the stone.

He felt it like a current through him.

It was like the time Tavitch had touched him. No, it was worse. He felt himself tumbling into memory, seconds stretching into minutes, everything slowed but his erupting guilt, a village in Brazil, bodies all around him but not dead: their pain and rage had survived them somehow, leaped at him now from this woman's hand.

Blinking, he saw Keller stand up. Keller, a bloody apparition who should have died . . . and maybe *had* died: who might be another ghost, another stubborn corpse come to make its accusation.

Gap-jawed, Oberg stood helpless in a river of ancient hate.

He felt the gun slipping from his hand.

Teresa's body pressed him against the wall of the shack. Her face hovered before him, transfigured with a kind of innocence he could hardly credit. In the world he inhabited, nothing like this existed. And it was another rebuke, luminous and terrible; he contorted away from her in a spasm of self-loathing.

Without warning, he understood the thing he was.

Monster, Ng had said.

The voice echoed down a twisted geometry from the gallows at Pau Seco. *Monster.* But it was true. He felt it in Teresa. She was unimpeachable, childlike, beyond lies. He withered in the fierce light of her hatred.

Screaming, he pushed her away.

The gun . . . but Keller had twisted the gun from his hand before he could raise it.

Oberg bolted through the open door.

3.   Keller raised the gun to follow, but there wasn't time to fire.

Panicked in the darkness, Oberg took two long strides toward the low chain-link fence and tumbled over it.

Keller ran out after him, blinking in the darkness. Dogs were barking; a few lamps had flickered on in the neighboring balsas.

He peered over the fence, down into the canal. Not yet dawn, but there was light enough to see Oberg's body spread-eagled at the base of a concrete riser . . . to see the dark canal water rise up and claim him, to see the stain of Oberg's blood washed into the slow swell, the rising and falling of the saltwater on this cold night.

A wind came off the tidal dam from the ocean. He turned to look for Teresa, and suddenly she was in his arms, the warmth of her against him, weeping.

CHAPTER 30

Later, after Wexler's quiet funeral in the Floats, Byron figured it was time to leave.

He had talked it over with Teresa days earlier. They said private good-byes, he held her briefly. She said, "You don't have to go." But he did. Time to get back into the world.

She gave him the stone.

"I don't need it," she said, and the new look was on her face: a smile that was almost childlike. "I've been there."

He walked with Keller a distance along the canal. It was a bright, clear day; the sky arched down to meet the hard angle of the sea. Byron shifted his duffel up his shoulder. Keller offered his hand.

Byron took it, though he saw Keller wince with the motion. "You all right?"

"Getting better." Keller essayed a smile. "You have the stone?"

He nodded. It was in his bag.

He was not certain why he'd taken it. Only this feeling—an instinct—that it might be useful.

Strange, he thought. Wexler had spent his life searching among these stones for something alien, some higher wisdom, a way out of the world. But finally it wasn't that. Byron had watched the change in Teresa since that night with Oberg in the float shack, some old brokenness healed. It was subtle, a lightness, the way she moved her eyes, but it was profound too; he had discovered he wasn't afraid for her anymore. So it was not a way out of the world but a way *into* it.

All debts paid. "She's doing all right." He added, impulsively—a little wistfully—"Watch out for her, Ray, all right? Do that for me."

Keller nodded.

He faced the mainland resolutely, but turned back a step later to take in Keller—Keller with his eyes full of old pain, Keller braced against a chain-link fence with one knee bent and the Floats rolling away behind him. He said, "You live here now."

And maybe it was true.

Keller walked back along the margin of the canal. He felt again this curious lightness. His Angel wires, he thought, severed from their socket, withering and dying inside him. But more than that.

You live here now.

He climbed a chain-link riser and saw the ocean out beyond the tidal dam. The ocean was implacable, dark, vaster than he could compass; and memory was like that, he thought, not video memory but his own memory, of Meg, of Teresa, of Byron, of his life: wide and deep and mysterious beyond saying. It contained him more than he contained it, and it would not brook betrayal; but there were days, he thought, like this one, when the ocean stood calm and seemed to augur in its tides some bright millennium.

He went down the boardwalk to the ancient float shanty, Teresa in the doorway waiting for him, calm in the sunlight. A breeze from the seawall made him shiver; she held the door wider. "Better come in," she said. "It's cold out there."

ABOUT THE AUTHOR

Robert Charles Wilson was born in Whittier, California, in 1953 but moved to Toronto at the age of nine. He has worked at a number of jobs, including film extra, and was most recently with the Ontario Human Rights Commission. His short fiction has appeared in *The Magazine of Fantasy & Science Fiction* and *Isaac Asimov's Science Fiction Magazine,* and he has published three other novels: *A Hidden Place, Gypsies,* and *The Divide.* He lives with his wife and son on Vancouver Island, British Columbia.

A Special Preview of

THE DIVIDE

the new Science Fiction novel by

Robert Charles Wilson

Imagine losing your personality . . . feeling it slip
and alter, steadily changing, until the person living
in your body is no longer recognizable as *you*. Imagine being able to understand what is happening, but
powerless to stop it. Imagine . . . and you will understand the feelings of John Shaw. **The Divide** is his
story.

Shaw was a "designed" child—the product of a clandestine research project meant to create a superior
human being. But when government funding ran
out, Shaw not only lost the only father he had ever
known—researcher Max Kyriakides—but was left without the monitoring his altered body required. Now,
years later, he is a grown man . . . but a man whose
mind is not entirely his own. . . .

Such an ordinary house. Such an ordinary beginning.

But I *want* it to be an ordinary house, Susan Christopher thought. An ordinary house with an ordinary man in it. Not this monster—to whom I must deliver a message.

It was a yellow brick boarding house in the St. Jamestown area of Toronto, a neighborhood of low-rent high-rises and immigrant housing. Susan was from suburban Los Angeles—lately from the University of Chicago—and she felt misplaced here. She stood a moment in the chill, sunny silence of the afternoon, double-checking the address Dr. Kyriakides had written on a slip of pink memo paper. This number, yes, this street.

She fought a momentary urge to run away.

Then up the walk through a scatter of October leaves, pause a moment in the cold foyer . . . the inner door stood open . . . finally down a corridor to the door marked with a chipped gilt number 2.

She knocked twice, aware of her small knuckles against the ancient veneer of the door. Across the hall, a wizened East Indian man peered out from behind his chain lock. Susan looked up at the ceiling, where a swastika had been spray-painted onto the cloudy stucco. She was about to knock again when the door opened under her hand.

But it was a woman who answered . . . a young woman in a white blouse, denim skirt, torn khaki jacket. Her feet were bare on the cracked linoleum. The woman's expression was sullen—her lips in a ready, belligerent pout—and Susan dropped her eyes from the narrow face to the jacket, where there was a small constellation of buttons and badges: BON JOVI, JIM MORRISON, LED ZEPPELIN. . . .

"You want something?"

Susan guessed this was a French Canadian accent, the nasality and the dropped "th" sound. She forced herself to meet the woman's eyes. Woman or girl? Maybe nineteen or twenty years old: a few years younger than I am, Susan thought, therefore "girl" —but it was hard to be sure, with the makeup and all.

She cleared her throat. "I'm looking for John Shaw."

"Oh . . . *him.*"

"Is he here?"

"No." The girl ran a hand through her hair. Long nails. Short hair.

"But he lives here?"

"Uh—sometimes. Are you a friend of his?"

Susan shook her head. "Not exactly . . . are you?"

Now there was the barest hint of a smile. "Not exactly." The girl extended her hand. "I'm Amelie."

The hand was small and cool. Susan introduced herself; Amelie said, "He's not here . . . but you can maybe find him at the 24-Hour on Wellesley. You know, the doughnut shop?"

Susan nodded. She would look for "Wellesley" on her map.

Amelie said, "Is it important? You look kind of, ah, worried."

"It's pretty important," Susan said, thinking: *Life or death*: Dr. Kyriakides had told her that.

Susan saw him for the first time, her first real look at him, through the plate-glass window of the doughnut shop.

She allowed herself this moment, seeing him without being seen. She recognized him from the pictures Dr. Kyriakides had shown her. But Susan imagined she might have guessed who he was, just from looking at him—that she would have known, at least, that he was not entirely normal.

To begin with, he was alone.

He sat at a small table in the long room, three steps down from the sidewalk. His face was angled up at the October sunlight, relishing it. There was a chessboard in front of him—the board built into the lacquered surface of the table and the pieces arranged in ready ranks.

She had dreamed about this, about meeting him, dreams that occasionally bordered on nightmares. In the dreams John Shaw was barely human, his head unnaturally enlarged, his eyes needle-sharp and unblinking. The real John Shaw was nothing like that, of course, in his photographs or here, in the flesh; his monstrosities, she thought, were buried—but she mustn't think of him that way. He was in trouble and he needed her help.

Hello, John Shaw, she thought.

His hair was cut close, a burr cut, but that was fashionable now; he was meticulously clean-shaven. Regular features, frown lines, maps of character emerging from the geography of his fairly young face. Here is a man, Susan thought, who worries a lot. A gust of wind lifted her hair; she reached up to smooth it back and he must have glimpsed the motion; his head turned—a swift owlish flick of the eyes, and for that moment he did *not* seem human; the swivel of his head was too calculated, the focus of his eyes too fine. His eyes, suddenly, were like the eyes in her dreams. John Shaw regarded her through the window and she felt spotlit, or, worse, *pinned*—a butterfly in a specimen case.

Both of them were motionless in this tableau until, finally, John Shaw raised a hand and beckoned her inside.

Well, Susan Christopher thought, there's no turning back now, is there?

Breathing hard, she moved down the three cracked steps and through the door of the shop. There was no one inside but John Shaw and the middle-aged woman refilling the coffee machine. Susan approached him and then stood mute beside the table: she couldn't find the words to begin.

He said, "You might as well sit down."

His voice was controlled, unafraid, neutral in accent. Susan took the chair opposite him. They were separated, now, by the ranks of the chessboard.

He said, "Do you play?"

"Oh . . . I didn't come here to play chess."

"No. Max sent you."

Her eyes widened at this Holmes-like deduction. John said, "Well, obviously you were looking for me. And I've taken some pains to be unlooked-for. I could imagine the American government wanting a word with me. But you don't look like you work for the government. It wasn't a long shot—I'm assuming I'm correct?"

"Yes," Susan stammered. "Dr. Kyriakides . . . yes."

"I thought he might do this. Sometime."

"It's more important than you think." But how to *say* this? "He wants you to know—"

John hushed her. "Humor me," he said. "Give me a game."

She looked at the board. In high school, she had belonged to the chess club. She had even played in a couple of local tournaments—not too badly. But—

"You'll win," she said.

"You know that about me?"

"Dr. Kyriakides said—"

"Your move," John said.

She advanced the white king's pawn two squares, reflexively.

"No talk," John instructed her. "As a favor." He responded with his own king's pawn. "I appreciate it."

She played out the opening—a Ruy Lopez—but was soon in a kind of free fall; he did something unexpected with his queen's knight and her pawn ranks began to unravel. His queen stood in place, a vast but nonspecific threat; he gave up a bishop to expose her king and the queen at last came swooping out to give checkmate. They had not even castled.

Of course, the winning was inevitable. She knew—Dr. Kyriakides had told her—that John Shaw had played tournament chess for a time; that he had never lost a game; that he had dropped out of competition before his record and rating began to attract attention. She wondered how the board must look to him. Simple, she imagined. A graph of possibilities; a kindergarten problem.

He thanked her and began to set up the pieces again, his large hands moving slowly, meticulously. She said, "You spend a lot of time here?"

"Yes."

"Playing chess?"

"Sometimes. Most of the regulars have given up on me."

"But you still do it."

"When I get the chance."

"But surely . . . I mean, don't you always win?"

He looked at her. He smiled, but the smile was cryptic . . . she couldn't tell whether he was amused or disappointed.

"One hopes," John Shaw said.

She walked back with him to the rooming house, attentive now, her fears beginning to abate, but still reluctant: how could she tell him? But she must.

She used this time to observe him. What Dr.

Kyriakides had told her was true: John wore his strangeness like a badge. There was no pinning down exactly what it was that made him different. His walk was a little ungainly; he was too tall; his eyes moved restlessly when he spoke. But none of that added up to anything significant. The real difference, she thought, was more subtle. Pheromones, or something on that level. She imagined that if he sat next to you on a bus you would notice him immediately— turn, look, maybe move to another seat. No reason, just this uneasiness. Something *odd* here.

It was almost dark, an early October dusk. The street lights blinked on, casting complex shadows through the brittle trees. Coming up the porch stairs to the boarding house Susan saw him hesitate, stiffen a moment, lock one hand in a fierce embrace of the banister. My God, she thought, it's some kind of seizure—he's sick—but it abated as quickly as it had come. He straightened and put his key in the door.

Susan said, "Will Amelie be here?"

"Amelie works a night shift at a restaurant on Yonge Street. She's out by six most evenings."

"You live with her?"

"No. I don't live with her."

The apartment seemed even more debased, in this light, than Susan had guessed from her earlier glimpse of it. It was one room abutting a closet-sized bedroom— she could make out the jumbled bedclothes through the door—and an even tinier kitchen. The room smelled greasy: Amelie's dinner, Susan guessed, leftovers still congealing in the pan. Salvation Army furniture and a sad, dim floral wallpaper. Why would he live here? Why not a mansion—a palace? He could have had that. But he was sick, too . . . maybe that had something to do with it.

She said, "I know what you are."

He nodded mildly, as if to say, *Yes, all right.* He

shifted a stack of magazines to make room for himself on the sofa. "You're one of Max's students?"

"I was," she corrected. "Molecular biology. I took a sabbatical."

"Money?"

"Money mostly. My father died after a long illness. It was expensive. There was the possibility of loans and so forth, but I didn't feel—I just didn't enjoy the work anymore. Dr. Kyriakides offered me a job until I was ready to face my thesis again. At first I was just collating notes, you know, doing some library research for a book he's working on. Then—"

"Then he told you about me."

"Yes."

"He must trust you."

"I suppose so."

"I'm sure of it. And he sent you here?"

"Finally, yes. He wasn't sure you'd be willing to talk directly to him. But it's very important."

"Not just *auld lang syne*?"

"He wants to see you."

"For medical reasons?"

"Yes."

"Am I ill, then?"

"Yes."

He smiled again. The smile was devastating— superior, knowing, but at the same time obviously forced, an act of bravery. He said, "Well, I thought so."

They talked for a long time.

Dr. Kyriakides had already told her some of this. He had kept tabs on John, but surreptitiously, since it was a violation of his funding agreements to do so . . . and he had no illusions about the source of his grants. Susan was able to anticipate some of what John told her. But some of it was new.

He said, "It depends on what you call a symptom, doesn't it?"

The research project ended when John was five years old. He was adopted out to a childless couple, the Woodwards, a middle-income family living in a bleak Chicago suburb. The Woodwards renamed him Benjamin, though he continued to think of himself as John. From the beginning, his adoptive parents were disturbed by his uniqueness. He didn't always do especially well in school—he was contemptuous of his teachers and sometimes a discipline problem— but he read beyond his years and he made conversation like an adult . . . which, the Woodwards told him, was very disrespectful.

"Jim Woodward was a lathe operator at an aerospace plant and he resented my intelligence. Obviously, a child doesn't know this, or doesn't want to admit it. I labored for eight years under the impression that I was doing something terribly wrong—that he hated me for some fundamental, legitimate reason. And so I worked hard to please him. I tried to impress him. For example, I learned to play the flute in junior high. Borrowed a school instrument and some books. I taught myself. He loved Vivaldi: he had this old Heathkit stereo he had cobbled together out of a kit and he would play Vivaldi for hours—it was the only time I saw anything like rapture on his face. And so I taught myself the Concerto in G, the passages for flute. And when I had it down, I played it for him. Not just the notes. I went beyond that. I *interpreted* it. He sat there listening, and at first I thought he was in shock—he had that dumbfounded expression. I mistook it for pleasure. I played harder. And he just sat there until I was finished. I thought I'd done it, you see, that I'd communicated with him, that he would approve of me now. And then I put the flute back in the case and looked at him. And he blinked a couple of times, and then he said, 'I bet you think you're pretty fucking good, don't you?' "

"That's terrible," Susan said.

"But I wasn't convinced. It just wasn't good enough, that's all. So I thought, well, what else is there that matters to him?

"He had a woodworking shop in the basement. We were that kind of family, the Formica counters in the kitchen, Sunday at the Presbyterian church every once in a while, the neighbors coming over to play bridge and the woodwork shop downstairs. But he had quality tools, Dremel and Black & Decker and so on, and he took a tremendous amount of pride in the work he did. He built a guitar once, some cousin paid him a hundred dollars for it, and he must have put in three times that in raw materials, and when it was finished it was a work of art, bookmatched hardwood, polished and veneered—it took him months. When I saw it, I wanted it. But it had been bought and paid for, and he had to send it away. I wanted him to make another one, but he was already involved in some other project, and that was when I saw my opportunity—I said, '*I'll* build it.'

"I was twelve years old. I had never so much as touched his woodworking tools. 'Show me,' I said. He said, 'You'll never manage it. It's not a beginner's project.' I said, 'Let me try.' And I think now he saw it as *his* big opportunity . . . maybe this would teach me a lesson. So he agreed. He showed me how to work the tools and he gave me some books on luthiery. He even took me to lumberyards, helped me pick out decent woods."

John paused to sip his cappucino. "I worked on the guitar that summer whenever he was out of the house. Because it was an experiment—you understand? This would be the communication, he would see this and love me for doing it, and if he didn't—all bets were off. So I took it very seriously. I cut and sanded, I routed the neck, I installed the fretwire and the tuning machinery. I was possessed by that guitar. There was not a weekday afternoon through July or August I was out of the house. I was dizzy with lacquer fumes half the time. And when he came home I would hide the project . . . I didn't want him to see it until it was ready. I cleaned the tools and the workshop every day; I was meticulous. I think he forgot about it. Thought I'd given up. Until I showed it to him."

Susan said, "Oh, no."

"It was perfect, of course. Max probably told you what his research had suggested, long before it was fashionable science—that the neocortical functions aren't just 'intelligence.' It's also dexterity, timing, the attention span, the sense of pitch, eye-hand coordination—things as pertinent to music or luthiery as they are to, say, mathematics. Jim Woodward thought he'd found a task that was beyond me. In fact, he could hardly have picked one I was better suited to. Maybe that guitar wasn't flawless, but it was close. It was a work of art."

Susan said, "He hated it."

John smiled his humorless, raw smile. "He took it personally. I showed him the guitar. The last varnish was barely dry. I strummed a G chord. I handed it to him . . . the final evidence that I was worthy of him. To him it must have been, I don't know, a slap in the face, a gesture of contempt. He took the guitar, checked it out. He sighted down the neck. He inspected the frets. Then he broke it over his knee."

Susan looked at her hands.

John said, "I don't want sympathy. You asked about symptoms. This is relevant. For years I thought of myself as 'John' while the Woodwards were calling me 'Benjamin.' After that day . . . for them, I *was*

Benjamin. I became what they wanted. Normal, adequate, pliant, and wholly unimpressive. You understand, it was an act. They noticed it, this change, but they never questioned it. They didn't want to. They welcomed it. I worked my body the way a puppeteer works a marionette. I *made up* Benjamin. He was my invention. In a way, he was as meticulous a piece of work as that guitar. I made him out of people I knew, out of what the Woodwards seemed to want. He was their natural child—maybe the child they deserved. I played Benjamin for almost three years, one thousand and eighty-five days. And when I turned sixteen I took my birth certificate and a hundred-dollar bill James Woodward kept in his sock drawer, and I left. Didn't look back, didn't leave a forwarding address . . . and I dropped Benjamin like a stone." He took a sip of cappucino. "At least I thought I did."

"What are you saying—that *Benjamin* was a symptom?"

"He *is* a symptom. He came back."

The Divide is a poignant tale of love and loss, of real people caught in frightening circumstances. It is a prime example of the evocative writing we have come to expect from Robert Charles Wilson—and an experience of the heart.

"Dan Simmons is a breathtaking writer."
— Harlan Ellison

Hyperion
by Dan Simmons

On the eve of invasion by intersteller barbarians, seven citizens of the Human Hegemony have come to Hyperion on a pilgrimage toward almost certain doom. They travel to the Time Tombs within the realm of the Shrike, whose powers transcend the boundaries of space and time, sharing their incredible stories in the hopes of unraveling the mysteries of the Time Tombs, of the Shrike and of Hyperion itself.

"Dan Simmons' **Hyperion** is some sort of extraordinary book. It's been quite a while since I've come across a novel that is at once so involving, so conceptually complex, and written with such style."
— *Isaac Asimov's Science Fiction Magazine*

And don't miss the stunning sequel to **Hyperion**
The Fall of Hyperion
by Dan Simmons
A Doubleday Foundation Trade Paperback
on sale now, wherever Doubleday Foundation books are sold

Buy **Hyperion** on sale now wherever Bantam Spectra Books are sold.